Previous selections of the
Universal Book Club

CAPER SAUCE
by **S. P. B. MAIS**

THINE ENEMY
by **SIR PHILIP GIBBS**

MARY OF DELIGHT
by **NAOMI JACOB**

WEB OF DAYS
by **EDNA LEE**

A FLOWER FOR CATHERINE
by **FRANK SWINNERTON**

THE BEND OF THE RIVER
by **GODFREY WINN**

AT SUNDOWN, THE TIGER
by **ETHEL MANNIN**

HONEY FOR THE GHOST
by **LOUIS GOLDING**

MART OF NATIONS
by **WINIFRED DUKE**

DEATH WITHOUT QUESTION
by **THOMAS MUIR**

Subscribers may receive, as additional books, any or all
of the Club's previous selections that are still in print.
PLEASE WRITE FOR ORDER FORM AND CURRENT
LIST OF PAST SELECTIONS STILL OBTAINABLE

STILL THE WORLD IS YOUNG

by

KATHLEEN HEWITT

5 & 6 ST. ANDREW'S HILL, CARTER LANE
LONDON, E.C.4

First published . . . August 1951
Universal Book Club Edition . August 1952

Printed in Great Britain
by The Anchor Press, Ltd.,
Tiptree, Essex

TO MY FRIEND

MEUM STEWART

For while a youth is lost in soaring thought,
And while a mind grows sweet and beautiful,
And while a spring-tide coming lights the earth,
And while a child, and while a flower is born,
And while one wrong cries for redress and finds
A soul to answer, still the world is young.

LEWIS MORRIS.

CHAPTER I

FROM the second-floor window over the lace shop a boy was watching the familiar kaleidoscope of the street. Though short and narrow it was usually lively, and through it, all day long, echoed sounds from the thoroughfares at each end. From Wardour Street came the whirr of traffic, from Berwick Street the clamour of the market. And after dark, cars and taxis would use this as a by-way to the night life of Soho.

In any cosmopolitan district children become prematurely sophisticated. The ten-year-old boy at the window, no more precocious than his schoolmates, was used to overhearing gossip—much of it in broken English—about the shadier aspects of the neighbourhood. These he accepted as a matter-of-course, like the wind or the rain, the foreign cafés, the loungers outside the pubs, the kerbside stalls, the women who crowded round displays of vegetables or stockings, and the street-corner bookmaker.

Along Sidley Street most of the ground floors had been converted into shops, some with glittering modern façades, others with inadequate windows in which the dim displays had not been changed for years. Loo Wong's Chinese Restaurant, with its faded orange signboard, and George's Restaurant—which relied for its décor on great dishes of fried sausages and onions—both contributed their odours to this sultry evening in 1938.

Many of the shopkeepers lived on the first floors, letting the upper rooms as apartments, and most of the side doors leading to these crowded tenements stood open all day. But the owner of the shop that displayed rainbows of lace had a flat in the East End; Mr. Linzer found it profitable to let the whole of the upper part of his premises to Mrs. Glatt, a ponderous middle-aged German woman, who paid her way by sub-letting all but the two rooms occupied by herself and her brother Karl, a jobbing tailor.

The attention of the boy at the upper window swerved from a sluttish female sitting on a doorstep, fanning herself with a newspaper, to a dog that was nosing along the gutter

7

as if trying to cool his nose on the discarded cabbage stalks and fruit peelings—the overflow of the litter of the market round the corner. Some children were dancing to a barrel-organ, radios were blaring from upper windows, a pedlar with tins of brass-polish was bawling incoherently, women held conversations from one doorway to another, two men were arguing raucously about a racehorse.

And through all these discordancies Vivian Mander could hear, behind him, the monotonous whirring of his mother's sewing-machine.

His rapt attention had not flagged for nearly an hour. The activities of his narrow world fascinated him, but in spite of his attitude of serious contemplation he would have been a perfect model for a study of a gipsy boy; beneath his mop of blue-black curls his features were firmly drawn, his skin had the dark bloom of a ripe peach, his brown eyes, over which the thick straight brows almost met, were lively even when he was in repose. Suddenly, as Mrs. Glatt came round the corner with a live eel curling itself out of her shopping basket, he laughed delightedly. Mrs. Glatt was broad and short, her perennial black felt hat was crammed on to her thick grey hair, her coat dragged back from the grip of its one button. She was unaware of the eel's movements until it curled round her bulging ankles, then she gave a leap that renewed Vivian's laughter.

"What's so funny?" His mother was raising her voice above the noise of the treadle. "Anyway, you're leaning out too far."

"Mrs. Glatt nearly lost an eel. Ooh, it's still wriggling."

"I'm sure I don't know how she can eat the things."

"She cooks lots of things we don't have. Foreign things, when I'm in bed I can smell them, the steam comes up the stairs."

"It's time you stopped sleeping on that top landing."

"I guess what they're having and next day I ask her. If I guessed right I score it on the wall. A cross for a win and a nought for a failure."

"As soon as she's got a room I'll see what we can do."

He protested. "But I like the landing. Through the sky-light I can see the stars."

Mrs. Mander was silent for several minutes, concentrating

on her work. She said suddenly, "There are two sets of scores on that wall of yours. What's the other one for?"

Vivian shuffled self-consciously. "One's for guessing what's being cooked."

"And haven't you told me that already. What's the other?"

"Oh——" He shrugged uneasily. "It's nothing special." The second column of scores registered how many boys he had conquered, not by fighting them but by forcing his will upon theirs. He had made boys perform all sorts of antics. Sometimes when he ordered them he had to break down their refusals, sometimes he dominated them just by staring and concentrating.

The whirring of the sewing-machine continued like the buzzing of a trapped insect. When it ceased he knew without turning that his mother was filling the kettle, setting it on the stove in the corner. Then she went on machining without having lit the gas, and that meant she was longing for a cup of tea but hadn't time to make it yet. What would it be like to be blind, to have to understand nearly everything through your ears? Vivian closed his eyes and was acutely aware of individual voices of people in the street below, of the rising and dwindling sounds of traffic near and far, but as he listened pictures of the familiar scenes shaped themselves beyond his lowered lids. He liked experiments, but this one was no good; when he opened his eyes he rubbed them as if emerging from a dream.

This was his mother's bed-sitting-room, kitchen, and workroom all in one. His own bed on the landing above was behind a screen with old theatre programmes pasted all over it. *The Wind and the Rain. Vortex. Hamlet. The Rose without a Thorn.* Some of the programmes were tattered and one of his games was guessing the missing words. On the landing he could hear all the friendly rhythm of the house, the soft pad-pad of Mrs. Glatt's slippers as she crossed her landing to argue with her brother, the clicking heels of the elderly typist who had the room opposite his mother's, the tired sigh of Dolly Hart as she paused on the stairs to get her breath. She was a waitress, and occupied one of the top rooms; the old Russian Wyganowski, had the other.

"Hi, Vivian!"

Tom Cray was shouting up as he raced along the opposite

pavement on his new scooter. Vivian made for the door, followed by his mother's caution, "It's nearly tea-time, you mustn't be long," and as he bounded into the street was met by a volley of boasts about the scooter. He said, "I've got something better."

"What?" challenged Tom.

Vivian shouted. "My window. My spy-hole on the world." A trio of Frenchmen passed, talking volubly. "Why do you think nearly everybody's foreign in this street?"

"Because it's Soho. Soho's always foreign."

"Yes," Vivian persisted, "but what started to make it foreign? Why is it suddenly English when you turn the corner into Regent Street?"

"Oh, you're always asking questions."

"If you get the answers you get more and more powerful."

Tom was obviously inattentive. He screwed up a ball of paper and threw it at the back of a passing policeman. "You'll never be powerful," he mumbled.

"But I *am*. I will people to do things. You've seen me do it, you've seen me ordering boys and compelling them."

"Not often," Tom grudged.

"But you know it's true." Two dogs began to fight and Vivian exclaimed, "It's not fair, the bulldog's bigger."

"You say you're so clever," Tom taunted, "what about willing the bulldog to give up?"

"I'm not clever, I never said I was, I'm powerful."

"Then stop them."

"All right then, I can." Vivian stared at the dogs, which were snapping and snarling on and off the pavement edge. They continued, and with a miserable awareness that he was failing just when he was anxious to demonstrate his talent, he muttered, "Stop fighting, stop fighting."

Tom guffawed. "You're supposed to do it without talking. You never said a word when you made Peter Swain climb that ladder. Anyway, they're not taking a bit of notice."

"It's because they're animals, not like people. Dogs are different, they haven't got the same brains, it's silly trying to compel dogs." Eager to justify his claim, Vivian added, "You ought to see my score. Every time I dominate anyone I mark it on the wall over my bed. I put a cross and that means a conquest."

"Well then, force me to do something."

"I don't want to. I only do it when I feel like it. I wouldn't do it now if you gave me a million pounds. I say, there's Johnny Johns. He's famous, you know."

"He's not. He's just an acrobat."

Johnny Johns waved to them. His act consisted of juggling with two swords while standing on his head, and his usual pitch for the performance was near the Irving statue in Charing Cross Road. Vivian had watched several times, but always slipped away unseen, having a respect for the pride with which Johnny bragged about his music-hall engagements. Who was to blame if they were only imaginary? "He's a great artist," Vivian asserted. "The agents keep trying to send him on world tours, to top the bills. Anyway, it's absolutely true he's been to Paris, he's got a signed photograph of Maurice Chevalier."

"I've got one of Douglas Fairbanks. It's in my room."

"You don't have a room to yourself?"

"I do, don't you?"

"Well, more or less."

Luckily Tom scooted away without demanding details. The top landing was more fun than a room, the two who lived up there usually stopped for a word as they squeezed between the banisters and the screen alongside his bed. Wyganowski lay in bed most of the day and went out at night. No one knew what he did for a living. He had shaggy grey eyebrows that were like moustaches and a great square beard, black as a stove, and throughout the year he wore a round astrakhan cap and long overcoat. Often he was in a talkative mood, rambling on about strange eastern harbours; he had described in detail how corn was ground in Lapland, how his grandmother used to say her prayers in a house by the Black Sea, how to cure a sick reindeer. All the information on scores of subjects flowed and gushed without prompting, or a single question would carry the monologue to the rice fields of China or some old social gathering in St. Petersburg. Life could never last long enough to hear all the answers that Wyganowski could give.

Dolly Hart, in the other room, worked at a café in Oxford Street. She was seventeen, with smooth black hair and a waxen complexion. In her pale pointed face the large hazel eyes were bright, as if with constant anticipation of fun, but she looked frail, and often exhausted. Vivian was sure that she was destined to catch the eye of some nobleman driven by the storm into her café. The storm would be necessary, because on a fine day the prices stuck on the windows might deter anyone of exalted rank.

Tom Cray scooted back. "I say! Over the road!"

"What?—Oh, Mrs. Vautel."

"She's not Mrs. Anything. Everyone calls her Tashy."

"That's short for Natasha," Vivian said. "She's Russian, but not the same kind as Wyganowski. He told me. Her father had a big estate, he was killed in the revolution."

"I expect that's a yarn."

"If it was, Wyganowski would have spotted it."

"Anyway," Tom persisted, "she's a bad woman."

Some obscure impulse prompted Vivian to defend her. "She's good at music. She knows all about all the music that's ever been made up. She's got a grand piano."

The questionable Tashy Vautel had come out of the door beside the gown shop, the smartest frontage in the street, with its gleaming chromium and plate glass and rosy neon lighting. She was a tall dark woman of thirty or so, handsome in a flamboyant way, with broad features made bolder by heavy make-up. She was walking with great self-assurance just a step ahead of her companion, a stout elderly man who moved stiffly and seemed breathless.

Tossing her silver fox cape from one shoulder, Tashy said, "One of these days I shall have a proper flat in a decent neighbourhood. I'll get away from these peasants."

Her sidelong glance set Eddie Roth wondering whether she was including him. "Peasants?" he echoed. "London people can't be peasants."

"People without brains are peasants wherever they are," she said arrogantly. "I want a new piano, that one I've got isn't worth another tuning."

Eddie puffed. "Pianos cost money."

"I thought they gave them away with packets of tea."

Yes, she was despising him. He said testily, "Times are bad enough without talking about pianos."

"When you think of anything original to say, be sure you let me know. You make me tired."

"Now Tashy, you know I love you. I do what I can——"
A girl on the corner gave a quick uncertain smile, and Eddie
touched Tashy's elbow. "Somebody saying hello, dear."

Tashy threw a scornful glance at the girl. "No friend of
mine. I don't stand about propping up the shop windows."

"No, no my dear. I know you don't." But a worried frown
deepened on Eddie Roth's forehead; he was puzzled. A woman
who was so uppish about her neighbours, who could play the
piano so beautifully—of course she was different. Tashy had
a bit of class about her. But you couldn't get away from the
fact that there were only two kinds of women, those who could
be bought and those who couldn't. Resentfully, Eddie Roth
wished that he could think of some scathing phrase. "You're
funny," he said, and her glance pitied his ineffectual comment.
Yes, she was exasperating. But he couldn't break with her,
for with all her tiresome ways she had a kind of magnetism
that was not entirely physical; the depths of her mind were
mysterious, she seemed to be both reckless about her own
interests and at the same time calculating. Whatever she cost
him, he would feel poorer without her.

CHAPTER II

TWO barrow men pushing the remainder of their stocks to
night-time store rooms collided, oranges were rolling in the
road and Vivian helped to collect them. He was given an
orange for his trouble, and exclaimed "There Tom, you see.
I've told you watching people is more fun than haring along
on a scooter. They're all different. The man in the cap was
swearing and the other one just laughed, though they were
both in the same mess. Here——" Vivian held out half of the
orange.

Tom accepted it scornfully. "People! You can have them."

As he scooted away again a bunch of girls came along.
They had just come out of the cigarette factory round the
corner and were pushing each other and squealing, then they
were pointing at the hats in the milliner's window on the

corner and laughing in shrill voices, pretending to deride what they coveted. Groups of women were arguing and gossiping, standing in the way of pedestrians. A couple were walking in the middle of the road as if to emphasize their aloofness, the woman lifting her cloudy blue skirts and smiling automatically at her escort's talk. They stopped to argue as to whether they were going in the right direction and the man exclaimed impatiently "All the streets going this way lead towards Regent Street, we can't be wrong if we zig-zag."

Evidently one of the factory girls had made some comment, for the couple glanced sharply in their direction. The woman shrugged her white-furred shoulders and the man said "What can you expect?"

Within a yard or so of Vivian the woman paused and mused aloud, "What can it be like, *living* in a street like this?"

They went on. What can it be like . . . ? The echo remained in Vivian's mind. Would living somewhere else be better? He had never before considered the point. The woman had spoken in almost a pitying way. But surely there was nothing terrible about Sidley Street? It had all sorts of advantages. When he had a few coppers he could get to Charing Cross Road in less than five minutes to search for treasures in the boxes outside the bookshops. There was plenty of excitement; only last week a gambling club over Loo Wong's restaurant had been raided, and before that two Maltese had had a fight on a top floor and one of them had been flung out of the window—landing, fortunately for his antagonist, on a cart filled with sacks of cabbages.

Vivian tried to think of some disadvantages. But he liked even his school, which was best on Wednesdays because on that day they were taken to the swimming baths. Sometimes he went to the pictures with other boys and they all had a sense of triumph when they slipped past a commissionaire to see an A-film—though why there was any attempt to exclude them they couldn't imagine, for they had never learnt anything from the adult entertainment that they could not have seen in real life. Husbands and wives going wrong, girls running away from home and taking to night clubs, men getting drunk—it all happened in reality often enough to be boring, and if you kept your ears open you heard things that would never get on to the sound track at any cinema.

On Sundays he and the gang sometimes went to Hyde Park, or when they had the bus fares, to Regent's Park. He never joined in baiting the keepers, for those who did so always looked silly when they were chased away. He had been to Brighton several times and once to Southend; he had the best pen-knife of anyone he knew, and an enormous stamp album that his mother had bought second-hand in the market. He had an orange box stuffed with books and labelled 'Mander's Library', and sometimes another boy would pay a penny for the privilege of borrowing a volume.

He went indoors and found his mother still thrusting at the treadle of her machine. He asked "Mother, what is it *like*, living here?"

"The questions you do ask!"

"Anyone could be unhappy, anywhere," he mused.

"Of all the old-fashioned ways to talk. I believe there's going to be a storm, the light's so bad. My eyes are tired." She leaned back, blinking as she pulled her work from the machine. Black rustling silk. "I've got to finish this by seven o'clock. Turn the gas down, we can't have tea for a few minutes yet."

Vivian lowered the gas beneath the kettle. "Is someone going to fetch the dress?"

"I'll have to take it." The words were nipped by the row of pins held in her lips.

"Where to?"

"Along to Curzon Street. Near Piccadilly."

"I'll take it for you."

"You will not. I'm not having you traipsing about at all hours."

"I haven't got any home-work. I could take a bus."

"You're not going to take it and that's that. Don't plague me. Anyway there's some money to collect."

"You know I'd take care of it. How much will it be?"

"Two pounds fifteen shillings. Two pounds ten for the making, I said, she can't object to five shillings for the binding and the bit of net."

"I'll put it in the pocket inside my jacket." Vivian spoke as if it had been decided that he should go. He wanted to act as messenger, to stand at the door of a rich house, perhaps be allowed inside it, to investigate further the problem of what living here, there, or anywhere else might be like. It was a fascinating problem; he was grateful to the woman in the cloudy blue dress for having started his speculations.

He mooned about the room, then sat on the bed and glanced at a fashion paper. The dullest thing he had ever seen; rows of ladies all the same shape. He rose and played with the things on the chest of drawers, two combs, a brush, a cardboard box of face-powder, several bunches of patterns of silk, a spring tape measure. In the oblong of mirror he could see his mother, her hair that was the colour of sand was drawn back into a knob. She had a small face, and perhaps she was too thin and pale, but he liked her as she was. There was a photograph of her with wavy hair put away in a drawer. One day Mrs. Glatt had a glimpse of it when the drawer was open, and exclaimed "My-my! Vot a pewtiful girl!" and his mother had given a queer little laugh as she said "It's me".

That was how he knew she was forty-one, for she had said it was taken twenty-one years ago, and Mrs. Glatt, still goggling at the picture, had guessed "You vos eighteen, maybe?" and his mother had said it was taken on her twentieth birthday. Then Mrs. Glatt said again that it was pretty, adding vaguely what a shame it all was.

Vivian opened the drawer a few inches and studied the picture that looked like someone else. No, he wouldn't want his mother to be like that now. For ever smiling. Her name was written on the corner. Norah. He asked "Where did you live when you were twenty years old?" (Another clue, perhaps, to the problem of living conditions.)

"In London."

"But what part?"

"Hampstead."

"Will you take me and show me the house?"

"No I will not. I've forgotten the house. Switch on the iron for me."

He knew that she remembered. "Was it your father's house?"

"The blessed boy!" she exclaimed. "No it was not. It was an apartments house."

"I only thought—— Lots of people live in their father's houses, even when they're twenty."

She leaned forward to drop the remainder of the pins from

her mouth, then turned and looked at him searchingly. "Has anybody been talking to you?"

"Talking? No, not specially, why?"

He had switched on the iron and was unfolding the ironing board.

"Your father was killed in an accident."

"I know."

"Then will you stop complaining because you don't live in his house?"

"I wasn't." Somehow, deep down, she was upset, or she wouldn't have twisted his inquiry that way. He recognized her mood and wondered—not realizing his own precocious sensitivity—whether a grown-up would have been able to discern the cause of it. It occurred to him again that he was always told about his father's death in just that same hard phrase. Killed in an accident. Other boys, Jimmie Simpson for instance, lived with their mothers in lodgings. But Mrs. Simpson had a photograph of a fierce-looking sergeant-major in a gilt frame, and attached to the frame there was a medal. That settled it that Jimmie's father had been in the army and had died of wounds in a foreign country. Tom Cray's father had died of pneumonia and his grave was in the churchyard of St. Anne's. In each case there was something to prove that those men had once lived. But his own father had neither a medal nor a tombstone; it was as if he had never existed.

Vivian began to lay tea on the end of the table not occupied by the pile of dress materials. His mother was now sewing by hand, and without looking up she said "You're a good boy."

"But I like setting the table. I'm a butler in a palace." He touched a plate with a pattern of blue spots and said "Inset with genuine sapphires."

"You and your fancies."

"Mother——"

"What is it now?"

"Tom Cray's mother said we must be Irish."

"And why does she think so?"

"Because of the way you speak."

"To be sure I'd never notice it. My father came from Dublin when he was a bit of a boy, more fool him. If it hadn't been for the London fogs, he might be alive today."

Even *her* father had a genuine death. "And Tom Cray's mother said the Irish get hobgoblins mixed up with the truth."

"Was she calling you a liar, then?"

"She said I didn't know where imagination began or ended. But that's all rot."

"You tell Mrs. Cray to mind her own business."

"The kettle's boiling."

"And can't I hear it? We're late. You can make the tea and cut yourself some bread and start. I shan't be a few minutes, it's just the press-studs on the belt—— No, you know better than that. Put the bread on the board, do, and use the knife downwards."

He ate bread-and-jam, watching her deft movements at the ironing-board. A grand lady would wear that dress, and she was welcome to the dingy black thing. He would like to see his mother in gay clothes. Hanging with everyday things in the cupboard in the corner there was a long dress made of soft stuff printed with roses and lilac trails. He said "The very first money I earn, will you dress up and let me take you out for the evening?"

"You'll have to learn to spend money properly."

"But we should both enjoy it. Isn't that the properest way to spend money?" Her smile encouraged him and he added, "It would be a sort of celebration, something for me to remember."

"Mercy sakes!" Her smile flashed off. "Sometimes you worry me, you do really. Talking about something to remember. That's middle-aged talk, it's old talk. Young things don't know that anything's worth remembering, they just take what comes."

"I want to store it——" Vivian laid a hand across his forehead, "in here. And I want to have so much, so much to store that my head will be stuffed bung-full."

"I'm sure I don't understand you. Pour me a cup of tea, will you?"

"There it is, didn't you see me put it handy? You're going to let me take that parcel to Curzon Street, aren't you mother?"

"Oh get on with your tea."

"But that's just why I was eating so quickly. To be ready."

She edged round the ironing board, turned off the switch,

and sat down. He pursued his advantage. "I'll get a bus from opposite the Palace, outside the fire-station. A penny ticket. Where do I get off? At this end of Piccadilly? Or half-way down? Or Hyde Park Corner?"

"At the Ritz. That's the stop after the one the other side of the Circus."

"That's easy."

"You turn up opposite Green Park. Half Moon Street would be best I think. You mustn't hang about. Really—I think at this time of the evening I ought to go."

"But it's settled." He rose and climbed on a chair to reach a box on top of the dresser. "This'll keep the dress from crumpling. I'll bring the box back."

"However you got that old head on your shoulders I don't know, you think of everything. Where's my purse?—Here you are, a penny each way. And you'd better take these two half-crowns, people never seem to have any change. If they give you three pounds, give them the five shillings. And write 'paid' on the bottom of the bill, and your name. And then put 'with thanks'."

He scrubbed his hands at the sink and ran a comb through his hair, wishing it would lie decently flat instead of springing back into curls. Then he was about to fold the dress when his mother leapt up.

"Take care. You may be a little Mister Clever but there are some things you can't do." She smoothed the silk, folding it over tissue paper, then she wrote the address clearly at the top of the invoice form. Vivian waited, smiling secretly. He was going to deliver the dress after all the argument about it at the start. He had made his mother obey him. That was another success to mark on the wall upstairs.

CHAPTER III

THE bus ride was all too short, for Vivian felt that in another few minutes he and the conductor might have become friends for life. Never had anyone answered questions more readily. But now they were passing the colonnade of the Ritz, slowing down. There was just time to inquire, "What part of London do you live in?"

"You're a one! What's it matter to you? Clapham."

"If you don't mind—— What's it like there?"

"Green Park!" shouted the conductor. The bus was at the stop.

"I mean, what's it like where you live?"

"'op off quick if this is where you want, son."

With an impression of Clapham as an expanse of parkland, Vivian watched the bus, an exciting boxfull of human beings, bobbing down the slope. Clapham might be all houses without a blade of grass. The question should have been asked earlier, and now he and the conductor would probably never meet again. A death parting—the phrase had come into a film; he was filled with a sense of self-importance as he felt that he had shared in this experience, for if they never met again—and death was surely ahead of both of them, some time—obviously that's what their shouted good-byes had been. After being such true friends for at least six minutes.

He waited for the traffic to flow by, crossed, and when he saw that Half Moon Street was just ahead, could not resist asking a policeman where it was.

"Up there on the right," said the policeman, adding genially, "Taking the washing home, eh me boy?"

Another friend—"Do I look like a washerwoman's son?"

"You'd better get along, whatever you are."

"My mother is the Duchess of the Wye Valley." That had puzzled the copper, according to plan. Now would it be possible to make him scratch his chin? That would make it a definite experiment. Vivian continued "Any time you go to Hereford you can see her name in the mosaic on a pavement opposite the Cathedral."

He was ready with further improvisations, but already the story had set the man scratching his chin. So this could be scored on the wall as a success. It was queer—he raked his mind for a word—how bendable people were. "I ordered you to scratch your chin," he said.

"Ordered?"

"Yes. Silently."

"Run along now, run along."

"One of these days I'm going to write my secret orders

down, in advance, then people will believe me." Vivian walked on.

A plump red-cheeked woman in a blue cotton dress opened the door of the house in Curzon Street. Her chin receded and the point of it looked like a button at the top of her festoons of flesh. "Yes?" she rapped. "This isn't the tradesmen's entrance, you know."

Vivian said importantly, "I've got a special delivery for Mrs. Trafford."

"All right. I'll take it."

"But I must give it to her personally. With my own two hands. And there's a document to be signed, sealed, and delivered."

"You play-acting little monkey."

"I'm responsible to my superior——" No, he couldn't expect to be believed if he said 'officer'. He substituted "partner".

"Oh come on in."

In spite of her tone the woman seemed amiable. Her wide hips waggled as she led the way into an immense room, and he was tempted to slap her behind just to see how she would treat such a piece of impudence. He refrained, realizing that his chances of observing this grand interior might depend on the woman's temper. "I'll take the dress to madam," she said. "You can wait here."

"There's two pounds fifteen to pay," he said.

"Madam doesn't go about swindling people. You can sit down if you want to."

She went out, closing the door, but he did not waste time by sitting down. Only in a museum had he seen such elegant pieces of furniture, and some of them were topped by ornaments fit—he decided—for a royal palace. Yet there was a kind of simplicity about it all. Of course these people did not cook and sleep and work in one room, in fact they never worked at all. Surely they got bored, just sitting and looking at the carpet that felt like velvet? Or at the mirror with a frame obviously made of pure gold? The chandelier was dripping with diamonds and the ceiling was a huge picture of women dancing with hardly any clothes on and trailing vine leaves. One of them was like Mrs. Collins, who scrubbed out George's Dining Rooms, the same broad pink face, but if you told Mrs. Collins she had a twin sister painted on a ceiling, wearing practically nothing, she would probably throw her bucket at you, to teach you not to be saucy. She had a shocking temper——

"Hullo."

Vivian started. In this magnificent and bewildering room he had thought he was alone. But a boy of about his own age was in a chair by the big fireplace. He was in pyjamas, with a shawl over his knees. Rather a feeble looking boy, with fair hair that was too long and freckles that seemed to have faded. "Oh, hullo," Vivian hoped he did not sound surprised.

"Who are you?"

It was queer how quietly the boy had been sitting there. Watching slyly—"That's my business," Vivian said. Then he realized that more might be gained by being civil. He inquired "What is it like, living here?"

"Awful. Rotten."

"Don't you enjoy—well, all this?" Vivian waved one hand. Then, feeling that the pure gold mirror must be included, he swung the other.

"It's the dullest, deadliest house in the world. I hate it. It's lousy."

"Well, you must be fairly decent or you wouldn't have told me. I was rather expecting you to boast, you know. My name's Vivian Mander. What's yours?"

"Philip Trafford. I'm eleven. How old are you?"

"I thought you were about ten." For a moment Vivian toyed with the idea of saying that he too was eleven. Or what about twelve? But then the other boy might say he was small for his age, and score a point. "I'm practically eleven."

"Do you go to school?"

"Of course."

"I wish I did."

"Don't you? I could put an inspector on to you." Vivian added hastily "But I won't, I'm not a sneak. I say, is it your bed time?"

"Not yet."

"Then why did you get undressed?"

"Some days I'm in pyjamas all day long."

"Tell me another."

"It's true," Philip insisted. "Mrs. Allberry won't put me to bed for another hour. That was Mrs. Allberry, who brought you in."

"*Put* you to bed?"

"I can't walk, you see."

Was this just a yarn? Vivian moved closer. With that pale face Philip was like a sick girl. He had a soppy sort of mouth, as if he was just ready to cry all the time. There was a table on each side of his chair. Games and jigsaw puzzles and a whole pile of picture books——

Perhaps it was true. "Why can't you walk?"

"I'm a mysterious case," Philip said almost proudly. "I stopped walking in the holidays after my first term at school. Mummy took me to Switzerland last winter. And since then Daddy's paid two hundred pounds for a doctor to come from Vienna. I have massage every morning. Do you know, I've cost thousands of pounds altogether."

"Well, what's wrong with you?"

"Paralysis. My legs."

"I thought only old people got that." Vivian found a stool and sat on it; all this was highly entertaining.

"I've got a wheel chair," Philip said. "I race it up and down the hall. My room's at the back, over the garden. I'll show you, if you like. It's got a balcony."

"I wouldn't mind seeing it." Vivian was seething with curiosity. "But I'd better wait and collect the money for the dress."

"Mummy has to save on clothes because I cost so much. People say she dresses very cleverly."

"Hang it all, it's *my* mother who dresses her cleverly, all yours has got to do is to fasten the hooks or something."

"I mustn't be annoyed because of my temperature."

"Blow your temperature."

Philip, offended, remained silent. Vivian rose to experiment with a cigarette box that shot up a row of cigarettes as it was opened. He'd have to tell Tom Cray all about this, it would make that scooter look pretty cheap.

"Mummy and Daddy are going to a dance," said Philip. "They call it going out to dinner, so they won't hurt my feelings, because it seems a shame if they can dance if I never shall. But I know it's a dance. Yvonne told me."

"Who's Yvonne?"

"Mummy's maid."

"What made you so you can't walk?"

"I was bathing. I came out of the sea. Dr. Turnbull says I might have stayed in too long. Then I had a scrap with another boy, a beast with red hair, his name was Alfred."

"My favourite name," Vivian decided on the impulse of the moment. Again he dropped on to the stool and sat with his jaw cupped in his hands, prepared to enjoy the account of the beast Alfred. "Who won the scrap?"

"I did, really. But I fell over."

"If you fell over, he won."

"I don't care who won. I called him a dirty swine and he kicked me. Hard. Right in the back."

"Then he *was* a dirty swine. Stinking. I made a mistake about liking the name, it's not really my favourite."

"I couldn't get up. They had to carry me into the hotel. Then they fetched a doctor."

To Vivian it sounded an unlikely story. "If anyone kicks you," he demurred, "you might feel a bruise for a day or two. I don't see how it can lay you out for ever." He added dubiously, "Where were you bathing?"

"Weymouth. Have you ever been to Weymouth?"

"Not very often." Vivian added quickly, "I prefer Southend."

"Oh. I've never been to Southend. There are such a lot of places you never see. It's awful."

Vivian took a deep breath. Here was another chap feeling exactly as he did, that it was essential to see everything, everywhere. "Yes, awful," he agreed in a hushed voice. "I say, could you and I be faithful friends, do you think?"

"Yes. Good-o."

"Then I tell you what, you can show me Weymouth and I'll show you Southend."

Mrs. Allberry came in to say that madam was trying on her dress. "Would you like a glass of milk, boy?"

"No thank you. And my name's Vivian." Why must she come butting in? If she stayed she might spoil a perfect friendship.

Mrs. Allberry remarked "Soon be bedtime, Master Philip. If you want to finish your story you'd better get on with it."

Vivian said "We're discussing geography."

"Oh my, what a Mr. Important!"

Mr. Clever, Mr. Important—why did they have to make that sort of remark? Fortunately Mrs. Allberry was bustling out. "It's fixed then. Southend in exchange for Weymouth."

"I hadn't agreed," Philip demurred.

"It's a fair swap." Vivian leapt up. "In fact I'm probably doing you a big favour."

"All right. Don't jump about, I'm not used to it."

"I want to see your room with the balcony."

"I've just remembered, I'll have to show it to you some. other time. They took my wheel chair down to the basement after tea."

"You promised."

"But how *can* I without the chair? Though I don't know, if you called down to Bennett he'd bring it up."

"Who's Bennett?"

"The butler. He's married to cook."

"A butler and a cook and Mrs. Allberry and Yvonne—— Do they all wait on your mother?"

"On all of us."

"Then how many makes up all of you?"

"Mummy and Daddy and me, of course."

"It's a lot of people to fuss over such a few."

"Yes, now I think of it, it is," Philip agreed. "I say, couldn't we kill some of them off?"

"Easy. We'll put a bomb under cook and Yvonne. That's unless you're just inventing them."

"I swear I'm not. We'll use gunpowder."

"With a time fuse, the sort burglars use for safes." As Vivian concurred he had a pleasant vision of two females disintegrating against the evening sky.

"My father's a colonel, he's in the regular army, he knows a lot about explosives."

Vivian improvised readily, "Mine was an admiral, an absolute expert."

"Oh!"

"What's the matter?"

"I've just remembered, it's Bennett's evening off. That's why Mrs. Allberry let you in."

"So what about me seeing your room?"

"It's a rotten shame," Philip said. "But you can't."

"I might."

"Well, it's the room right at the end of the hall."

"You've got to show it to me."

"I've told you, I've told you, I can't."

Obstinately, Vivian contended "If you don't show it to me, then I don't see it."

CHAPTER IV

THE argument had become a battle of wills. Vivian changed his tactics, saying with affected carelessness, "I don't care whether or not I see your rotten room. I'm not interested. But you could show it to me if you wanted to. It's just that you're a stubborn pig."

Philip's girlish mouth trembled. "I wish Mrs. Allberry would come back, she'd stop you talking like that."

"You're stingy, that's the trouble. You're too stingy to use your feet."

"Don't be a swine."

Vivian walked to the door, making a pretence of departure. "If you're a stubborn donkey I'm finished with you."

Philip was on the verge of tears. "I'm not stubborn. I can't even stand."

Now Vivian's affection of rage became almost a reality. He swung round, "Of course you can stand, you liar!"

"Shut up! Shut up!"

Yes, it was silly to shout. If they made a row someone else might come in and that would be the end of this experiment. Vivian said more quietly "Of course you can. You're only fooling everybody. You can't fool me. My mother was a princess in St. Petersburg, she's taught me not to be taken in by dirty little cads." This was getting results; Philip's face was twitching and he was gripping the arms of his chair as if about to rise. Vivian continued ruthlessly "Stand up! Stand! Get up! Of course you can, you can, you *can*."

"I can't. I'll prove it. If I hurt myself——"

Vivian was now completely entranced by the situation. Everything but the urge to conquer this boy was forgotten. "Hurt yourself!" he hurled back. "Cowardy-custard. You're ashamed, you're dodging, you're scared I'll find out there isn't a balcony to your room. You sleep in the coal-hole, you sleep in the lavatory. You're pretending you can't walk to stop me finding out you're a liar. Liar, liar!"

"I'm not!"

"Liar! Get up, you fool."

Blubbering, Philip tried to lever himself up. He let go with one hand to wipe his pyjama sleeve across his wet face, and staggered sideways.

"You're cheating," Vivian accused. "Let go with the other hand. Straighten up." He moved from the door and stood in the centre of the room. "Let go, didn't you hear me?"

Philip held out both hands. As he stood unsupported his mouth was agape with fear. He swayed and regained his balance.

"Now walk."

"Don't make me. *Please.*"

"You do what I tell you."

"I'm frightened."

"Come here, it's only about ten steps. I'll measure." Vivian walked across, counting. "All right, it's twelve." He touched Philip's pleading hands. "Only twelve steps." He moved back. "This is the spot. In fact, I've given you half a yard."

Philip took two faltering paces and stopped in bewilderment. "I *can* walk! I didn't know, nobody knew."

"Didn't you hear me tell you to come over here? You haven't come half—not a quarter of the way. Get a move on, will you?"

The two boys were utterly absorbed in their own drama, Vivian already exulting at his conquest, Philip astonished and trembling. Their eyes were fixed on each other as they waged their strange contest, and neither heard the door open, neither saw Philip's mother stopping as if appalled, clutching at the woodwork.

Mrs. Trafford was in middle age and still beautiful, though her beauty was threatened by gauntness. Her hair was dark, expertly dressed in smooth waves, and on her long, clear-cut face the cosmetics were cleverly applied. Her stylish appearance was of the kind to command attention anywhere, and her reputation for dressing in original styles was enhanced by her evasions about the origins of her wardrobe. It was seldom suspected how truly she spoke when she dismissed inquiries by references to a 'little woman round the corner'. Now she was staring in astonishment at her crippled son, tottering towards the son of her most resourceful 'little woman'.

Vivian was counting Philip's steps as he took them. Six. Seven. Philip made a gesture of helplessness and Vivian merely beckoned. Two more steps, and now it seemed that Philip would fall. Mrs. Trafford held a hand across her mouth as if to check some exclamation. She half-turned and saw her husband. He too seemed to be transfixed where he stood. She heard his tense whisper, "Good God!"

"Shift a bit," Vivian ordered. "Do you think I can wait here all night? I take back what I said about you being a liar, you really are rotten on your feet. Come *on*, will you?"

A last step, and Philip had reached him, falling forward, gasping and making sounds that might have been laughter, then their four hands were gripped tightly together.

"There!" Vivian said. "You got here. But you'll have to speed up a lot before I'm satisfied."

The two in the doorway came to life. Mrs. Trafford darted forward and fell on her knees, taking Philip in her arms. Vivian saw that she was in the dress his mother had pressed so carefully. Dragging it all anyhow, crumpling it. Her husband had come in and was mopping his brow, then he was tugging at his dinner jacket as if it was too tight. He was a short square-built man with bushy grey eyebrows, one of which was cut in half by the scar of an old wound, his forehead was furrowed into three separate ridges; his hand dropped from his short grey moustache to his side and now he looked as he were standing at attention at some parade.

"You saw him? Oh Arnold, you *saw* him?" Mrs. Trafford looked up, her thin face beautified by her delight. Vivian relaxed. At first he had feared that he was in for a scolding. He should have been thinking about collecting the money for the dress, not playing games with this blubbery kid.

Mrs. Trafford was still kneeling, holding Philip. Her husband said "Here, let me take him," and lifted Philip, pressing him against his shoulder, then with his free hand he helped his wife to rise.

Philip mumbled "Pretty good, wasn't it? I came alone, right across the room."

"I saw you, old chap," his father said gruffly. He cleared his throat noisily, whisked out his handkerchief. "Splendid, splendid."

Mrs. Allberry bustled in and was assailed by the three of them telling her the astounding news. "Well of course, Colonel," Mrs. Allberry said, "we're all pleased." Vivian tried to attract their attention, kicking the bureau as if by accident. Were they never going to come to their senses and settle up? Another kick, just to remind them.

The Colonel exclaimed "Who *is* this boy?"

"He brought my *frock*, dear. I just couldn't believe my eyes."

Mrs. Trafford had a way of emphasizing a word or so in nearly every sentence. "Please," Vivian said, "could I have the two pounds fifteen? I've got the bill——" He brought it from his pocket. "I'll write paid on it."

They were not listening. The colonel had taken Philip back to his chair. Mrs. Trafford was saying she felt faint and Mrs. Allberry offered to run for a glass of water. Vivian shifted from one foot to the other; he had been told not to loiter and now it seemed as if he had been here for hours. When the glass of water was brought Mrs. Trafford put it on a small table, and knocked it over. The tinkling of broken glass seemed to emphasize the enormity of delay.

"Get me a drink, a real drink," Mrs. Trafford said.

"Please——" Vivian began again.

But Mrs. Trafford was still talking. "I'm all to *bits*. I didn't know I was such a weakling. But *really*, Arnold, it's such a *thrill*."

The Colonel asked Philip, "Could you stand up again, old chap, and show us how you do it?"

Philip shook his head, a lock of fair hair jumping away from his forehead.

"But if you did it once——"

Still Philip refused. To cut the argument short Vivian said "Perhaps he's tired. After all, if he's not used to—— What I mean is, this is a pretty big room. He could do another

walk tomorrow." He just remembered to add, as he caught a
glowering glance from under the heavy brows, "Sir."

To his wife the Colonel rapped, "*Who* did you say this
boy is?"

How slow they were. Mrs. Trafford was taking a small
glass from a tray, sipping it. Vivian said "I'm Vivian Mander.
My mother's waiting and if I don't get back she'll be anxious.
Please could I have the money?"

"The money!" The Colonel spoke explosively. "Of course,
of course, we're not thinking about——"

Mrs. Trafford interrupted "After this, how can we possibly
go out and be all social? I'd be gibbering."

"We'd better ring Turnbull," the Colonel said. "I mean
we must do everything to maintain the—the cure, the
improvement." He made a gesture towards the telephone at
the far end of the room. "Mrs. Allberry, you might ring up
Lady Podswell, her number's there somewhere. Tell her we're
extremely sorry—er—— Not to wait for us. We may be there
later. M'm, I don't know. Oh tell her anything."

"Yes sir."

Vivian walked to the door and came back to fix his eyes
significantly on Mrs. Trafford.

"Arnold, dear. The boy's *still* waiting to be paid."

"Paid, paid? How much is it?"

"Two pounds fifteen, please sir. Here's the invoice."

"Invoice be blowed. One, two, three. There you are, give
your mother three pounds. And there's another pound for
yourself, just to mark the occasion. You don't realize what
this evening means to us, me lad. I expect you like toy
soldiers or some such nonsense."

"I don't like toy soldiers," Vivian spoke stiffly. He picked
up three of the notes that had been flung on the gilt and
ebony table. "Thank you all the same, sir. There's your
change. I'm pretty sure my mother wouldn't want to be
tipped anything extra." He put down the two half-crowns
and fumbled for the pencil to write the receipt.

Ignoring the coins, the Colonel had moved back to Philip.
"You all right, old chap?"

Philip was asleep. Mrs. Allberry had been making excuses
on the telephone and was now beside the Colonel. Both of them
were gazing anxiously at the boy, who, now that his pale face

was devoid of all expression, looked more babyish than ever. "I'll carry him to bed, sir. He ought to rest soundly tonight." Mrs. Allberry glanced at Vivian. "I'll see him out first."

Vivian handed over the invoice, receipted with extravagant flourishes. "Thank you, sir. I must hurry."

"What?—Oh yes. Look, you're leaving the odd pound. Take it, and the five bob, there's a good lad. Buy your mother something."

"Well," Vivian was struck by a sudden idea, "yes after all, thank you sir." He picked up the money. "And please can I have the box back?"

"Box?"

"The dress box."

But the Colonel was incurably inattentive. It was Mrs. Trafford who told Mrs. Allberry, "Leave Master Philip for a minute, and *get* the box."

Mrs. Alberry went out and the Colonel began to pace backwards and forwards. "Absolutely extraordinary—— Mind you, Dorothy, I always felt sure it would be all right, Philip's basically healthy. But it's devilish queer how it's happened."

"Yes. Very strange."

"A bit of a surprise. H'mm. For both of us, eh?"

"Yes, Arnold."

"Poor darling, you do look shaken."

"After *all* we've done, after *all* the disappointments."

"It's miraculous."

Vivian could stand no more of this. He said clearly, "Philip walked because I told him to. I wanted him to show me his room. He says it's got a balcony and I've never been on a balcony, only sort of looked up at them. It was only an experiment."

The silence that followed his explanation made him feel awkward. He went to the door, but swung round at the Colonel's sharp challenge.

"What do you mean? An experiment? You 'told' him?"

Vivian met the Colonel's eyes and felt relieved. The questions were quite straightforward, not hidden threats. The short square man looked almost unhappy. "You see, sir, if you tell people strongly enough, I mean if you tell them and really mean it, and you're prepared to die if they don't obey, they do obey."

"Well I'm——!" The expression ended in a puffed out breath.

"It's my own game. I call it dominating. I make my mother obey. I've made a lot of people obey. Sometimes they don't know I've done it, but they've been conquered all the same. I made Philip obey. Really he was fairly easy. We'd just agreed to be friends for life, through thick and thin."

The Colonel seemed to be struggling for breath. Vivian gave him a chance to reply and as no words came he moved again to the door, where he turned to give a courtly bow, so deep that the pencil in his pocket dug into his ribs. That sort of thing went with enormous houses and grand people in evening dress—and anyway, it was one more gesture to puzzle them. Phew! The hall was as big as Loo Wong's restaurant. Mrs. Allberry was running downstairs with the cardboard box. What luck. He might have forgotten it, after all. He patted the notes in the inside pocket of the jacket that was too small for him, and made a dignified exit.

CHAPTER V

THE side door was usually closed at dusk, but as Vivian approached it he saw that it was open. And his mother was there, waiting. "Mercy!" she exclaimed, "you've been a time. Whatever kept you? I thought you'd been run over."

"I haven't been so long." He knew that his voice was sulky.

"It's just on two hours," Mrs. Mander rapped.

"Sorry," he growled.

She took the cardboard box. "Was it satisfactory? Did she try it on?"

Vivian improvised "Oh yes. She wanted me to tell you, she'd never been so pleased with anything in her whole life."

"Really?"

They were in the hall, and as his mother struck a match to light their way he saw the gleam of pleasure on her pale face. At that moment he wanted nothing more than to be able to invent some stupendous tale that would make her happy, not for a fleeting minute, but for ever. This was the moment to take a chance. "Mother——"

"Run on up. Stop dragging your heels."

"I'm tired."

A door was standing ajar, yielding a glimmer up the second flight. Mrs. Glatt was in her brother's back room and they were jabbering in their own language.

Home. So much better than rooms full of gold and diamonds. "Mother——" Again he had to stifle a yawn.

"Did she pay you?"

"Here it is." He brought out the three pounds, the two half-crowns, and then his own note. "The gentleman wouldn't take your change and he gave me a pound for myself."

"Whatever for?"

"Oho." Vivian yawned. "They've got a boy, a really cissy-boy and he's an invalid or something."

"Whatever's that got to do with it?"

The sharpness of the inquiry, the touch of suspicion, filled Vivian with a sense of injustice. But he knew that the truth would be forced out of him if he failed to give it readily. "Philip, he's called. He hasn't been able to walk for—oh, I don't know how long. Years."

"Well?"

"Me and him—I mean he and I, we had an argument. In the end I told him to walk and he did. That's all."

"Oh Vivian, Vivian!"

What was wrong? His mother sounded as if she were despairing. After all, he hadn't done any harm. She had dropped on to the chair by her machine and was looking as if the end of the world had come. Then she was plucking, as if automatically, at some fluff in the spool-holder. "Oh Vivian, I don't understand you."

Yes, she looked quite miserable. He edged round the table and patted her arm. "There's nothing to fret about. Mrs. Trafford put the dress on and she liked it awfully, and they were all extra pleased because of Philip."

"You—you really made a cripple walk?"

"He's got two legs. I expect he wasn't as ill as they all made out."

"Oh Vivian my boy, if only——"

B

She broke off, shooting the spool back into the socket, sliding the chromium plate that covered it. He always cleaned and oiled the machine on Saturdays and its brightness filled him with pride. "Mother, I didn't take the pound at first. Then I had a spiffing idea. I'm going to give you a treat."

She wasn't listening. She was staring at the machine as if she had never seen it before. And now the wall. Then she picked up a length of muslin and was rolling the edge automatically. "You're going to dress up," he said, "and I'm going to take you out to dinner."

"No." She threw down the muslin and forced her attention with a visible effort. "Don't talk nonsense. I'll get you something to eat. It's time you were in bed."

"Let's go out in the evening tomorrow."

She was silent for a full minute before she said "Sometimes you frighten me. I don't understand you. You're my own boy and I don't understand you."

"Well, if you'll say what it is you don't understand——"

"I'll get you a slice of bread and jam." She rose and went slowly to the cupboard, then made a gesture of distress as if she wondered why she was there, with one hand on the catch.

"Will you dress up tomorrow evening. In that dress in the other cupboard, the long one with flowers on it? I've never seen you in it."

"The two-piece chiffon, they're not wearing them now." She seemed to be musing aloud, for her tone was different as she asked "You're not lying to me? You really did make that child walk?"

He nodded.

"He's never walked since he was six years old. He's been a grief to the Traffords, a terrible grief and worry. And all the expense. She's spoken of it many a time."

Vivian was at a loss. His mother was sighing, making helpless movements with her hands instead of getting out the loaf and the butter. Anyone would think he had committed a crime. He teetered on the edge of the bed, feeling wronged. As his mother gave him the slice of bread and jam she said suddenly, with brightness that he knew was affected, "It's seldom enough I get out. All right. You can spend that pound taking me out."

"When?"

"Perhaps tomorrow."

"That's what I suggested. Where shall we go?"

"We'll see."

This was a thrilling end to an exciting evening—exciting in spite of all the fuss over that soppy boy. "Tomorrow," Vivian said, "Tuesday."

"Get on or you'll never be up in the morning. There's a kettle of water, finish your jam and get your jacket off. Your nails are terrible. Sure and I'm going to bed early myself."

He hurried over his washing. He had achieved a triumph with Philip, had escaped too severe a scolding for his delay, and his mother had been surprisingly amenable about the idea of having dinner out. It was success enough for one day. He put on his pyjamas. "I'll leave the door open, then I can see. Good night, Mother."

"Good night, Vivian love." She kissed him and, still holding him, said musingly, "You're a strange boy, to be sure."

"Mother——"

"And what is it now?"

"There's a programme on my screen. It's 'The Duchess of D-A-N-Z-, and the end of it's torn off. What's it meant to be?"

"The Duchess of Danzig, I suppose. It's a very old thing."

"When somebody made the screen, were they trying to make a picture out of all their ideals?"

"The nonsense you do think of."

"Oh well. Good night, Mother."

He climbed the top flight of stairs, seeing his way by the light from the open door. He could have walked up these stairs blindfolded, but he liked to see the silhouette of his mother as she watched him. The Duchess of Danzig, he repeated to himself. He would seize the first possible chance to claim the Duchess as a near relative. He edged round the screen and slid into bed and heard his mother close her door. Mrs. Collins who cleaned George's place over the road was going to have a baby; Nina Roberts who lived over the barbers was certain about it, and Nina was thirteen—an age at which she was hardly likely to be wrong. Tashy Vautel's new friend had a cream car and a chauffeur, but he always left the car in Golden Square and walked to Sidley Street, then he would ring the bell beside the gown shop and though no one could be seen the door opened. About an hour later, out they would come, and walk till they found a taxi. Did they think they were carrying on secretly? The chauffeur would wait till his master was safely indoors, and then come along and go into Loo Wong's for a feed. And always took jolly good care, before he came out, to look over the curtains to see his master wasn't about.

I like Tashy Vautel, Vivian thought, but she'll be a million by the time I'm grown up, so even if I've got a cream car and a chauffeur she'll never be mine. Never be mine—— The skylight was a square of pale illumination. It was never really dark, with the lights of the West End so near.

Suddenly he reared up. He had nearly forgotten to mark the score. The policeman. Philip. Mother. Three conquests in one day. Pretty good, that. As he fell asleep he was congratulating himself. No one in the world could be better placed, not even a boy who had a room with a balcony. He wished he could meet the woman who had queried so condescendingly, 'What can it be like, living in a street like this?' He was in a gorgeous restaurant, with liveried footmen in powdered wigs waiting upon him, and opposite sat a young woman in cloudy blue. He was saying "Living in this street is like immortality because no one knows when the first breath was breathed here and anyway you've got a face like a silly doll." Tomorrow mother was going to dress herself up like the Duchess of Danzig.

CHAPTER VI

CARRYING a parcel, Tashy Vautel went in at the side of the gown shop. Among the letters stuck behind a gas-pipe in the narrow hall there was one for her. A French stamp and her daughter's bold childish writing.

Tashy went up and on the first floor landing fumbled for her key. The large front room overlooking the street was in disorder; the bed was only casually made and the clothes she had worn for the last week were slung here and there. Only the grand piano was comparatively free from a clutter of oddments—and even on that there was a bottle of crimson nail varnish, standing on a scrap of tissue paper. Tashy pulled off her hat, threw it on to the muddle of powder boxes, jars, and bottles on the dressing-table, and ripped open her parcel.

Five yards of silk, vividly patterned. She unrolled it and held it up to her chin, studying the effect in the mirror. If only she had ever learned how to sew, she would have made it up herself; as it was, she ruined a stocking if she tried to stop a single ladder, and a hook that came off had to stay off. As she was admiring herself a sudden doubt assailed her. Was she beginning to look middle-aged? She was thirty-two, too young to have those lines under her eyes. She dropped the silk and smoothed her skin upwards with red-tipped fingers, wondering whether a course of face massage would be worth whatever it would cost. She would have to do something about her figure, her curves were getting out of hand. But how she loved rich food, one course after another, with the right wines and liqueurs. It was strange that the English were so slap-dash about their meals, two courses and that was that with most of them, no skill, no art about it. She picked a crystallized peach from the box that Eddie Roth had given her yesterday and ate it slowly, relishing the flavour. How, she wondered, could anyone smoke and blunt the palate to such delights?

The letter lying on the table caught her eye. She tore open the envelope and found a photograph in the fold of note-paper. Olga was nearly nine, and her likeness to her father was growing more pronounced. Etienne had been much too handsome, with his beautifully cut features and fair hair and blue eyes; their marriage had lasted for less than a year and no woman would hold him for long. He might be anywhere by now. Tashy sighed, remembering his gaiety, his escapades, his excuses—always so plausible, and the charm he could produce as easily as another man would pull out a handkerchief. Everyone loved him, she had loved him, but he had the temperament of a spoiled matinee idol, and this, combined with his childish, appealing simplicity, made him impossible to live with; he was always wrong yet never wrong.

Dear Mother, Olga wrote, *Thank you for your letter and the £1 note enclosed. Sister Marie changed it for me and she is taking care of all but fifty francs. I hope you are quite well. On Tuesday we went to Paris by bus, we went into Notre Dame, it is wonderful. The other girls are going home next week for holidays, some time will you let me come home——*

Tashy frowned at her tawdry room, then her expression softened as she glanced at the row of crosses beneath the signature '*your loving daughter Olga*'. The kid was going to be a problem in a year or so—and in less than that time there would probably be a war. Oh well, it was no use crossing bridges before reaching them, the heat was exhausting enough without trying to solve problems that had no answer. The afternoon sun struck right on to the windows, making the room like a hothouse, the noise from the street was even louder than usual.

The doorbell rang and almost automatically she darted to the mirror to slap on powder and lipstick. Who could it be? Not Eddie, surely, for she had seen him only yesterday and he had said he was off to Birmingham. She ran down, opened the street door—"Why, Eddie!"

"Surprised to see me?"

"Yes of course. What about Birmingham?"

"I changed my plans. Hope I'm not interrupting?"

She led the way up, furious at his leering suspicious inquiry. "Interrupting what?"

"Oh nothing. Just thought I'd give you a surprise."

She controlled her expression as they reached her room. All along she had felt Eddie's mistrust, resenting and despising it. This would be the end of him. Yet he was hanging his jacket on a chair, putting a parcel on the table, just as if the place belonged to him. She said "It's too hot for tea, I think I've still got a drop of gin."

He tapped the parcel. "Bottle of Liebfraumilch. Nice cool drink for a day like this." He slid a penknife under the string. "You're all dressed up, aren't you?"

"I've been shopping."

"Better slip into something comfortable."

"I'm comfortable enough." She saw his expression, reflected in the mirror. He was puzzled, but she would not give him any cues that would lead to a quarrel. Disputes were exhausting.

She'd let him stay for half an hour, or long enough to dispose of the wine. "I'll get the corkscrew."

"Aren't you wondering why I didn't phone to let you know I'd be along?"

How men tormented themselves! He was unsure of her yet he had had to manœuvre an occasion that might have given him pain. For in his own way, Eddie was in love with her. The affair couldn't have been of the permanent sort, but while it lasted she was an important part of his life. And here he was, sneaking along, expecting and fearing that he would find someone else here. She said casually, "It's lucky I was in."

"Who's the kid?"

He had picked up Olga's photograph. "Oh, that. The daughter of a friend of mine."

"She's pretty. Yes, she's lovely. Blonde." He glanced at Tashy, back at the photograph. "No relation? No likeness at all, she's got a heart-shaped face."

Tashy took the photograph and slipped it into her handbag. She dropped into the armchair and Eddie said, "You'd be more comfortable with your feet up."

She ignored the suggestion. "I'm ready for my glass."

"You're funny this afternoon."

"Maybe it's the thermometer."

"We ought to have a run down to the coast some time."

"M'm." She took her glass, the wine reflected rainbow colours from various articles in the room. Eddie sat by the table, his shoes half-slipped from his feet. "Good luck, Eddie."

"Been shopping, have you? Anyone go with you?" he asked.

"No. I never need any help when I'm choosing things."

"I thought you might have a boy friend who'd give you some ideas."

There, he had come out with it. "I've known you for four months, Eddie. Do you think I've played around with anyone else in that time?"

He shrugged. "How do I know what you get up to?"

"But we made an arrangement."

"Sure, sure." He tipped up his glass. "But I'm not the first friend you've had.—Ready for some more?" He was holding out the bottle.

"Thanks. Fill it up and I'll drink up. You do the same."

Surprised, he drank his wine as she did, at a draught.

"And again," she said.

"This isn't the way to drink."

"It is when I'm impatient."

He misunderstood and leaned over to embrace her. "No," she said, "I'm not impatient in that way."

"You're in the funniest mood. Can't understand you at all."

"That's the truest thing you ever said." Tashy rose and held the bottle to the light. "Just a drop between us." She poured it out. "Tie your shoes up. You're going now."

The colour drained from his face. "Then there is someone else."

"Put it that way if you like."

"But this isn't treating me fair! I knew I'd catch you, you're expecting someone! You——! I come along with a nice bottle of wine, there's never a cross word between us, and you tell me to get out! I won't have it, understand?"

"There's never been a cross word because I don't quarrel. I think it's a waste of time. I've always taken care to smile when I was furious."

"What have I ever done to make you furious? Tell me that."

"Now Eddie," she spoke patiently as she might have done to a child, "I'm not being caught in an argument. I've been furious often enough. Let's call it my fault. I'll only remind you of one thing, because it fits in now. How often have you made the remark, that there are plenty of other women? You've said it to annoy me, and it's never annoyed me— because come to that, there are plenty of other men. So we'll both be all right. I can't think why you've stuck as long as you have. I play Bach or Beethoven when you want Blue Heaven and do-do-de-o-do."

He exploded. "You're untidy and slipshod and immoral."

Her slight shrug accepted the accusations. Already, to her, this affair was a thing of yesterday, and Eddie no more than someone she had known and rather pitied. As he continued to rail at her she sat down, giving him the advantage, for he was able to shake his fist down at her. He would do neither her nor her home any injury; he had always feared scandal. Probably in his own neighbourhood he was regarded as a pattern of respectability; some of his ready-made catch-phrases were worthy of any mothers' meeting. But now he raged and swore, accusing her of every kind of deceit, of every vice he could rake up from the muddier depths of his mind. It seemed that his collar would burst as he made wild gestures, his voice grew hoarse and his accent lost its veneer of gentility.

"Well?" he challenged as his invective ran out.

She rose. "You put your foot up on the chair and I'll tie the lace."

He dropped back, staring at her in horror. Then with a deep gulp he lifted one foot and tied the lace, and hastily knotted the other. He snatched up his coat and dragged it on, and paused as if trying to think of some acid phrase of farewell. But none came, he was silent, with the expression of a snarling animal, before he went out. Of course he slammed the door, that was to be expected. Tashy took the bottle and two glasses to the section of the landing that was supposed to serve as a kitchen. She dropped the bottle in the garbage-bin, washed the glasses, and put them in the cupboard that stood where a stove would have been, if she had ever done any cooking. Then she went back to her room, slid out of her clothes, and lay on the bed. She felt curiously exhausted, as if the torrent of abuse had been a physical assault. None of it had wounded her, though some of it had been truth, for Eddie had never been close enough to her heart to inflict a wound; her secret pride, her secret shame, had always been immune from his inept attempts to explore them. Tashy closed her eyes, and presently she was sleeping tranquilly.

It was nearly six o'clock when she woke, refreshed, and with a deep sense of relief. Little over half an hour later she folded her dress material into a parcel and took it over the road. Mr. Linzer was just about to close his shop.

"Oh Mr. Linzer—if you don't mind. You'd know a good dressmaker, wouldn't you? I don't want to pay a fortune."

The lace merchant jerked his thumb upwards. "You don't haf to go no further. Mrs. Mander, second floor. Front room."

"Thanks a lot."

"I got some time to spare this efening. Heh?"

"I haven't," Tashy said. She was used to Mr. Linzer's suggestions, they were repetitive but not progressive. His idea of an evening out, according to Mabel, the barmaid at the Duke of York's, was a meal at the Corner House with the display of snapshots of his family as entertainment. Tashy smiled over her shoulder as she turned into the doorway.

A tap on the second-floor doorway, and a boy whom she knew by sight emerged. Vivian, that was his name. This evening his brown eyes were even brighter than usual, as if with anticipation. His hair was wet and obviously he had made an attempt to brush it flat. "Mother's busy," he said. "At least, she's changing. So you can't come in for a minute. I'm taking her out to dinner."

"Starting young, aren't you?" Tashy smiled.

"Well yes, Mrs. Vautel."

Tashy grew serious. "How did you know my name?"

"I've heard some of the other boys—I mean, I just happened to know it."

"You tell the brats to mind their own business."

Mrs. Mander called "Who is it?"

Vivian opened the door an inch or so. "Mrs. Vautel."

Instantly Mrs. Mander was at the door. She was in the long floral chiffon dress that had hung in the cupboard ever since Vivian could remember. "Oh," Tashy exclaimed, "you do look nice."

"What is it? What do you want?" Mrs. Mander was abrupt.

"I've got a length of material. I thought you could make it up for me. It's lovely stuff, pure silk."

"You'll have to get it made somewhere else."

"What, have you got so many orders?"

"Enough."

Vivian stood by impatiently. If these two went on talking he and his mother would never start. Each minute as it passed was something lost for ever. He wondered if he might master Tashy, make her go away, by staring at her. But she was too busy unwrapping her parcel, displaying the silk as if the sight of it might induce a change of mind, saying, "I'd pay you whatever you asked."

"I'm not asking," Mrs. Mander said.

"What's wrong? It's your business, isn't it? I'm not in a hurry, I'd wait a few weeks."

"I don't want your order, Mrs. Vautel."

"So you know my name too! And you pick and choose. It's just too bad I'm not in Debrett." There were plenty of dressmakers, weren't there? But this rejection was humiliating.

Mrs. Mander stepped back into her room, dragging Vivian with her, and closed the door.

Through the door came Tashy's exclamation, "Stuck-up nobodies!" Vivian asked "Mother, why don't you like Mrs. Vautel?"

"She's not our kind."

"But Mrs. Glatt isn't our kind, and Johnny Johns isn't our kind, and Mrs. Cray's different. What *is* our kind?"

"For heaven's sake!"

"Are you nearly ready?"

"Just my hat." Mrs. Mander patted her sandy hair. "It's not in the fashion but it used to suit me."

"You look nice. You look beautiful. I've got my pound note."

She smiled. The irritation of Mrs. Vautel's intrusion was evaporating and now Mrs. Mander was stung by something near to compunction. The woman's affairs had kept her neighbours' tongues bubbling with scandal. But the same man had been about for some months and it might be a permanent affair, not one of a degrading sequence of liaisons. Mrs. Vautel might be settling down, and even if her status wasn't entirely respectable she might be no worse than many who passed as such. But her flashy appearance, her assurance, her peculiar individuality, were a subtle challenge to one's sense of what was decent. "Where's my bag? You're sure your nails are clean? Now we're ready."

Vivian leapt down the stairs two at a time, raced out, then steadied himself to his mother's pace. They turned down Wardour Street, and when they came to St. Anne's Church Mrs. Mander paused to gaze at it. "I like churches."

"Yes, I know. Perhaps some day we could live opposite one."

"We can't pick and choose. But I could spend days looking at them. Perhaps it's the feeling of all the prayers that have been said in them. When I was your age I used to look out of my window at the cathedral, Armagh Cathedral. The kings of Ulster used to be crowned there, two thousand years ago. Oh, the orchards! And the rose gardens all round." Mrs. Mander broke off and sighed. "I suppose they're still there. One day I'll have to go back and see."

"Why don't they have kings of Ulster now?"

"It's all in one with Britain, and loyal they are. Oh it's no use remembering and dreaming, my mother used to say 'Norah', she'd say, 'you'll spend your life dreaming'. Little did she know what my life would be. And there, I've never been inside a church for years, and you only get the religion they give you at school, you're no better than a little heathen."

"I suppose," Vivian ventured, "however rich you were, you couldn't buy a church."

"Dear me no. They're all owned by—it might be the Archbishop of Canterbury. No, he wouldn't exactly own them but—— Oh, come on, do."

She took his hand as they crossed Shaftesbury Avenue. "You haven't told me where we're going."

"To the Adriatic Restaurant."

"Are you going to drink champagne?"

"The idea! We'll just have the dinner. You're to mind your manners."

He smiled. As if he didn't know what to do. He would walk in, snap his fingers just as Clark Gable did, and half a dozen waiters would dart forward to serve them, bowing low, offering the menu.

They had turned into Gerrard Street. "Here we are," his mother said.

CHAPTER VII

LACE curtains were looped across each other within the windows. There was no brilliantly lit portico, no gilded commissionaire to open the door, and to Vivian the exterior of the Adriatic was disappointing. But as he walked in his hopes were revived by the smell of rich cooking, the soft glow of the pink lamps on the table—though the daylight was still bright outside, and the soft hum of conversation that suggested an infinity of exciting secrets. The entrance that he had rehearsed was not materializing; four people at a table just within the door were staring, reminding him that he was a beginner, and he almost slunk behind his mother.

After all, it was correct to let her go first. And now she was saying good evening to a short man with a puffy sallow face and a nearly bald head on which the black side whiskers looked artificial.

"Madame?" As he spoke the greeting formally his expression changed to one of genuine welcome. "Why, excuse me, for a moment I did not recognize you."

"Hullo, Benito."

"Such a long time it is! Oh, a pleasure indeed."

They were shaking hands. They were old friends. "How's your wife, Benito?"

"Oh very well. This evening she is with Lisa. Lisa's daughter is now nineteen, how the years run away."

"I always think of her as a baby."

Benito laughed. "She has a young man, so perhaps I become a great grandfather soon, eh? I ask you, do I look even like a grandfather?—This way, please."

Above the oblong of the main part of the restaurant there were two alcoves at a slightly higher level. Benito led the way to one of them. "A special table, ha? Your own table."

"Fancy you remembering."

"Oho, I remember. Those were the good days. How long, h'mm?" Benito's plump hands were never still and now he was reckoning on his fingers. "Ten, eleven years?"

"That's about it. Benito, this is my son.—Say how do you do, Vivian."

Vivian's hand was shaken as his mother dropped on to the seat against the wall. He had imagined himself sitting opposite, but there was no room in this shallow alcove and, feeling slightly disgruntled, he sat at the side. In this outing, which he had meant to manage in a masterful way, every detail was taken out of his control, for now Benito was proffering a wine list and insisting, "You accept a bottle, madame," and the menu, produced with a flourish, was almost unreadable. French. Probably some of those strange words stood for things with delicious flavours. Vivian sank down in his chair, acutely conscious of his age in this worldly environment, and Benito was making it all worse by saying that he would arrange their dinner. "I know what you like, madame, I remember." Then he called out, "A bottle of thirty-one."

"Half a bottle, Benito."

"It is ordered. I take a glass with you. And your son—the name again?—Ah, Vivian. Monsieur Vivian, he too take a little wine."

"No Benito. He's only a kid, he's got to go to school tomorrow."

"I'm ten," Vivian said, for they were behaving as if he'd just fallen out of the cradle.

"Ten years old, eh? Then of course, Monsieur Vivian, you will have some of the Chambertin. Just so." Benito measured two inches between finger and thumb. "Ah, excuse me." He went to greet a couple who had just arrived.

"I didn't know," Vivian said, "that we were coming to a place where—I mean, he's a friend of yours."

"Lisa—his daughter—was with me in a workroom in Bond Street. She married a Greek and they've got a restaurant in Bloomsbury."

There was so much of the world to be explored. "Did she marry before you did, or after?"

"Just before. Fancy her girl being nineteen." Mrs. Mander was reminded of her envy of Lisa during the years in which she herself had almost given up hoping for a child. A waiter, shuffling on flat feet, brought the wine. "Why Antonio, you're still here!"

A smile flickered over his long grey face. "Forty-two years, madame. I was here before Mr. Benito came from Italy." Antonio changed the small vase of flowers on the table for a larger one. Then he drew the cork and ceremoniously poured a spoonful into Vivian's glass. "All right, monsieur?"

Vivian sipped and nodded approvingly. Just like William Powell in that film with Myrna Loy—but he caught an amused sidelong glance from his mother as she chatted to Antonio, and in the same moment was assailed by doubt as to what he should do later on about tipping. Perhaps it would be better just to give up. He slipped his pound note from his pocket and slid it under the table on to his mother's knee.

She exposed the note and Antonio gave a great toothless laugh. "Ho-ho, a rich son, eh?"

"I shall be," Vivian said grimly.

"Ho-ho-ho. He has determination, the little one."

Little one. This was outrageous. Vivian silently renounced the struggle. It was not his party. It was his mother's and

Benito's and Antonio's. It was the party of the immense man with the giggling blonde in the other alcove. Anybody could have it, he would merely eat his meal, taking care not to look sulky, for that would be open confession of defeat.

"If I can make the money," his mother was saying, "he'll go in for a profession."

Cups were set before them. They contained what looked like jelly, and Vivian controlled his surprise on discovering that it tasted like soup. Throughout the meal he was on his guard about his behaviour, copying others, using his fingers for asparagus—which seemed a messy business, as the stuff was swimming in butter, eating a helping of chicken cooked with paprika without pulling a wry face at a flavour he thought revolting.

But he grew more cheerful towards the end of the meal. Nearly all the other diners had gone and Benito was sitting opposite to him, making him feel big with every turn of the conversation. Benito and his mother had finished the wine and now were having a minute quantity of a white sticky-looking drink in tiny glasses. His mother was laughing, she was the prettiest woman in the world, prettier than all the film stars rolled into one. On his one glass of wine Vivian was light-headed, the universe was singing, and in this alcove above the level of the other tables he felt more than physically exalted. Benito, who had the sense not to inquire about his school and what his favourite subject was, and what he intended to do when he was grown up, was now remarking seriously, "And you, Monsieur Vivian, I expect you have many interests?"

"Oh yes. Lots."

"Indeed. Yes, of course. As for instance?"

Vivian realized that his sudden uncontrollable belch might have undermined his dignity, but Benito was rising to bow good night to a departing patron. "I beg your pardon—— You were saying?"

"Oh," Vivian remarked airily, "I've got friends, you know. Colonel Arnold Trafford, for instance."

"Oh yes?" Benito was obviously impressed. "His wife is one of the best dressed women in London."

Mrs. Mander interpolated, "On nothing. I design and make most of her clothes."

"Well well, Monsieur Vivian, this indeed is interesting."

"As a matter of fact, it's their son who's my closest friend." It was flattering that Benito had dismissed the financial relationship, and Vivian elaborated "I've done them a terrific favour. Philip—that's their son, he's a cripple and I made him walk. They were jolly grateful, I can tell you."

"Yes. They should be."

Was Benito's expression rather too solemn? "I'll bring them all in some time."

And on this pleasant note of patronage the outing ended. Antonio brought the bill, but Benito tore it up.

"No, Benito. Really——" Mrs. Mander opened her bag, Benito reached over to close it.

"It is a pleasure. You are my guests. Oho, it reminds me of the good days, the happy days."

Several times during the evening Vivian had sensed what seemed to be almost a conspiracy. Benito and his mother had known each other when—no, before he was born. Benito was perfectly respectful but he conveyed an impression of being on intimate terms with her, and many of their references had been obscure. It was as if there were some vague ghost who had been dear to them, yet they mentioned no name.

Vivian emerged from his nebulous speculations and concluded that the restaurant proprietor probably knew the answers to the questions that he himself had never dared to put directly to his mother.

Then they were all shaking hands and wishing each other "Au revoir". Again Vivian promised to bring along his fashionable friends from Curzon Street, and Antonio came forward, looking melancholy and cynical, to bow them out. On the whole the evening had been a success. Vivian yawned all the way back to Sidley Street.

There was a car outside the lace shop and as they approached a woman got out, followed by a squarely-built man. Colonel and Mrs. Trafford. It was as if they had heard the presumptuous claim to friendship. Yet, Vivian reflected, he could hardly score it as a conquest, for he had not so much as imagined he would ever see them again.

"Oh—Mrs. Mander." Mrs. Trafford stepped forward, with the feather in her tiny hat quivering like a battle plume. "Could we have a word with you?"

"Yes, of course."

"We won't keep you long, but it's *rather* urgent."

"It's extremely urgent," Colonel Trafford interpolated, "as far as we're concerned."

"Come in. I'm afraid it won't be very tidy. It's not often I go out in the evening." Mrs. Mander glanced down at her flowered chiffon, feeling suddenly self-conscious. Getting all dressed up in a thing that Mrs. Trafford would know hadn't been fashionable for the last ten years!

Vivian slunk in behind them, feeling utterly bewildered. They were saying they were most grateful, "We're throwing ourselves on your charity——" Had the world gone topsy-turvy? What would they think of this after Curzon Street? But Mrs. Trafford had been here before, for fittings.

Mrs. Mander was striking a match, apologizing for the absence of electric light on the stairs. "The trouble is, if there is one, people *will* leave it on."

The room was in no great disorder, though both of them had changed hurriedly. Vivian grabbed the shirt and trousers he had worn for school and folded them away. Mrs. Mander scooped a pile of unfinished work from the table. The Colonel said "Please don't bother. We realize it's an intrusion."

And a minute later Vivian was dismissed to bed. He went with a feeling of grievance, hardly balanced by the fact that the visit spared him the usual routine of washing. What had those two come for? Something to do with Philip, of course. The Colonel wouldn't have come if the call had anything to do with dressmaking, and that precious boy seemed to be the only other thing that mattered to them. Vivian stripped off his best suit, letting it fall on the landing floor. The square of skylight was dimmer tonight, his scores on the wall were invisible, but there were no new conquests to add. He remembered that he should have brought his pyjamas upstairs, and just as he was thinking what a good excuse this would be to go down again, to try to discover what was afoot, his mother called out and threw them up. "Good night, Vivian love."

Mrs. Glatt had been cooking goulash. Lying in bed, Vivian sniffed deeply, and then felt sick. Perhaps he had eaten too much, but each course had been exciting, even the thing with paprika in it. Was it the glass of wine?

A door was opening. Wyganowski was on the landing, humming softly. His light snapped off. "Mr. Wyganowski——"

"Hello there!"

"I've been out to dinner in a swell restaurant."

"Well well. Excellent." Wyganowski was moving the screen. "To eat and drink well, that is the second best thing in life. No, it should come third."

The huge Russian was a vague shape against the darkness, with the faint glow from the skylight on his astrachan cap and beard. He had no features, no limbs. "Then what ought to come first and second?" Vivian inquired.

"To love. And to be an artist."

"But if you can't draw?"

Wyganowski made a clicking sound. "There is also music. Once I could sing, always I hear music. There is acting, or dancing, writing. You can be an artist even in reading, even in thinking, in your attitude to life."

Vivian stifled a yawn. He was always delighted when Wyganowski stopped to talk, but tonight sleep was threatening the conversation. He pinched himself awake. "What I really want to know is, what's the best way to get rich?"

"To be an artist."

"But you——" Vivian cut off what would have been a tactless comment.

"I am very rich, because I am independent. Listen, little boy, you must not let them make you one of the mob. Don't be a butcher's boy, a mechanic, a clerk."

"Someone's got to do all that."

"Millions can do all that. You are different. You are an individual. I know, I always recognize an individual, even a small one. The butcher's boy becomes a butcher, perhaps he makes money, and what then? Thirty years later he is still cutting chops, or perhaps he retires, and in his dreams he trims the fat from kidneys because meat was the whole horizon. No, no. The clerk—— He becomes perhaps an employer, a bank manager, a shipping magnate. Until he dies he is scribbling little figures in his mind. The rich people, the great people, they are so rare. They are the artists, the aristocrats who, whether or not they can afford to, live in their souls and minds."

"I'd like to be a doctor."

"Yes, yes, there is science. Perhaps you are a scientist, that is something that even artists respect."

Wyganowski lit a match to look at his watch. The tiny flare seemed to pick out the huge hook nose, the vast black beard, the moth-eaten state of the astrakhan collar of the long overcoat. A fire engine was clanging nearby. Then it was a faint dwindling warning about something that did not matter. Wyganowski's voice was like the sleepy purring of a cat that had somehow learnt to use words. "The secret of happiness, Vivian, is to be completely selfish. No one is completely so, so no one is happy."

"But—oho-oho—sorry, it's rude to yawn, isn't it supposed to make you happy, helping people?"

"Who," Wyganowski purred, "can help the whole world? While anyone is in difficulty, the helper is still miserable. The opposite, to be selfish—yes, that may be difficult. One betrays oneself, responding to impulses."

Why, thought Wyganowski, do I babble to a small boy who is nearly asleep? Is it to find out what I really believe? Or to ease my mind by plain lying? Or trying to persuade myself? He said fiercely "I am happy, understand? I know what I am talking about." Here he was, babbling, and people he had known were dying in concentration camps, and the British doing nothing about it, pretending not to see so that they should be safe. If only one could save just a few, any of them, friends or strangers. "Be an artist," Wyganowski said hopelessly, "or a scientist or some sort of a creator. Good night, little boy."

Wyganowski was lumbering down the stairs, trying each one cautiously. The faint flare of another match far below. Only after the front door had slammed did Vivian realize that he might have resented that 'little boy'. Why did the queer old man always go out at night? Was he as poor as his shabby clothes or as rich as his cigars? Vivian rolled over, making his bedclothes into a sleeping-bag. Decent of Benito to stand them the dinner. That meant his mother was a pound in pocket. What was happening between her and the two visitors in the room below? Fantastic speculations on this point, mingled with the determination to show Tom Cray, at the swimming baths tomorrow, how a somersault dive was done by an expert, extended into the blur of oblivion.

CHAPTER VIII

MRS. TRAFFORD was doing most of the talking, with her usual touches of over-emphasis, while the Colonel slipped in staccato phrases to reinforce her explanations. They were sitting stiffly at the table as if at an office conference; there was only one armchair. The window-curtains flapped inwards with the breeze yet the room, to the Traffords at least, seemed airless.

"You see, Mrs. Mander, this means *everything*," Mrs. Trafford was saying. "My husband and I, well, there hasn't been a single waking minute in *years*, when the anxiety has been out of our thoughts. Of course everything *possible* has been done. I can't *tell* you how many doctors. *And* a psychiatrist, one who's been *most* successful—— He said Philip didn't *respond* and we were wasting our money paying his *enormous* fees. Not that the money *mattered*. Our present man, Dr. Turnbull, is *absolutely* sound. We saw him last night, after Philip was asleep, and he called again this morning."

"A very good man with children," the Colonel remarked.

"Oh yes, *wonderful*. So patient. But this morning—and then it was only after a *lot* of persuasion, after trying for over an hour, Philip couldn't move a *step*. He just managed to stand for a minute, no it can't have been more than *half* a minute. He fell over and was *terribly* upset, crying and begging us to leave him alone. We took the doctor's advice and didn't try to force him any more."

"You see," Colonel Trafford said crisply, "after yesterday evening, this was most disappointing."

"To be sure," Mrs. Mander agreed, "it must have been."

"It was Arnold—my husband here, who had the *brain wave*. He said 'If that other boy had such a good effect, let's get him back here'."

"No no," the Colonel said, "not quite as baldly as that. I did say it would be a good thing—for Philip—to throw them together. Much the same age, gives them a lot in common. A kind of—m'm—sympathy. Let nature work it out."

The glance between husband and wife suggested that neither version was the complete one. Mrs. Trafford was haggard under her make-up, her restless hands betrayed the state of her nerves. "We may as well put it *directly*," she said, "would you let Vivian come and *stay* with us?"

"I couldn't. I'm sorry, I'm sure, but this is his home."

"Of *course*, we understand." Again husband and wife were exchanging glances, then Mrs. Trafford said "This really is terribly—it's *absolutely* vital to us. Would you consider coming *with* him? There are two rooms on the top floor, one of them's quite *large*, we'd do everything to make you feel it was a home."

"I couldn't. It's very kind of you. But this is my place and I'm used to working here. I shan't always be here, I'm making plans, and I couldn't carry them out if I move here and there and lose my business connection."

"Of course," said the Colonel, "we should show our appreciation. I mean to say, we'd want to make it worth your while. Whatever you suggested."

"But I've always been a very independant nature."

"Please don't misunderstand——" In embarrassment the Colonel brought out his cigarette case, then hastily thrust it away. After all, this was the woman's bedroom as well as sitting-room. "We're asking you the favour, it would be our privilege."

"Do smoke. I don't mind smoke at all."

The Colonel offered a cigarette. "No thank you, I don't. But I like the smell of it." Mrs. Mander rose to get matches, but already Mrs. Trafford had snapped her gold lighter. They both seemed more at ease with the cigarettes going.

"You both seem very sure that Vivian would do your boy some good."

"He proved that he could. That's why we're here."

Again Mrs. Mander rose, to give a twist to the tap over the sink. The drip-drip was making her as edgy as Mrs. Trafford seemed. "I wasn't surprised," she said.

"It's an extraordinary business, surely."

"Vivian's got a special kind of—perhaps you could call it a kind of magnetism."

"Magnetism?" the Colonel echoed. His suspicion of the word was obvious.

"A kind of power. He can dominate other children. Yes, and grown-ups too. I don't like it, it worries me, it's not——" Mrs. Mander hesitated before the word 'normal'. "It makes me uneasy," she finished lamely, "I don't know how it'll develop."

There was an uneasy silence. Mrs. Trafford glanced at the clock; she was longing for a drink and wished, now, that she had not refused the offer of tea. It would at least have relieved the thirst that reminded her of her craving. She said "You mustn't worry, at least your boy *is* sturdy and healthy."

"A kind of power," her husband ruminated. "Yes, no one could deny that. I do wish you'd reconsider your decision."

But Mrs. Mander was following her own line of troubled thought. "Usually it's just boyish tricks, but of course this is different. Often it's just to make someone look silly. This might have done some good. All the same I don't know whether I ought to encourage it."

"He's probably psychic," Mrs. Trafford commented.

Her husband suppressed a protest. He hated the very word psychic. Yet surely enough Vivian's peculiar gift was inexplicable by any reasoning that he himself knew of. Even Dr. Turnbull, most reliable of medical men, had been impressed by the boy's command of Philip, and had agreed at once that he would be a helpful companion. Even, the doctor had added humorously, if the Soho child made Philip precocious and gave him a cockney accent. Oddly enough—considering the locality—both Vivian and his mother spoke well, and her occasional touch of brogue was charming.

The discussion had so taken a turn that now it seemed as if they had met to discuss Vivian's welfare, not Philip's. "He's my responsibility," Mrs. Mander was saying. "I don't always understand him, but I shall manage him. I sometimes wonder—— It's not a thing I'd tell everybody. There's been a lot of religious feeling in my family, deep religious feeling, and my grandfather and his brother both went queer with it, but they got thousands following them, they had such a way with them, such a persuasive way. All the same——" Mrs. Mander smiled half-apologetically, "they didn't believe in what priests and clergymen said, they had their own ideas about God and heaven and forced people to swallow them."

"Heredity," the Colonel said. His wife concurred, "That *sort* of thing runs in families, I suppose, like any *other* characteristic. Don't you think that if Vivian came to us he *might* get rid of the habit that worries you?"

"It's not a 'habit'."

"I'm sorry. I *do* express myself so *badly*."

"Good or bad, it's a dominating power. I don't know whether it's a kind of hypnotism, or magnetism or mesmerism. I don't really know the difference, so I can't put the right word to it."

The Colonel suggested "In another place he might forget all about it. Find new interests."

"Interests!" exclaimed Mrs. Mander. "He's got so many, I often wish he'd be uninterested."

"An alert mind, obviously." The Colonel rose, stood upright for a moment, and sat down. "So sorry. A touch of cramp." What could one expect, he thought, with one's chair jammed between a table and a dresser? "Suppose you let him come and stay with us for a few weeks?"

"There's his school to think of. And he'd grow away from me." Seeing Mrs. Trafford's hopeless expression, Mrs. Mander added, "if it's any good, he could go and see your Philip. At the week-ends. Or perhaps sometimes after school, so long as he was home by eight o'clock."

"Of *course* it would be some good," Mrs. Trafford spoke fervently. "We'd be most grateful, tremendously grateful."

"We certainly should," her husband agreed. "Even a few hours ought to have some effect, to judge by yesterday evening——"

Mrs. Trafford interrupted "We'll send the car."

"You will not. I'm sorry, I didn't mean that so sharply. But Vivian can take a bus. Riding in a car, why, he'd be getting bigger ideas than he's got already."

"This is splendid, splendid." Colonel Trafford stood up again. "You're doing us a great favour, Mrs. Mander. Philip has really taken to your lad, I know they'll be good friends. I see that you won't discuss—er—any question of repayment. But there may be something we could do for your boy. Perhaps later on."

There was an awkward silence. Then Mrs. Mander said quietly, "Thank you, but I'm not doing this for anything we'll get out of it. I'm as certain as I'm sitting here that my Vivian can persuade your Philip to get on his own feet. If he did it once he can go on doing it. But I don't want to encourage him in his dominating—as he calls it—and it's only for the sake of your poor boy that I'm agreeing now."

For a moment or so neither of the Traffords found any reply. Then Mrs. Trafford said "We're more than grateful. Would you let Vivian come tomorrow?"

"It's the day for the swimming baths. He's so keen, he always comes home tired. It's the one evening I don't have to force him to go up to bed. Saturday would be better."

"Saturday," Mrs. Trafford agreed eagerly. "Could he come in the morning?"

"Yes, that's all right. I might want him to do some shopping for me. He's very useful and quick, and of course I'm always busy. He could go along, let me see now—about eleven."

"And stay to lunch, of course."

"Well, thank you, yes."

Mrs. Trafford rose, and again expressed her gratitude. The Colonel felt the irony of the situation; that they should have argued for so long, in this cramped makeshift room, pleading for companionship for Philip! Asking one of his wife's dressmakers a favour, tiptoeing around her sensitivity on the point of payment, feeling that their future happiness, their peace of mind, depended on the agreement of a woman who twiddled a sewing machine almost on top of her bed!

He said again "It's very good of you, Mrs. Mander." Indeed her favour was incalculable. The boy who had worked the magic of getting Philip across the drawing-room floor would surely get him out and running about.

Mrs. Trafford picked up her fur. Now to get home, now for a drink. Mrs. Mander was edging round the table to open the door, saying "If only I'm doing the right thing——"

"Oh—I never mentioned the dress. It's perfect."

"I'll take you down." Mrs. Mander left the door open to light the way, and struck a match at the turn of the stairs. "The dress? Yes, I got your message."

"My message?"

"You *did* say you'd never been so pleased with anything in your life? Or was that a bit of Vivian?"

Outside, stepping into the car, Mrs. Trafford exclaimed "I never even *mentioned* the dress to him."

"I hope he's not going to be a liar.—Home, Evans." The Colonel dropped heavily beside his wife.

"But what a *relief*, Arnold. That the boy's coming."

"It certainly is. I'm dam' glad. I'm sure everything's going to be all right. Pray God it is." He took his wife's hand. "But I say—funny set-up, that. I rather thought, with such a first-rate chance, she might be grasping. Not that I'd have grudged anything."

"She's never been grasping. I don't tell her so, but I'd have had to pay enormous pric s to get her styles. She designs them herself, you know."

"All dolled up, wasn't she?"

"You heard her say, she'd been out to dinner."

"But with the boy. It's funny, isn't it?"

"I don't know. I don't *care*. I want a drink."

"Dorothy"— something in his tone set her on the defensive, —"if Philip does get better, wouldn't it be a good sort of thank-offering to try to slow down a bit?"

"I might."

"I know it'd be an effort."

"I've been so completely miserable, I know I've rather let go."

"That's just what I mean. Things are going to be better. You're a lovely woman, I don't want you losing your looks."

His tactfulness touched her. "I'll try," she said. "I must say this evening's been *rather* shattering. I thought she was going to refuse."

"Struck me as very straightforward. In a way, very dignified. Wonder what happened to the husband?"

"Oh, she's a widow. She sheers away from any sort of reference to him."

"Later on we might take those two boys down to the cottage."

"But with all this war scare——" Mrs. Trafford broke off.

"Sussex would be fairly all right. But it looks as if Chamberlain can handle that German pip-squeak."

"George Cawdell says a war's inevitable."

"If he's right," the Colonel said, "I'll be busy and you and Philip will get out of London."

The car swung into Curzon Street and slowed down.

In the room over the lace shop Mrs. Mander slid out of her unaccustomed, out-dated finery. She hoped that she had made a wise decision, but she wasn't sure. How could she be sure what was best for a boy with a wild imagination whose father had died with a rope round his neck? Vivian had the same fantastic flights of fancy which with Harry had turned to ruthless ambition. Details of the shame and tragedy of over ten years ago sprang to her mind, wounding as if they had happened only today; a shameful grief, she thought, grows more bitter with time. Those visits to the prison—and three days before Vivian was born she had gone, as if compelled to do so, to the gates to read the notice posted up, and so had learnt that the last chance of seeing Harry ever again was gone. She had danced with him in the very dress that she was now hanging in this cupboard——

The dress slid from the hanger and she was suddenly convulsed with misery, her throat was choked with sobs as tears drenched her face, her body was swaying uncontrollably and her wild hands beat against the wall. Then suddenly she was quiet, overcoming her hysteria—as once, for the sake of her unborn child, she had mastered her frenzy of fear in the months of waiting between the arrest and the trial, in the weeks between the trial and the end.

When at last she lay exhausted in bed her mind was still ranging feverishly over the past. The fields of Armagh and the grandfather who went about in a shirt of sacking, with bare feet, telling everyone about the flames of hell. The journey to London with her father, who was lured by the high rates of pay earned by munition workers. Her meeting with Harry, back on leave from the Somme and all eager to pack every moment with gaiety before he went back to the mud and brutality of the trenches. So handsome, so gaily sure of himself; no wonder he had risen from the ranks to be a captain, no wonder she had been crazily in love. He proposed three days after they met and they were married four days later, only a few hours before she saw him off at Waterloo. Again she heard the farewell yelps and whistles from the grey troop train as it slid away into the fog.

Then after the delirious armistice, demobilization and no job. Maybe, she reflected now, he would have been steadier if they had had a child, but so many years passed before she felt the first thrill of expectancy—and then it was too late. Nine hectic years of riches and poverty in which Harry had run around with his former fellow officers, with desperately bright young women, who all took the possession of money for granted. Why, Harry had argued, should he starve trying to sell vacuum cleaners, or be a garage hand? How he had maintained his spurious veneer of prosperity she had never known. He boasted, schemed, and ranted when he met shameful disasters which merely made him more stubbornly averse to any steady occupation.

The pose had become an obsession; he felt it his right to be wealthy, to lead an adventurous existence in which his vanity could be fed by the admiration of his associates—to whom, in the uncertainty and cynicism of the 1920's, he figured as an inspired leader of revels.

Perhaps she would have had more power to control his waywardness if she had not been so deeply in love with him. Often she had found it difficult, when he was gay and triumphant, to question the methods by which he had achieved some particular success. She had assured herself, while every waking moment was tainted with fear, that eventually he would settle down. At times he was in the depths of melancholia, feeling the agonizing pain of the head wound that had kept him out of action for four months in the last summer of the war. The wound had healed, the doctors said it would have no after-effects.

No after-effects . . . She had known him as an ardent, impetuous lover who would kneel at her feet to present flowers and perfumes, while she laughed at his claims to be the Duke of this or the Prince of that. Later, it seemed, he could not distinguish between his play-acting and reality.

Jim Lassiter had been his downfall. Lassiter was older, a confidence trickster with a world-wide range, and Harry, fascinated by his exploits, still more by his big talk, had been lured into a kind of partnership.

Why had they quarrelled? It might be that Harry had come to his senses, but the details of that final tragedy could never be known, for Lassiter was dead and Harry had gone to the gallows—he who might have died as a hero—without attempting to explain or defend himself.

That last terrible interview. Harry saying "I'm as good as any of them, I'll prove it yet." Had he thought, even then, that he could evade the processes of the law, escape miraculously? Was Vivian, now sleeping overhead, blessed, or it might be cursed with the power his father had so often claimed, the ability to dominate others? If it could heal it was indeed a blessed gift. It was the wound that had driven Harry crazy; maybe Vivian would atone for all his father's transgressions. The sins of the fathers . . . But had some translator of centuries ago made an error? Could it not be that the sins of the fathers were not visited upon, but expiated by their children? If Harry had been alive he would have known some translator who could have explained this point. For Harry had known all sorts. And he himself—her somnolent thought was blurred—had been all sorts. Unconsciously, Norah Mander flung her thin arms wide, as if to receive an embrace.

CHAPTER IX

WEEK by week Philip Trafford became more active, though his progress was variable and obviously dependant upon the companionship of Vivian. Almost reluctantly, Mrs. Mander agreed that Vivian should spend part of his summer holidays at the Traffords' cottage in Sussex. The change would be good for him, he was eager to run wild in the country, but where— she speculated uneasily—would this strange friendship lead?

When the two boys returned to London, Colonel Trafford decided that Philip should go to boarding school in the autumn. Philip protested and pleaded, finally agreeing that he would go happily enough if Vivian could go with him—but now Mrs. Mander took a firm stand.

"I'm not having Vivian at any boarding school," she declared. "He'd get ideas above his place in life. He must finish at school where he is, then if he takes a scholarship he'll have earned it, or if I can see my way he'll have the extra education."

Colonel Trafford argued, "If that's what you're trying to achieve, isn't it simpler just to accept it? If you don't mind my saying so, it would be an enormous advantage to the boy to mix with others from—how shall I put it——?"

"It doesn't matter how it's put. What you mean is, he'd be mixing with boys of a class a cut above his own. Well, I don't want that unless he works his way up." Mrs. Mander finished with a flash of bitterness that the Colonel found puzzling, "Making him a jumped-up gentleman. It might be the ruin of him."

So in August a tutor-companion was engaged for Philip, and Vivian continued to visit the house in Curzon Street. Mr. Barmbie was thirty or so, pallid and imperturbably amiable. He spent almost as much time polishing his thick spectacles as wearing them, and the slight activity seemed to be a mute apology for his lack of forcefulness; he had an obsequious manner, which persisted even when his pupil was deliberately slow, or the shock-headed boy from Soho more than usually impish. With Mr. Barmbie the boys went on jaunts to theatres, exhibitions, to Windsor Castle, to the coast, to the Tower of London and the Zoo. When Mrs. Trafford was not using the car she let them have it, with Evans to drive them, and Mr. Barmbie would polish his glasses and smile vaguely while the boys contended for the privilege of sitting in the front seat. Vivian rarely lost the argument, but Philip sometimes won the seat by bribery. Both preferred Evans's lively conversation to the tutor's instructive comments, and sometimes the chauffeur could be persuaded to make a detour through Soho, when Vivian would all but fling himself out of the window to attract as many recognitions as he could.

He developed the habit of boasting to his contemporaries about his extraordinary luck, while in describing the outings to his mother he omitted references to anything that might emphasize the superior wealth and social position of his benefactors; instinctively, he was aware of her sensitivity, of her incomprehensible fear.

At home one day, unaware of the fact that she was just outside the door that was standing ajar, Vivian was telling Tom Cray about a visit to Hampton Court. "Of course," he said, "I always see that my chauffeur gets a good lunch."

"*Your* chauffeur!" Mrs. Mander swooped in. "I suppose it's *your* Daimler."

"It's as much mine as it is Philip's," Vivian retorted airily, and was surprised to feel himself gripped—who would have thought that his mother had such strength in her arms?—

and smacked soundly with a slipper, while Tom stood by smirking.

"I suppose"—the scolding kept time with the beating—"you think you're one of the smart set? I'll cure you of that. Lies and pretences, they only lead to misery."

The incident provided Tom with repartee when he had to listen to further bragging. But as the weeks wore away each was overshadowed by some new phase of international tension, and when Colonel Trafford took a post at the War Office he arranged for his wife and son to go as paying guests to a manor house in Stannet, a Berkshire village. The ineffectual Mr. Barmbie departed for a school in Cheshire.

Mrs. Mander refused to allow Vivian to go to Berkshire, and he expressed his own opinion to a circle of his Soho friends. "I'm glad to be rid of Philip. He's a mug. Soft, soppy, a cry-baby."

"What about the Daimler?" Tom Cray sneered. "Don't tell me you've let him take the car with him?"

"If there's a war," another boy said, "we'll all be slung out of London, my dad says so, because the Germans will drop millions of tons of bombs and there won't be anyone left alive."

"*I* should be left alive," Vivian declared. "*I* should be deep under the ruins, I'd creep out, and everything would belong to me. Piccadilly and Buckingham Palace and the conjuring department at Gamages."

"Don't be daft," said Tom. "It'd all be ruins. Anyway, you wouldn't dare go in Buckingham Palace, nor Gamages, if you hadn't got your precious little gentleman to take you and pay for you."

Late in September Mrs. Mander stopped her treadle machine as she heard a newsboy shouting, and hurried downstairs. Across the way a taxi had stopped, Tashy Vautel was fumbling in her bag for the key while her escort took his change from the driver. That woman, thought Mrs. Mander, breathlessly overtaking the newsboy, was a disgrace to the street; since the evening when she had called with her length of dress material she had become quite scandalous. No longer could she be credited with a position vaguely between respectability and the other thing.

Headlines flared across the front page of the paper. Hitler

was making a sensational claim to friendship with Britain and France:

We want peace with England, we want nothing from France, absolutely nothing, only peace. I have assured Mr. Chamberlain that there would be no more international problems. Dr. Benes can choose either peace or war. If he does not accept our demands we shall liberate our Germans. I now step ahead of my people, I shall be the first soldier ahead of them . . . Stand to attention! Ready, march!

From a radio in the next house the nine o'clock news reinforced the threat. The landlady's brother ran up from his room and with a pitiable expression asked to have the latest developments explained to him. He had the bowed figure of an old man and a fringe of grey curly hair that looked like feathers gummed to his scalp. "Please—could you tell me? What says the newspaper?"

"You can have it, Mr. Glatt."

He made an elaborate gesture. He could not read.

Mrs. Mander did her best to explain. "It is war," Glatt wailed. "My sister and I—what will happen to us?"

The Glatts were German. Mrs. Mander said "You've been in this country for years, you'll be all right."

"Since nineteen thirty-four only. A terrible year. Five sisters I had, now only one. And Magda's two sons—all, all are gone." Mr. Glatt went out, stumbling blindly against the door post.

Twenty minutes later Mrs. Trafford arrived. "Arnold takes a terribly serious view," she said. "I've left Philip at The Manor, but as *always* when he's without Vivian he's *pining*. I go back in two days' time. We may have to close the Curzon Street house. We've had *awful* financial set backs, Arnold's *utterly* absorbed by his work. I *tell* him he's overdoing it, it's not as if he's *young* any more." Mrs. Trafford was using emphasis even more lavishly than usual. "Won't you change your mind? Vivian would be so *much* safer out of London, wouldn't he?"

"I don't know what to think." Mrs. Mander blinked at her work-littered table, at the dress that had to be finished by next morning, at her sketches of a cape and a cocktail party outfit.

"*Imagine*," Mrs. Trafford pursued, "if there were a *sudden* hail of some devilish weapon we can't even *imagine*. If what they're calling an 'emergency' really happens, all the children would have to go away, and isn't it *far* better for Vivian to be with people he knows?"

"Well—yes. If only . . ." Mrs. Mander broke off.

"You were going to say?"

"If only he doesn't get to think he has the right to live in a big house with people who aren't his class. It's not that I'm not ambitious for him. I am. But I want him to rise the steady way. I've a special reason."

"But," Mrs. Trafford's puzzlement twisted her face, making hollows beneath her cheekbones. "Who could be steadier than *we* are? There's lots of *discipline*, though Mrs. Gould-Vane is the *kindest* woman. It's the greatest stroke of luck she's taking us at all, I suppose you *know* they were frightfully rich before the Wall Street crash. And really it does seem a *shame* to keep those two boys apart when they're so—well, really, devoted."

How could Mrs. Trafford guess that Vivian was inclined to despise Philip, valuing the friendship only for the excitement it provided? In a mental flashback Mrs. Mander saw her husband, so 'devoted' to his rackety but useful associates. "I'm worried," she admitted, then after a long pause, "yes, he can go. It's very good of you. I suppose there's a school somewhere near?"

"They'll go in to Reading, for the time being. Of course, later on, Philip must go to a public school and the varsity."

"Later on," Mrs. Mander echoed, thinking that she must take a workroom, must employ an assistant, and advertise. Later on Vivian must have advantages equal with Philip's, but to provide them as if they were a matter of course would be to deny him the necessary toughening of his character.

Confused as were most of the public by the futility of the Munich meeting, Mrs. Trafford stayed on at The Manor with the two boys. Six months later, when arrangements were being made for their return, Colonel Trafford, exhausted after a day at the War Office, called in at Sidley Street and persuaded Mrs. Mander that an extension was advisable. "The emergency may be staved off," he said guardedly, "but no one can foretell developments. It's important for the youngsters to be where they're safe."

Mrs. Mander sighed, "To be sure you treat Vivian as if he was your own son. I'll be feeling he's a stranger. It's all so unsettling. The last time he was home the other boys made a joke of him, because of his accent and his clothes. I want him home in three months, and that's definite."

Frowning absently, his scar showing white between the two branches of one grey eyebrow, the Colonel agreed. In three months there might be no choice for anyone. The tension, the inevitability of cause and effect were obvious to all who could read the writing on the wall. So Vivian's return from Stannet was deferred and again deferred, and after the first portentous Sunday in September he no longer spent odd days in London. Instead, his mother visited Stannet on occasional Sundays. Why, he speculated after one of these meetings, did she seem so different each time? For years she had had no new clothes, yet now her rather severe outfits were both new and stylish: she had an air of assurance.

"Sometimes," Vivian complained on one of her visits, "I get fed up with sponging on the Traffords."

"How can you say such a thing? Look what you've done for them. I know when we're sponging and when we're paying our way. Mrs. Trafford promised to send me some customers, she's never done so, and if they come now they can pay twice the old prices. Seems to me the war's sent women clothes-crazy. We're packed up with orders and I still work till all hours, though I'm thankful I've the machine at home run on electricity. That girl Amy's gone into the Waafs but I've got a soldier's wife to take her place, Violet Bracey, she'll need a lot of training——"

To Vivian the day-to-day affairs of Sidley Street and its neighbourhood seemed unreal, and even the stormy phases of the war were like a preposterous melodrama being played beyond a lowered curtain. He heard of the death of a former schoolmate, Artie Howes, in an air raid, of the devastation in the market where his mother did her shopping, in Shaftesbury Avenue and Brewer Street, but he felt that he would return to find those places as they were, with Artie still scribbling indecent words on the walls. No bombs fell near enough to make any personal impact; life at The Manor

C

became a dull routine of going to school, salvage collecting, helping with the National Savings drive, listening to Mrs. Gould-Vane's laments about shortages. The army camp nearby was an enclosed world of its own, but Mrs. Gould-Vane's nephew, a Flight-Lieutenant, spent two days of his leave in the house and his casual flippancies were—for Vivian—more realistic than all the newspaper reports. If only he himself were old enough to don a uniform! Instead, he was coming out in spots and going through the childish tedium of measles with Philip as his sole companion.

The boredom was only slightly relieved by his mother's visits and a sequence of friendships made impetuously and broken off when they fell short of anticipation. He had performed his tricks of domination over one after another of his schoolmates, and had even had a success with one of the masters. At sixteen his impatience was spurred into action by the allied invasion of Europe; if he did not make a move now he might miss the whole show! Again he pleaded to be allowed to return to London, but again his mother and Mrs. Gould-Vane harped on the intolerable reminder of his age.

He was a fraction under five-foot-eight, by adopting a frowning expression he could look less boyish—— On a summer morning he slipped away from Philip at Reading station, when they were on their way to school, and took a train to Paddington. But at the army recruiting office he was turned away with a smile, before he had any opportunity of adding two years to his age. He took a bus to the East End, but fared no better, though he jostled in an entrance hall with a gang of youths who were resenting the necessity of being there. A third rejection late in the afternoon set him thinking that he might get a job in a munitions factory, but by now his self-confidence was undermined and he was hungry. In the doorway of a Lyons branch he swung round and darted for a bus slowing down for traffic lights. Fifteen minutes later he was in Sidley Street.

How different now was the front room on the second floor! It was well furnished, almost elegant. A desk now stood where the bed had been; his mother told him that she now occupied the whole floor, sleeping in the back room.

She was in a strange mood. Why did she always conceal any agitation by attending to details that couldn't matter?

Tidying a few papers, rearranging some cornflowers in a vase, unpicking the cleaners' label from a cushion-cover—— His absence had been reported by telegram, for Philip had sneaked as soon as he reached their school, yet all she said was "There you are! Is there ever to be an end to you worrying the life out of me?"

"I'm not a kid any more. I'm going to work in a factory."

"Sit down and eat something, do."

He was startled, as he wolfed the meal, by the ringing of the telephone. This too was an innovation. His mother was snapping "Don't be silly, Violet. We can't take on any more.— Oh well, if she comes back, say twenty guineas. That'll put her off. And she couldn't have it for two months."

As the receiver was put down Vivian said, more boldly, "I'm going to the Labour Exchange in the morning."

She gave him an enigmatic look. "You haven't even heard a flying bomb."

"Yes I have."

"Miles away from you, dropping in a field or a pond. While one's going over you can hardly breathe, then the mechanism stops working and that awful silence, then the *cr-rump* and perhaps you hear the crash of the houses, and it's all very well to feel safe for a little while, but you can't help thinking of the poor souls who got it."

Across the road there was scaffolding where the house next to the gown shop had been. But that had been one of the bombs in the first few weeks of the raids. "How's Tashy Vautel?"

"What makes you ask?"

"Well, she was injured, wasn't she?"

"Only a few cuts and shock. She was back in no time. She's no friend of ours."

Vivian leaned back, his hunger satisfied, studying his mother with a sense of discovery. She was so slim and neat in her black dress, she didn't look middle-aged, her face was smooth and her hair, now expertly waved, was still bright. If she had been a stranger, he thought, he might have imagined she was deaf, so attentive were her eyes. "You're not afraid to stay in London," he remarked, "and you never go to shelters."

"No." Vaguely, she wondered if her comparative indifference to danger lay in her past experience of the limits of fear. Or was she, instinctively, a fatalist?

He reverted to the topic uppermost in his mind. "I've had enough of school, I've passed enough exams, other chaps of my age are doing jobs—in another year I'll be in one of the services."

"In another year the war will be over. They're saying it'll finish in September."

"What's Tom Cray doing?"

"You needn't envy him. He's employed at Pedro's, rides a bicycle delivering drinks to some of those terrible clubs. He ought to be ashamed. His mother's on munitions."

"Well, I'm not going back to Berkshire."

"I'm not arguing about it. You've got to go, this very evening. I'll phone them and let them know you're on the way."

"I'm not going." Vivian walked across and faced his mother, silently using all his power to force her to acquiesce.

It was a full minute before she muttered "Well, perhaps tomorrow morning."

"Is the bed still on the top landing?"

"No it isn't. You know we had two fire bombs through the roof."

"Then I'll sleep on the floor." She had given way much more easily than he had anticipated.

"I don't know whether I've got extra blankets."

"I'll only want one, in this weather——" Already his mother was telephoning, waiting for the connection to Stannet, then she was sweeping the receiver away from her ear, as if to avoid voluble rejoicings at his safety.

"Yes, he'll be back tomorrow," she said.

"Not tomorrow," he interpolated.

"By an early train," Mrs. Mander spoke firmly into the telephone. "I'll time it so he can meet Philip at Reading and they can go on to school together."

"School!" Vivian exclaimed, not caring if he made Mrs. Gould-Vane at the other end inaudible. "I can get a job, I *ought* to get a job——"

Down went the receiver. "You'll do as you're told. Don't you try any more of your tricks."

He was about to protest further, but saw his mother's

profile sharp against the dresser, now painted cream, and was suddenly and poignantly reminded of a moment of years ago. Then, he had watched her in just that position and had drawn a pencil likeness on a length of pale blue linen lying on the table, all ready to be cut out as a dress. The trouble she had had to remove that drawing! It had been erased completely, but his memory retained the picture which now, again, she posed all unwittingly. "I liked you with your hair drawn back," he said. "It's how I always think of you."

"It was easier." She sighed. "You can't always afford to do what's easy. Now don't stand about. There's that ottoman, you could clear it out for me, it's full of your old rubbish. Toys and books and I don't know what. I've got to go back to the workroom, Violet'll be wondering what's happening, there's work enough for half a dozen waiting."

"Can't you take one evening off?"

Her reply was to depart. He opened the ottoman, turned over the top of its jumbled contents, and closed it again. The childish reminders jarred with his determination to be a man. For some time he stood gazing from the window, his old spy-hole on the world, but few of the passers-by were familiar, then he went out and down Frith Street to the entrance to his mother's workroom. The first floor was hers, but as he stood on the landing and heard the sound of whirring sewing machines he had a sense of exclusion. They were busy; everyone except himself was busy. He did not belong here, nor to his school desk; he belonged nowhere. In this mood of resentment he mooned up to Oxford Street, and was glad of the chance to help some A.R.P. men moving a pile of sandbags.

At half-past nine he returned to Frith Street, but the black-out curtains prevented him seeing whether or not anyone was still on the first floor, and the side door was shut. As he waited, wondering if he might ring, his mother came out with a second dim figure beside her.

"Vivian! Hanging about like this!—Oh Violet, this is Vivian, he's just up for a few hours."

As Vivian shook hands he discerned, vaguely, a round pleasant face, a rather squat figure. His mother said "She's had bad news, her husband's wounded." And then, to Violet she said "You run along, you'll get better news, don't you worry," and the other hurried off along the dark street.

He slept in the armchair in the sitting-room, and at dawn was awakened by a rough shaking. His mother was in a severe black coat and a kind of beret. "Come along, I've got a taxi and I'm taking you to Paddington. Get up, get your clothes on, just wash your hands and face. I've got to be at the workroom by eight-thirty, Violet might not be there and Peggy—she's the new learner—she just lazes about if there's no one to start her off. I'll want some breakfast before then. Here's a cup of tea, I've packed you some sandwiches."

Startled, still half-asleep, he stumbled to his feet, realizing that her haste and urgency were self-defensive measures. She was giving him no further opportunity to pit his will against hers. Handing him his clothes, as if he were a child, she urged, "Hurry, do. The trouble you give me, turning up like this and worrying the life out of everybody."

"There's no need for you to bother. I can get myself off, but——"

"Hurry do, and stop arguing."

So he was back at Stannet, still going off to school with Philip, taking part disdainfully in activities purporting to be of national importance, and having a cubbish flirtation with the daughter of an estate agent who, at fifteen, was as resentful as he was at not being eligible for military service. In less than a year now, in a few months, he would have a chance of escape. He exercised diligently, stretching his muscles, gloating when his measurement taken against the wall registered a quarter of an inch short of five-foot-ten.

At Christmas a war-widow, said to be recovering from a nervous breakdown, came to stay at the Manor. Daphne Langley was thirty-two, with blue-black hair cut like a boy's and regular, almost classical features. Her pallor, her large melancholy eyes, her habit of sitting by herself apparently lost in thought, her refusal to be drawn into the general table-talk, all impressed Vivian, and to his adolescent imagination she was a romantic, lonely creature, bereaved by the war and probably wronged in other less obvious ways. He concentrated upon trying to attract her attention, performing small services, acting the gallant by holding her chair for her, opening doors and so on, ignoring the amused glances that passed between Mrs. Trafford and Mrs. Gould-Vane, dismissing Philip's sarcasm as envy of a superior technique in chivalry.

Daphne Langley remained impervious. It seemed that she was completely absorbed in her secret reveries. Mrs. Gould-Vane's niece, a lumpy young woman with an unfortunate resemblance to a parrot, laced her gossip about the lovely widow with hints of drug-taking. "She's doped, that's what's the matter with her. Never stirs herself to do a hand's turn anywhere."

To Vivian the whispered suspicions merely enhanced Mrs. Langley's glamour and mystery. Would she never notice that she had a fervent secret adorer? At Christmas he used his gift from Colonel Trafford to buy a small silver case to hold a book of stamps, but lacked the courage to present it. Impossible to place it among the other gifts on the breakfast table——

He slipped upstairs after his return from church with the others and, assuming that she was not in her room, opened the door an inch or so and slid his gift in over the carpet. It bore no message, but surely she would know? Then, somewhat dismayed, he realized that she was there, now, holding his tiny package.

"Just a little thing," he said awkwardly, "I expect you've got one already."

"But no. Why, it's lovely. How very kind of you."

"It's nothing," he said, backing away, almost tumbling down the stairs. The glow in those beautiful eyes was more than he could stand; wildly he imagined that he and she had fallen desperately, irrevocably in love.

All through the midday meal—and the smell of roast turkey was later to be a reminder of his emotions—he could hardly take his eyes from the face of his beloved. Logical reasoning, all sense of the ridiculous, were lost in his confused mood of mingled exaltation, anticipation, and despair. Everyone else helped to clear the table. Mrs. Langley, as usual when there was a general scene of co-operation, drifted away, but Vivian, carrying a few pieces of cutlery as an excuse, rushed into the hall after her. She smiled slowly and with a light touch on one of his wrists murmured "I'm going to my room. My head"—the slim white hand went to her forehead—"come up and see how I am, there's a dear boy."

So she understood! She too felt this compelling urge!

Of course he would kneel at her feet and, if she allowed it, just kiss the hem of her gown. Or did the invitation hold more ardent implications? Vivian made a perfunctory show of helping with the rest of the clearing-up, then rather ostentatiously he pretended to read in the lounge. Mrs. Trafford detained him, it seemed for hours, but at last he was able to slip furtively upstairs, trying to smooth his rebellious hair with his hands, pulling his collar straight. Too late now to remember that he should have scrubbed the ink from under his nails.

Mrs. Langley's room was nearly dark and he tiptoed across the floor, feeling suddenly afraid. She might be genuinely, desperate ill. She was on the bed and so still she might be no longer breathing. He leaned over her. "Are you all right?" he whispered, his lips dry and shivering. Her hand gripped his, pulling him down, he was aware of her exotic perfume, and in a sudden frenzy of excitement he was covering her bare shoulder with kisses. As the eiderdown slid away, he realized that she was naked. An almost derelict gas fire wheezed on the far side of the room. "I'm cold," she whispered, "so cold."

Mrs. Langley did not appear in the lounge at tea-time or at the supper-table. Vivian was deterred only by his promise to her not to rush up to her room. Was she in an agony of remorse? Or hiding because she too felt the inevitable tragedy that hung over their doomed love—doomed, because the stupid world would never understand that the sixteen years or so between them mattered not a jot? Late at night, when the house was sleeping, he tried her door and found it locked.

The agony lasted into Boxing Day, for still Mrs. Langley did not appear. Then the doctor from the village strode through the hall and Vivian, startled, could not restrain the query "Is she going to DIE?"

The doctor laughed. Oh, the grossness of humanity! Vivian waited at the foot of the stairs and was further stung by the doctor's comment, as he came down. "She's certainly going to die—but probably not for another quarter of a century. Maybe more than half a century."

Vague reports fluttered through the house. Mrs. Langley had taken sleeping tablets—three, four or five, when her prescription ordered one. Then Vivian was appalled to see an

ambulance at the door. To avoid the unbearable sight of his
stricken beloved being borne out, without the chance of one
last intimate word, he darted to hide himself in the lobby
where the tennis equipment was kept.

Too bad, everyone was saying, that Mrs. Langley had had
to go back to the nursing home. Philip was openly jubilant.
"I'm glad she's gone, I got sick of her reeking perfume."

"It was French and frightfully expensive." Thus solemnly
and ludicrously Vivian defended her choice.

"And of course," Philip added, "she was always trying to
lead me on."

This statement, Vivian felt, was too absurd to need
contradiction. He would not demean Daphne Langley's
memory by engaging in a vulgar dispute; instead, he applied
himself to writing what he hoped were immortal sonnets to
his lady love's eyes. He never saw her again but from time
to time, inescapably, the memory of those two hours of
bewildering emotion would set his pulses throbbing.

In the following summer he returned to Sidley Street.
During the war the Traffords had moved into a flat in West-
minster, and Philip was grumbling about its limited accommodation; he was to go to Cambridge in the autumn. With an
introduction from the Colonel, Vivian found a post at Trimble's,
an old-fashioned bookshop not far from the Traffords' new
home

After the spaciousness of the Manor House the second floor
in Soho seemed to have shrunk. Two houses in the street had
been demolished, the rest were all more or less scarred by the
bombing, and the lack of fresh paint and general renovation
gave them an aspect of decay. The petty activity of the locality,
which years ago had been full of interest, now seemed dull
and sordid. On the eve of his first day at Trimble's, Vivian
wondered whether he would ever be able to settle down here,
to fall into the pattern.

His mother, busy with her accounts, stirred from her
preoccupation to say, "Now you'll be able to go steadily,
without always fretting to get away from where you are. It's
lucky that top floor room was vacant, and the roof's been
patched up well enough. Out of your three-pounds-ten a week
you can give me half and I'll settle with Mrs. Glatt. When
I'm not back in time there'll always be something for your

supper, and if you haven't forgotten how to be handy you can serve yourself."

"Thirty-five shillings——"

"Yes, that'll leave you enough to cover lunches and fares. It'll do you good if you walk most of the way. You're well fixed up with clothes and as you get on you'll be able to buy your own."

"I'm still growing you know."

Mrs. Mander said sharply, "I shan't let you go shabby, or looking ridiculous."

Vivian reckoned up his possible day-to-day expenditure and as he did so he noticed the invoices on the desk. Twenty-two pounds, seventeen guineas—— His mother had been making money; she was still doing so. Yet she had haggled over the telephone with a hairdresser about the price of a permanent wave, she had complained when he himself had bought a volume on book-collecting, using part of a five pound note given him by Colonel Trafford. Was she becoming a miser? Why, in the last few years, had she become so absorbed by the development of her business, when formerly she had been so ready to preach that wealth was not the basis of happiness? What were her ambitions?

As the months passed she remained enigmatic, concentrating on her affairs, driving hard bargains, profiting from the prosperity that was the hang-over of the war. Only rarely did she show any flashes of her old tenderness, and even when she did she would quickly regain her almost impersonal manner. Yet Vivian felt no doubt of her love; it was as if she were on her guard against the emotional relationship.

At the end of a year at Trimbles he was receiving four pounds a week. Tom Cray, with whom he spent occasional evenings, was contemptuous of such earnings. "I'm on a much better lark," he said. "Doorkeeper at the Blue Eagle. Five quid a week and tips and what I pick up on the side."

"On the side?" Vivian echoed. Was Tom, who had been rather dull as a boy, going to develop as an easy-money racketeer?

"I keep my trap shut." Tom had developed the habit of talking in a husky undertone, as if every sentence he spoke might incriminate him. "Plenty of business is done in the club, I sometimes mind parcels for the big boys. Not my business to know what's in them." Tom smirked, his face curving into more lines than it should have had at his age. His spiky fair hair was now plastered down with an oily dressing, his bright blue suit had shoulder-pads that made it look as if he had put it on hanger, and all. "Four quid a week, chicken feed!" he remarked.

"But I like the job. We get a lot of interesting people——"

"Lot o' bookworms. If you want to get anywhere these days you've got to be in with the wide boys." Tom opened a fat wallet to pay for two beers and cigarettes. "Blimey, I could give your salary away and never miss it. There's a new lark that's going to bring in a packet. Nylons. Straight off of the ships, three quid a pair, and all the blondies rushing for 'em. Smashin'."

Another twelve months passed and Mr. Trimble raised the salary to five pounds. At about this time Vivian had become interested in Lorna Drew, who was in charge of the children's books. She was a plain girl, with frizzy brown hair, small eyes, and a rather coarse mouth that she emphasized by painting it bright orange. But surely such lack of physical beauty must be compensated for by spiritual qualities? On this common error in logic, Vivian built up a picture of a soul-mate, and to celebrate his promotion, invited her out for an evening.

Over a meal at the Corner House he expressed his interest in the housing problem. "In fact, I think we ought to go and have a look at Abbey House."

Lorna's small eyes glittered blankly. "Abbey House?"

"Didn't you see the news? A whole lot of squatters have taken possession of the place, it's a huge block of flats. They feel they have the right to homes."

"Oh," said Lorna. "What's it got to do with us?"

Rather pompously, Vivian said, "It's interesting from the point of view of social progress."

"Couldn't we go dancing?" Lorna sulked.

But she allowed herself to be piloted to a bus to Park Road, where demonstrators were chanting outside the invaded mansions and police were trying in vain to move on the watching crowds while guarding the two gateways that led into the private road in front of the block. Lorna soon tired of the spectacle, of the marching columns of supporters shouting in chorus, "The squatters want blankets, the squatters want water and blankets." Evidently the police allowed a contribution of blankets to pass, for people at the windows shouted "Twenty-five blankets are not enough," and the phrase was taken up by those outside, who presently changed it to "The doctor wants more blankets."

"What doctor?" Lorna yawned.

"The one who was allowed to take in blankets for the children."

A man at a window shouted "Pregnant women want blankets." Press-men were taking flashlight photographs and passengers in passing buses were staring. At the report that no more blankets would be allowed in, and that there was still no water in the block, the outside contingent organized a sit-down strike in the road. Lorna said irritably, "It's too late to go dancing now, it's a wasted evening," and went off.

Vivian stayed on, watching the traffic come to a standstill as more and more figures surged forward to sit or lie down on the road. Drivers, exasperated, used car-horns in a discordant chorus and one who tried to drive on came to a halt when he realized that his vehicle was carrying about a dozen young men who were swarming over the bonnet and roof. All around the stationary traffic the crowd jostled and chanted, watching the windows, in some of which fires flickered behind the vague silhouettes, and over the strange scene floated the intermittent voice from a loud-speaker "Support these plucky people. The people want blankets and water." It might, Vivian reflected have been the cry of cave dwellers of thousands of years ago —and this was civilization, with Lorna and thousands of Lornas wanting to dance away their thoughtless evenings. But was he any more effective in relation to a problem that should have shamed any but primitive people? Should he concern himself with humanity and not only with his personal life?

The speculation was to recur again and again, though only a week later, on a bus, he was responding to the provocative glance of a girl whose natural beauty was hardened by expert make-up. Teresa claimed to be a film actress, but he soon realized that the extent of her activities was an occasional day or so of crowd-work at various studios. Her demands were expensive and though he found her sophistication fascinating he became clear-minded at their fourth meeting.

All this prattle about clothes, cosmetics, expensive restaurants, and money—"I'm a waste of time for you, Teresa," he said, and after a long wide-eyed gaze she agreed in a matter-of-fact tone. "Of course you are. All my girl-friends say I'm being a fool and time *is* so valuable. But just for a little while—well, a girl can let herself off the lead some-times, can't she? You're so refreshing, so very young, so much younger than I *ever* was."

Yes, at twenty-three she was tough and experienced. The thought of glowing fruit already rotten at the core darted through his mind—yet Teresa wasn't such a delusion, for she admitted that she was obsessed by her ambitions. Her heart and brain were welded into a mechanism designed for climbing. He had had enough, now, of being the personification of youth for her old, old spirit, and as he made short, auto-matic replies he was urging her, silently, to go away.

Suddenly she said, "Darling, would you mind terribly if I went and telephoned?"

"Not at all." He had to make an effort not to smile at having conquered her so easily. Then he watched her walking through the cafeteria, slim and modish and arrogant, with all the men looking at her, and knew that she would not return.

On his way home he was considering his prospects. His call-up papers would be arriving shortly, and he looked forward without enthusiasm to the military diversion. Mr. Trimble had promised to keep his post open for his return. Philip had been rejected by the doctors, he was far from robust, and had all the airs and affectations of a young man of fashion in some more leisurely age. His taste in dress was effeminate; he excused his laziness by references to his early handicap, and his lack of filial sentiment by adopting the attitude that his parents had favoured the interloper. Vivian had spent several week-ends with the Traffords at their country cottage; on one occasion Philip had been there, and his patronizing manner was so offensive that afterwards Vivian was careful to accept invitations only when he knew that Philip would be away.

CHAPTER X

VIVIAN'S call-up papers had arrived just as he had a week-end invitation to the Traffords' cottage when Philip would be there. Previous refusals had been timed so obviously to avoid him that they were likely to be offended—but the authorities had solved the problem for the time being. The first three months of army life had dragged by; then as the routine became less irksome through familiarity, Vivian began to enjoy it. Early in his training he found a congenial spirit in Collinson, a lean, sallow man who was painfully aware of his own slightly grotesque appearance, of the lack of balance of his high forehead, prominent nose, and receding chin. By a combination of luck and wangling, they had remained together throughout their period of service, until Collinson returned to civilian life a fortnight in advance.

And there he was at Waterloo station, waiting with a Rolls-Royce and a chauffeur, making a characteristic reply as Vivian commented on such luxury. "Typical of my private life, old boy. Trouble is, the frame's so much better than the picture it contains. Hop in."

"It's decent of you to meet me. If I'd had a chance to put you off——"

"That's why I left the wire till the last minute." Collinson began talking about his father's theatrical business. "Expects me to go into it, of course. Ugh! First nights, bouquets and tantrums, fixing up tours. He can keep it."

"It's a ready-made career for you." Vivian spoke absently, thinking of his own return to Trimble's. Or should he try some more adventurous occupation? If so, what? He would never be an astute money-maker, in most situations the financial angle would occur to him only as an afterthought. Trimble's seemed to be the answer.

Collinson was saying, "You know, with your thought-transference act, you could be a top-liner. If you like I'll put you in touch with the right man——"

"Twice nightly!" Vivian exclaimed. "Skip it."

"Hundreds a week, waiting for you on a dish——"

"Not my dish. I'd get the jitters and leave the audience

flat. Just the feeling that I had to do it at a given time would stump me. Forget it."

"Pity. I could dine out for months on what you did to Sanders in the canteen. What a treat for the boys, seeing the sarge look such a fool."

"He asked for it."

"Sure.—Say, are you as glad as I am to be done with all that?"

"I don't know. It's been a break. New angles, with such a mixed lot. I always liked angles." And at least, Vivian reflected silently, he had sprung clear of the Traffords. From now on his life would be his own. "Put me down here, I want to stretch my legs."

"Don't forget today week."

"I won't. Scott's bar, seven o'clock. So long."

A few minutes' walk brought Vivian to Sidley Street. How squalid it was, after all! The door beside the lace shop was open and the odour of the house, once so agreeably familiar, now struck him as unpleasant. In a moment his mother was running down the stairs, falling into his arms, and her welcome made him feel that she had changed, had become demonstrative. But up in the second-floor room she was just as she had always been, controlled and watchful, as she completed the preparations of a meal. A nerve under one of her eyes was twitching, her hair had faded to a dull cream colour; she was as alert as ever, still conveying the impression that she was ridden by some secret enthusiasm—but what that might be he had never known.

Two days later he returned to Trimble's, and, by the time he kept his appointment with Collinson, it was almost as if he had never been away. Yet, as habit reasserted itself, there were moments when he felt stifled, caged, vaguely resentful. Self-discipline, he realized now, could be more difficult than mere obedience.

Leaning against the wall at the far end of the downstairs bar Collinson was glowering as he ordered two light ales. Well tailored and carefully groomed, he seemed to have acquired a new personality, but a few minutes in which his comments were all characteristically acid restored their familiarity. Vivian asked. "How's the theatre world?"

"I couldn't care less."

"Then you must be a terrific help to your father."

"Sarcasm's *my* line, old man. I'm not trying to be a help. I'm emigrating, as soon as I can get a passage. Australia, for choice."

"What'll you do there?"

. Collinson shrugged. "Three guesses, yours or mine, couldn't cover the possibilities. The old chap's raging, of course. But he was enterprising enough in his day and now I'm showing I'm a chip—no, call me a nasty splinter—of the old block."

They had two more ales while pooling their limited knowledge of opportunities in various colonies. Collinson said "Of course it's not easy to get a passage, but I can pull a string or so. I never cared to think of this country as a concentration camp. Why not team up and join in the get-away?"

"It's an idea." At the prospect of parting, Collinson's friendship seemed more than ever valuable. He was sensitive, courageous; his habit of bitterness was rooted in some inner dissatisfaction rather than in any desire to wound. Vivian brooded for a minute or so before he added, "You'll be leaving a prosperous father and a couple of sisters. Far be it from me to go all sloppy, but my mother's alone except for me."

"Persuade her."

"I couldn't."

"You mean you wouldn't."

"How right you always are."

They discussed their doings in the last week and Vivian mentioned the Traffords. "The Colonel came into Trimble's to ask me to dinner. I refused. Polite as polite, of course. He's a decent old stick, but I hope he took it as the sign-off. Let's go somewhere and have a sandwich."

In the bar in Haymarket Collinson changed his orders from beer to double whiskies. He was staggering by ten o'clock and had to be taken back to his flat in Brook Street. "Look at it!" he challenged, flapping a limp hand at the elaborate lounge. "Decor for a young man of fashion. Always had bew'ful backgrounds, old boy. Had to go away and come back before it turned my sh-sh-stomach. Handwoven velvet. Brocade. Wrap me up in my tarpaulin jacket, I'm pickled."

Vivian let himself out, ignoring Collinson's invitation— only just articulate between gulps from the bathroom—to have another drink. He walked to Soho marvelling that anyone should be driven to exile by an excess of money and luxury; if a spartan existence was preferable it could be found without travelling half round the world. Collinson had some queer twists in his mind.

And there he was again next day, bounding into the bookshop to report that he had had a stroke of luck in wangling a passage to Sydney. He bought four volumes of plays to read on the voyage as if the theatre were still his main interest. "Going in a couple of days. Have to pay some duty visits and all that, sisters with shiny new babies." Collinson was being almost too deliberately off-hand. Equally casually Vivian said "Good luck. Send me a line, some time."

"Sure. Funny postcards. Cheeroh." Collinson walked out quickly without glancing back, and Vivian was left with a sudden keen sense of isolation. They had been no more than camp-comrades, yet there was a quality in their friendship that seemed outraged by this abrupt termination. Automatically, Vivian attended to a woman who wanted advice about gardening books.

Colonel Trafford was dressing while Dr. Turnbull packed his bag and wrote a prescription. I'm puffy, getting old, he thought as he faced the mirror to adjust his collar, and it may have been some kind of envy that provoked his comments on Vivian. "He's incredibly fit. Fine upstanding young fellow. Brown as the proverbial berry, all muscle and no fat. Army training's done him a world of good."

"H'm, yes. You do understand you'll have to take it easy? When you're tired, give in and take a rest."

"He was always a handsome young blighter." The Colonel was inattentive. "Can't help making a comparison with Philip."

"I didn't realize Mander was back. As a matter of fact I'd like to see him. A colleague of mine is interested. Baumgartner. Top-notch psychiatrist. He went from Berlin to New York and came over here two years ago——"

But Mrs. Trafford appeared to say that tea was ready, and in the lounge the three of them discussed various topics, including Philip's progress at Cambridge, before Vivian was mentioned again.

"Of course," Dr. Turnbull said, "even old-fashioned blokes

like me have to realize there's more in physical and mental welfare than can be dealt with by stuff out of bottles and surgical enterprise. That paralysis of Philip's began as a physical condition, it might have continued indefinitely as a neurosis."

"It isn't only Philip——" Mrs. Trafford seemed to be defending her son against the implied accusation of special frailty. "Vivian's worked what seems to be miracles on plenty of others. At school for instance, the masters knew about his domination of the other boys. And he does seem to have the gift of—what can one call it?—of faith healing. A boy called Fairlie sprained his wrist quite badly, but Vivian concentrated on it and the pain went. Even the swelling next day—— And then there was an absolutely amazing thing with one of the masters."

"Oh lord yes." The Colonel chuckled. "Carter, the Latin master, he——"

But Mrs. Trafford felt that it was her story. "The poor man was driven nearly mad with nettle-rash. In a terribly hot spell at the end of the summer term. Vivian went to his study and offered to cure him. Well, the master was irritable—it's such a childish complaint, I always think—but he'd heard of some of the things Vivian had done, so after his first explosion of annoyance he challenged the boy to prove his words. Vivian cured the nettle-rash. The head wrote to Arnold, he felt it ought to be put on record. Such a definite instance."

"That brings me back," Dr. Turnbull said, "to what I was going to suggest. Dr. Baumgartner—I told you, he's a specialist—seems surprised that so far no one has made any serious test of the young fellow's capacity. He doesn't doubt the reports, but he suggested a demonstration. I promised to put the idea forward. Through you, of course. You've always been *in loco parentis* there."

"I don't know that I am," Colonel Trafford demurred. "Vivian's pretty independent, like his mother. He won't even come along and have dinner. And of course I'm under a sense of permanent obligation."

"Should have thought it was the other way round," the doctor observed. "You spent plenty on him."

"A few hundreds, neither here nor there when we had more than enough. But for him, Philip might still be in a

wheel-chair. I found Vivian a job as soon as he left school
and he's stuck to it, barring the national service diversion."

"Baumgartner's very keen to investigate."

"Well, Vivian was never disobliging. We can try."

Half an hour later the Colonel and Dr. Turnball were being
greeted by Mr. Trimble in the bookshop, which was full of
customers and browsers. The proprietor was an elderly man
with a permanently worried expression; his pince-nez gave
him constant trouble and when he was not adjusting them he
was plucking one side of his chin, as if feeling some invisible
scar.

"I'm afraid the visit's personal," the Colonel said. "Don't
let us keep you, we'll bide our time."

Vivian was serving a spectacled young woman who was
sniffing at books as if they could be chosen by their smell.
Colonel Trafford waited for the conclusion of the transaction
before he approached, "Hullo Vivian. Can you spare a
moment?"

"We're just on closing," Vivian suppressed a flash of
resentment. Was he never to be free of the Traffords? "Then
my time's yours."

Already Mr. Trimble was at the door, letting customers
out, shooting the bolt each time a few departed. Vivian was
switching off lights as Dr. Turnbull said "I wonder where
there's a telephone. Oh—sure to be one at the cash desk."

The grey-haired woman counting out piles of silver handed
him the instrument, but he hesitated before he dialled. Was
he wise, after all, to go ahead with this project? He himself
had no fancy for experiments, he liked conventional methods.
Baumgartner, on the other hand, was unorthodox, and his
moods were as unpredictable as were those of some of his
patients. His originality could be deplorable. Yet he was
patient, assiduous, generous. Dr. Turnbull dialled the number.

Vivian, too, was hesitating. But suddenly, in the dimmed
lighting, he was struck by the Colonel's changed appearance.
The old chap was getting on and he looked ill. Of course one
had to agree to whatever he wanted; it was obvious that this
was not just a casual call. So long as Philip didn't come into
the picture—"I'm ready," Vivian said.

But there was a slight delay on leaving. Mrs. Trimble
had turned up and introductions seemed inevitable. Her

husband removed and replaced his pince-nez a dozen times in quick succession; he seemed disconcerted as he told her "Of course I was coming straight home, my dear."

The Colonel, climbing into the car, remarked "Rather significant, that."

Vivian protested loyally "Trimble's a pattern of respectability."

Turnbull started the engine. "It's a wise employee who knows his own boss."

CHAPTER XI

So that was what they were planning. Vivian demurred "I'm not sure that I want to be investigated. I admit I've brought off a few stunts, but it's all catch-as-catch-can."

"Which suggests"—Dr. Turnbull swerved round a stationary lorry—"that it's time to apply some definite measurements."

"But in the last year or so I've almost dropped it. It didn't fit in with army routine, but at least it taught me one thing. Most chaps are scared of what they don't understand. Not inquisitive, or ready to praise or blame. Just dead frightened. Like a lot of wild-fowl who think they're being caught. So suspicious they can't even enjoy a joke, unless it's one they know by heart."

Turnbull laughed. "You're giving me quite a lesson in psychology. I believe you're right. The primitive instinct of fear is often a make-weight for lack of reasoning power. Quite a useful defence for fools who mistrust their own logic. Or haven't any."

The car was running through Portman Square as Colonel Trafford leaned over from the back seat to tap Vivian's shoulder. "Your mother must be pleased to have you back. My wife tells me she's busier than ever."

"So she is. She's at the workroom till nine or ten o'clock, most nights."

"Can't you make her keep reasonable hours?"

"I've tried. It's no good." Again Vivian was trying to assess his inability to influence his mother. Even when he had succeeded, her yielding had been due to her own relaxation. He had to conclude that their close relationship undermined the power that, with others, had been so effectual. Collinson's suggestion of emigration had provoked reflections on this point; it needed something like that, Vivian thought now, to make him realize how firmly bound he was; he would make his own life but she was inseparably part of his spirit. Yet she had none of the petty possessiveness that would have irked him.

The door of the house in Cavendish Square was opened by a maid and, as they were admitted, Dr. Baumgartner came down the wide stairway. Vivian found himself facing a man of his own height, probably twice his age, and much more heavily built. The psychiatrist had a square head with wiry brown hair brushed up in the German style, protuberant blue eyes, and a puffy mouth. Introductions were made and shaking his hand was like squeezing a flabby football. They were led up to the first floor, into a spacious room in which the curtains, armchairs, and carpets were all of a subtle shade of blue-grey. The armchairs were the only furniture and the one ornament was a tall grey vase on the mantelpiece in front of a curved mirror. It contained exotic scarlet flowers.

"Hibiscus and African lilies!" Colonel Trafford exclaimed. "And by jove they're real."

"I grow them myself," Dr. Baumgartner said.

"But how? Where?"

The puffy mouth, smiling, became a surprisingly wide arc. "By will-power," Baumgartner said, and Vivian felt that the flippant reply was a thrust. The daylight had scarcely began to fade, but a touch on some concealed switch illuminated the room with fluorescent lighting and, apparently automatically, the grey curtains swung across the tall windows. Evidently the host had some ingenious ideas. A strip of lighting ran round the curved mirror and now the brilliance of the flowers and their reflection was enhanced. A manservant came in with a tray that held a bowl of ice, a steaming jug, and one cup and saucer. "My cocoa," said Dr. Baumgartner.

"Cocoa?" Now it was the Colonel who sounded slightly scornful.

"Don't be alarmed. I do realize it's not popular as an aperitif." Baumgartner slid a panel in the wall and drew out a cocktail-bar from which, with flourishes like those of a conjurer, he detached four small chromium-and-glass tables. "Well now," he said, when he had served drinks and poured out his own cocoa, "this is a conference, ha? How do we begin?"

"Well——" Dr. Turnbull broke off and there was an awkward silence. "Perhaps Vivian would describe some of the—er—incidents."

Vivian was thinking, Let them ask the questions. Then he caught the Colonel's eye and had a flashing memory of that kindly man puffing and blowing as he fielded to make up a game of cricket with only three players, encouraging Philip at the wicket. Play the game—— "Of course," Vivian said. He found himself talking easily, explaining his delight when first he discovered that he could dominate his playmates in Soho. Then there was Philip, in the big house that seemed so incredibly luxurious, so exciting; a cripple who became a challenge.

"In fact," Vivian added, "there always seems to be an element of challenge in these events."

Dr. Turnbull turned to their host. "You'll remember the main points about Philip. He recovered, then seemed to be becoming altogether too dependent. He went off to the country without Mander, and was helpless again after only a few days."

"I remember perfectly." Dr. Baumgartner shrugged. "Possibly a hysterical condition."

Turnbull spoke with asperity. "He couldn't stand, that's definite. I tried some simple tests when I went down. Philip was in a chair in the garden and asking for a drink of water. I fetched it myself and left it just beyond his reach. He couldn't have known anyone was keeping watch. He called out, but of course I'd given instructions that no one was to answer. He tried to get to his feet, he did his best to reach that glass of water and ended up by sobbing himself to sleep. Vivian came down the next day and set him up again. After that they were in Berkshire together and Philip finished his schooldays normally enough."

Dr. Baumgartner's blue eyes glinted in Vivian's direction.

"Well, that's victim number one. What about the rest of them?"

"Oh, nothing so definite as Philip. I used to score off boys at school, every now and again. In fact I was in hot water more than once for making them break the rules. There was a bully called Vanek. He tried to be funny about my mother being a dressmaker——"

The Colonel put in sharply, "How did he know what she was?"

"Oh, I can't remember."

"But if it annoyed you so much—— You mean Philip told him?"

Vivian shrugged. "I was often a swine to Philip, when I felt he was hanging on to me too much. It was my fault, really. When he wanted me to go to the tuck-shop with him I told him he needed a nanny and he'd better go back to Mrs. Allberry. So he said I'd better go back to my slum and the sewing machine. Six of one, half a dozen of the other. I had the last laugh. Vanek kept on about the sewing machine and one day out at Caversham I made him jump in the river in all his clothes."

The three others laughed and Baumgartner urged "Go on."

"There was a washerwoman who used to come to The Manor—down in Berkshire—twice a week. She had an eternal backache. I took hold of her one day and willed with all my might that the pain should stop. It did. Mrs. Gould-Vane caught me with my arm round her waist—or nearly round it, I was only fourteen and she was awfully fat. Then a boy called Fairlie sprained his wrist. I got it right in no time. There were plenty of other examples. Since then of course I've been in the army, and I might have been unpopular if I'd done too much of that sort of thing. Certainly I did one or two stunts, and was suspected of having confederates. But an N.C.O. who thought he was a super-Montgomery——" Vivian wanted to laugh at even the recollection, "I gave him an awkward ten minutes, and that had them beaten."

"You tell us of results," Dr. Baumgartner demurred, "but what we should like to understand is the method."

"I don't know that I can explain it."

"You must be aware of the processes in your own mind."

"Well—yes. That's not to say I can describe them. Particularly to an expert in these matters. It's not as if I'd ever trained myself, or studied the subject. However—— I find I relax completely, physically and mentally. That's perhaps for less than a minute before I concentrate. Then I concentrate as absolutely as if my little finger were hooked on to a rope over a chasm, when hanging on would mean life or death. I have a feeling of—h'm, I hope it's the right word? —transmutation. I become the other person, he and I for the time being are a single entity. In some way that must account for the obedience, usually without any spoken instructions. As for the healing of pain"—Vivian shrugged—"perhaps for the time being the victim takes over my own roaring good health. Maybe that's why the subject needn't concentrate, declare his faith, or what-have-you. All I ask is the other's relaxation. Or rather, usually I don't ask but just hope for it, for that sort of request gets some people all tense and strung-up."

Dr. Baumgartner replaced his empty cup on the saucer, doing so with great care, as if fearing to make the slightest sound in the silence that followed. As he rose to refill the glasses Vivian added. "I think the trick, or whatever you like to call it, amounts to transposition, substitution. That's as clearly as I can put it."

The down-curve of Baumgartner's fleshy mouth implied scepticism, and Colonel Trafford remarked, "It's all beyond normal experience, anyway."

"What about the after-effects?" Baumgartner's inquiry was in a purring tone that seemed in keeping with his catlike movements. "Do you do anything to release your subjects from control?"

"The release seems to be automatic. Or perhaps it isn't. It depends on the case. I'd never worked it out before, but I realize now that there's a point at which I deliberately let go, break up the unity."

"And you yourself—do you feel any after-effects?"

"Not always, not if it's been some trivial effort. I've always had a terrific amount of reserve energy. But if I've put up a real effort I feel a sort of numbness, as if my senses weren't functioning normally. As if they've been keyed-up too high and have gone all slack. It doesn't last long. At times

I've been dead tired, whacked. Luckily"—Vivian smiled at Dr. Turnbull, poised on the edge of his chair as if waiting for some explosion—"I'm a good sleeper. I've never had a hangover of tiredness or nerves or anything the next day."

Vivian sipped his second glass of sherry. Surely he had explained sufficiently? The other three were silent, as if expecting further details. "As a matter of fact," he said, "there are times when putting on my act leaves me on top of the world. Exhilarated. As if I'd got a monster prize in a competition. Perhaps it's just self-satisfaction, a sort of gloating over my own cleverness."

"Do you feel a compulsion to—as you express it—put on your act?"

"Lord no! When I do it it's just to please myself, or because I happen to be sorry for someone. It needs no preparation and costs me no more than a few after-yawns."

"You prefer to perform in private? Or do you enjoy making a display?"

Vivian laughed. "I used to like showing-off years ago. When I was a kid. Now, I don't know. Or do I? I find it irritating if people make too much fuss about what seems to me so simple."

Evidently Colonel Trafford felt that further examples might be helpful, for he rose suddenly and said, "You haven't mentioned the case of the Latin master——"

"He was just one of them." Vivian was growing impatient. His mother would be wondering why he was late. "At least that affair had plenty of witnesses. There's no corroboration of one or two efforts that have been much more dramatic."

Baumgartner suggested, "Shall we have a demonstration now?"

"I'd so much rather not," Vivian said quickly. "You see, I've always acted on an impulse of my own, not to order."

"But," Baumgartner said smoothly, "you claim to be omnipotent."

"I don't! Why, it would be ridiculous——"

"Let us say," Baumgartner cut in, tapping his fingertips together as he gazed at the ceiling, "that Philip Trafford reacted to you because he felt some particular sympathy. It happens often enough between young people. An emotional reaction. You give an account of your 'miracles' without very much substantiation. Nettle-rash! Bah! It can subside with or without treatment. In most cases, as far as we're concerned your word is the only evidence. Shall we say———" The doctor moved towards the object of his attack, his sentence unfinished.

Both the Colonel and Dr. Turnbull were protesting. Vivian sprang up. "*I* didn't want to blather about it, I merely wanted to oblige."

There was a prolonged silence. Then Dr. Baumgartner's voice came softly, tauntingly, through his wide contemptuous smile, "Shall we say that you are a boaster and a liar?"

Now Colonel Trafford had risen. "I can assure you, from my own personal knowledge———"

A gesture from Dr. Turnbull silenced the outburst. Vivian's stare returned to Baumgartner and remained on him. He steadied his anger, maintaining his concentration. Baumgartner's expression changed; his smile faded and his beefy face seemed to go flabby. Vivian lifted his right hand, cocking a finger as he walked to the mantelpiece, silently ordering the other to follow him. Baumgartner moved slowly, as if he were sleep-walking.

For a moment stood passively, then he took the scarlet flowers from the vase and strewed them one by one about the room. With extreme solemnity he stuck one in the V of Dr. Turnbull's waistcoat, and was left holding a single flower, at which he gazed incredulously as he blinked himself back to reality.

Vivian was at the door. "Now," he said, "you know whether I'm a boaster and a liar."

He ran downstairs, but walked more slowly towards Oxford Street, for he had a sudden sense of exhaustion. But to think of the three men in that beautiful room with flowers starring the grey carpet, and Baumgartner coming to his senses gripping one last blossom!

Next day Dr. Baumgartner dropped in at Trimble's. "I provoked you deliberately," he said. "You'd said something about provocation, challenge, so I felt it might be the only way to persuade you to perform."

"Well, I bought it!"

"I could have resisted, but to what extent, and how much greater compulsion you could have exercised, I don't know.

The point is I felt your compulsion, understood your directions. You certainly have an extraordinary faculty."

"You were quite easy," Vivian said.

"I told you, I didn't resist. We must have another session, with both of us using all we know."

"I thought it was a conquest," Vivian smiled. "We'd better call it a draw."

"Oh, it was certainly a conquest. I was completely under when I decorated Turnbull. I'll never hear the end of that."

Vivian was aware that Mr. Trimble was watching them. "I mustn't stand about chatting, or I'll be having to dominate the boss."

"You can sell me an expensive book. Your gift must be a great asset in salesmanship. You show the customer something and it's sold."

"I don't play tricks in business hours."

Baumgartner ran on. "You see a beautiful girl and she's yours, you——"

Vivian interrupted "And when I want a horse to win I'll just order it to go at sixty miles an hour. No, it's a very uncertain faculty and the less I exercise it the better."

CHAPTER XII

On Saturdays Trimble's closed at one and Vivian reached Sidley Street about half an hour later. Mrs. Glatt was waddling along with her shopping basket, Johnny Johns came out of George's Dining Rooms carrying the two swords with which he juggled on various open-air pitches, Mr. Linzer was unrolling a length of lace in the doorway of his shop and praising its quality to a woman who was plucking and criticizing. Mr. Linzer's suits all had elaborate pleating at the shoulders, the coats extended nearly to his knees, and the extra fullness exaggerated his animated gestures.

Vivian went into the tobacco shop and when he emerged Mrs. Glatt was talking to Johnny Johns, who exclaimed "Vivian knows me, he'll say I'm O.K."

"Of course," Vivian agreed. "What's the idea?"

"I want a room," Johnny said, "I'm settling down. No more dodging off to fairs an' race meetin's. I'm goin' into a reg'lar business." He turned to Mrs. Glatt, "I'll give you a week in advance."

Vivian occupied the top-floor back room that had been Wyganowski's and the vacant room was next to it. He said "Of course, I've known Johnny since I was a kid——"

"Lodgers or no lodgers," Mrs. Glatt puffed, "I haf to finish my shopping."

She went on, followed by Johnny, then someone called "Hi, Vivian!"

He swung round and saw Philip Trafford. "Philip! What the devil are you doing in London?"

"Just slipped up for the day. Good lord, you *do* look full of pep. The maiden's dream, and no mistake."

"Come on in," Vivian said.

"No. Let's go somewhere and have a drink. I'd rather not meet your mother."

"She's probably still round in Frith Street."

"My old things don't know I'm up." Philip brushed away a thread of fluff that had settled on the lapel of his lavender-grey suit. "Where shall we go?"

"The Swiss? But wait a moment—or I'll follow you. It's in Old Compton Street." Vivian ran upstairs and opened the door on the second floor. His mother was there. "I just thought I'd let you know, I shan't want lunch."

"But it's ready." Mrs. Mander pointed to the cold meal on the table.

"You'll have to eat my share."

"What are you up to?"

"I shan't be long." He went out hastily to avoid having to invent explanations. On the way to the pub Philip remarked that he was meeting a girl at a quarter past two.

"That means I'll have to hurry. I'll do it in a few minutes in a taxi. But I've come away without enough ready cash. You can change me a cheque, can't you?"

"For how much?"

"A tenner."

Vivian shook his head. "That's what I earn in a fort-night." They turned into the bar.

"Well, eight pounds? Or a fiver?"

"I can manage a fiver, I was paid yesterday." Vivian ordered two half-pints.

Philip had his cheque-book on the bar. "Who shall I make it payable to?"

"I haven't a banking account."

"Oh. I'll leave it open then."

Vivian counted out the notes.

"By the way," Philip cautioned, "don't mention you've seen me. The old birds would be mad, thinking I was neglecting my studies and them and all that."

"Well, are you?"

Philip smirked. "All part of my education, old boy." He drank his beer in one long draught, said "Sorry I can't stop," and dashed out, leaving Vivian waving the cheque to dry the ink.

Mr. Linzer was still in his doorway, watching for a chance to tout for custom. Vivian asked if he would change the cheque and the lace-merchant drew a great bundle of notes from an inner pocket. "Of course," he said amiably. "Very pleased. Ven you get young lady, you pring her to look at my lace. Lof'ly quality, all colours, best price."

"Thanks, Mr. Linzer."

Vivian went up the stairs two at a time and received the greeting he expected. His mother said "Whatever are you playing at? You come dashing in, you don't want any lunch, then just when I've cleared away, here you are. Do you want any or don't you?"

"I'll get it. Don't bother."

But already she was spreading the cloth. "What made you change your mind?"

"I thought I'd go out with a chap. Then I didn't want to."

Her expression told him that she knew he was hiding something from her, and he added, "After all, I don't have to explain every moment."

She sighed. "No. You're a man and men always do what suits them, no matter if everybody else is put to inconvenience."

He patted her arm and made her smile. "Something else has upset you, what is it?"

"No. Only—sometimes I think we've lived too long in this street."

"Flats are hard to find."

"Do you have to tell me that? Sit down, do. It's corned beef." She tossed the salad in its dressing.

"What about yours?"

"I had it."

"You didn't take long. You eat about enough to keep a sparrow alive." Vivian noticed that the ottoman was open, and some of the contents stacked on the floor. "Have you been having a turn-out?"

"Some of your old things." Mrs. Mander picked up an exercise book. "I never knew you kept a diary."

"Oh that. It was ages ago."

Mrs. Mander opened the book and read *"Vivian Mander, aged ten, 32 Sidley Street, London, England, the World, the Universe, Space——"* She glanced down a page. "How well I remember Mrs. Weston coming to see me!"

"Mrs. Weston?"

"You made her Bertie eat three bananas with the skins on them."

"So I did. I'd forgotten."

"And this——" Mrs Mander read another entry aloud, *"I tried to stop a lady crossing the road, but she crossed. A failure."*

"Go on," Vivian said, "confessions are good for the soul."

His mother gave him a long non-committal look before she turned a page. *"February twenty-fourth, an exciting day, there was a blizzard——* Blizzard with only one Z in it."

"I remember! A woman slipped off a bus and broke her arm and I got her in a doorway and after a few minutes she didn't feel a thing. I took her home. All manly and chivalrous, I suppose."

"How do you know her arm was broken?"

"Doesn't it say?"

Mrs. Mander read *"The doctor from the next door flat came and said her arm was broken and he could not understand why it was not hurting. Got home, Mother in a stew. A definite success. I would rather stop pain than make people do silly things."* Mrs. Mander paused. "A good thing you knew that much. Then there's a long piece about Bill Ogden."

Vivian took the book and glanced at the account. Bill Ogden, who had taken Dollie Hart's room after she left, had been troubled with insomnia. Playing a violin in an orchestra till dawn, his days were almost as restless. But how easily he had succumbed to persuasion, and after three days had needed no persuasion.

"I never knew you wrote it all down," Mrs. Mander reached for a piece of sewing and was threading a needle. "I never did understand you, and that's the truth."

"Mother——"

"What is it now?"

"Did I get any of this from my father?"

She threw down the scrap of silk, exclaiming bitterly, "Your father thought he was the cleverest man in the world. He was always smarter than the next. There wasn't a question he didn't know the answer to, he had plans to reach the moon, to the moon and the sun——"

Her tone was becoming shrill, almost hysterical. Vivian leapt up. "I'm sorry. I didn't mean to remind you of anything that would—— Here," he offered his handkerchief.

"I'm all right." She straightened herself abruptly. "I'll clear up the things if you've finished. Do you want a cup of tea? If you do you'll have to make some fresh. I'll have to go back to Frith Street, there's an order that won't be finished by Tuesday if I don't get on with it. Violet being away—oh, I didn't tell you, she's got 'flu. And I've still got my week-end shopping to do."

A trail of breathless sentences dragged over an old sorrow to hide it—Vivian said gently, "I'll come and carry for you."

"You're a good lad, Vivian."

"Oh, I like the market, it's so lively."

"Come on then." They went out and along Berwick Street, weaving their way through the crowds round the gaily coloured stalls.

CHAPTER XIII

THE sun was striking through the early morning haze when Vivian came down to breakfast on Sunday, to be startled by his mother's cryptic exclamation "Taking in street beggars!"

"Who is?"

"Mrs. Glatt. That fellow who hangs round the pubs and scrapes a living on the pavements, the one with the two swords —she's letting him have that other room on the top floor."

"Johnny Johns. He's all right. He certainly earns all he gets. Juggling's hard work."

"This is just a house for ne'er-do-wells. It's only that it's central, or I'd have got out before the war. I'm sure I never thought I'd be living all these years in the middle of riff-raff."

"Johnny's going into business. I heard him telling Mrs. Glatt."

"If idle talk came true we'd all be millionaires. Get on with your breakfast, do, unless you want me to be standing about till midday clearing it up."

Vivian sugared his grape-fruit. Nowadays, he reflected, his mother made a habit of acid comment, yet her nature could never be otherwise than kindly. "Dolly Hart had that room," he mused, "I often wondered what happened to her. What a life! Fifteen shillings a week for being a waitress in a place where hardly anyone left a twopenny tip." He had a sudden clear recollection of Dolly's pale despairing face. She had borrowed a shilling from his money-box to make up her rent one week, and had given him some bull's-eyes when she repaid it.

"If she's wronged in this life," his mother was saying, "she'll have her reward in the hereafter."

How easily religious faith could smooth out every problem! But did the Almighty lash the weak with misfortunes merely to give them a lovely treat in the hereafter? Did the same power allow the twisters to flourish in order to give them hell later on? What proof was there that any sort of re-adjustment lay ahead? No proof, only faith—and perhaps a capacity for faith was the greatest natural gift anyone could have.

He turned from his ethical reflections to read the paper. But he felt restless, and presently he suggested "I'd like to go up the river. Would you come with me?"

"You know I've always plenty to do."

"Isn't it time you started sitting back sometimes? We'd get some fresh air, after being stuck indoors all the week."

"You know well enough, I was never a one for gadding

about. Running here and running there, people tire themselves out."

He did not press the subject, fearing to exasperate her. But how relentlessly she drove herself, grudging herself even small luxuries. Had she what was sometimes labelled an anxiety complex? It took him a minute or so of reflection to realize that if this were so, it would be anxiety on his behalf. As if he couldn't look after himself. "I wish now," he remarked, "I'd fallen in with Tom Cray's idea. He's gone on a steamer to Clacton."

"He's no friend for you, the bad lots he mixes with."

"Yes, he does seem to have got into a different crowd," Vivian agreed, "the big-money racketeers."

His mother took up the comment with asperity. "Is that another way of saying you're dissatisfied?"

The room seemed hot and stuffy. Across the whole front page of one of the newspapers lying on the table ran a headline about the Haigh murder trial; the acid-bath horrors had kept the public shuddering all the week. Vivian went upstairs and as he opened his door Johnny Johns called from the next room.

Johnny was unusually smart in a new suit. His luggage seemed to consist of his two swords and one broken suitcase, and now he was fixing the swords in the shape of a cross on the wall. "My fam'ly crest," he grinned.

Johnny's cheerfulness, even his stunted and twisted figure, seemed like a reproach to depression. His buoyant disposition had not subsided through all the vicissitudes of his vagabond existence. "What's this business you're going into?" Vivian inquired. "Or was that just a yarn for Mrs. Glatt?"

Another bright grin. "No yarn, I give you my word. I've saved a few nicker an' I'm goin' in with Ginger. You know Ginger Parly, 'e's fed up with the ice-cream lark an' we're openin' a club."

"Where?"

"Old Compton Street. The Two Swords, that's its monicker. Ginger knows the business, 'e was barman on one o' them big liners. We got talkin' about what a lot o' money there was in drinks, an' 'e's got a bit put by for the ante, so there we are an' Bob's your uncle. We open Wednesday, you got to be there you know."

D

"I'll be there but I shan't stay till breakfast time."

"Nor will nobody else, see? We're goin' to keep to the hours. We don't want to put our bit into a show an' 'ave the busies comin' in an' closin' us down, before we got a chance to get the money back. You trust ole Johnny!" He winked knowingly. "Well, I got to go an' meet Ginger. Got to buy a few small tables."

"On a Sunday?"

"East End. Open till about three. Come with us?"

"Well—no." Vivian invented an appointment, realizing again how far he had outgrown the companionship that Sidley Street offered.

He followed Johnny down and from the second-floor window saw Johnny limping energetically along the dusty pavement. Tashy Vautel was over the way, and now crossing the road, with a very beautiful girl beside her—a girl with flowing golden hair and a creamy skin. Even from this height, as she looked up, he saw that her eyes were greenish-grey. His mother, busy behind him, rapped "What are you staring at?"

How surely she sensed his interest! He said "Tashy Vautel."

"Haven't you seen her often enough? You might find something better to do than gaping at her."

Two minutes later there was a tap at the door and Tashy was there with the golden-haired girl. Mrs. Mander checked her surprise and bit out the word "Yes?"

"Could I talk to you for a moment?"

"What is it?" Grudgingly, Mrs. Mander admitted them.

Tashy was wearing less make-up than usual and was quietly dressed. But Vivian's attention was upon the girl, now standing timidly just inside the door. Her face was heart-shaped and her mouth was like that of a cherub in an old painting. One hand was thrust into a pocket of her light linen suit, a crucifix hung on a slender gold chain at her throat.

Tashy said "This is my daughter. Olga."

"Your daughter?" Mrs. Mander was not concealing her antagonism.

"Say how d'you do to Mrs. Mander, Olga," Tashy rapped.

Olga extended a hand and withdrew it quickly when she realized it was not going to be taken. Her "How do you do, madame?" had a trace of French accent in it. Vivian moved over to her, took her hand, and was aware of his mother's sharp disapproving glance, though his own eyes did not veer from Olga's face.

"She's been at a convent near Paris," Tashy was saying. "She was there all through the war. But she's come back for good now. She's learnt to do beautiful sewing and embroidery and I want to get her a job."

"You can sit down," Mrs. Mander said shortly.

Tashy flounced on to a chair. "You're in the dressmaking business. I thought perhaps you'd help."

"But I've two assistants already, I don't need any more."

"I thought you could tell me how to get her into a good firm. That's the idea, isn't it Olga?"

"Yes, please," Olga said. "It would be very kind of you."

Mrs. Mander's glance softened as she studied the girl. "The best thing for you to do would be to watch for the advertisements in the papers."

"Oh yes. I will do that. But London is so strange. So enormous."

Her gaze returned to Vivian, who said "You'll get something, easily enough."

"Take samples of your work when you go to apply," Mrs. Mander advised. "How old are you, eh?"

"Nineteen, madame."

Tashy said "Haven't I told you, Olga——? We don't use that 'madame' stuff here. Oh, Mrs. Mander, there's another thing. They haven't got another room over the road. I suppose you don't know of one?"

"I don't. Mrs. Glatt's full up here."

"I want it to be somewhere respectable," said Tashy, and her words seemed to echo with implications of her own dubious position.

"Yes. Of course."

Tashy rose. Impulsively, Vivian seized the chance just as they were going out to ask Olga "Are you doing anything today?"

"Doing anything?" Olga seemed puzzled.

"Would you come up the river with me?"

Olga glanced at her mother, who laughed, "Why not?"

"But I should like to, very much," Olga said.

"Then why shouldn't we go right away?"

Again Olga looked at Tashy, who said, "It's O.K. by me."

Vivian snatched up his tweed jacket, not caring that his

mother's whole attitude signalled disapproval. At the door he turned to say gaily "If we're late, don't wait up," and followed the two down the stairs. Outside, the sun was brilliant.

"Well, good-bye Tashy," he said, and as he and Olga walked off, he had to answer Olga's questions about the nickname. "It's what she's usually called. Among friends, I mean."

"But her name is Natasha."

"I ought to call her Mrs. Vautel. It's just my cheek——"

"Your mother dislikes her. There is no friendship there."

"That's only because they don't know each other very well. Oh, here's a bit of luck. A taxi."

"You are extravagant," Olga smiled.

"I feel extravagant." In the taxi he asked her how long she had been in France.

"Since I was six years old."

"That's just about when we moved into Sidley Street."

"You're lucky," Olga remarked. "You live with your mother."

"Yes." Vivian felt awkward. There were obvious reasons why Tashy might find a daughter an embarrassment.

Olga was saying "My mother's work is so different."

"Oh—yes. Yes." He was at a loss.

"I mean, working in night clubs. She plays the piano.— You have lived so near for all these years, surely you knew that?"

"I'd forgotten," he lied. "I was away for quite a while."

"She does it for me. I've had a very good education. For her, a real musician, jazz cannot be amusing."

Lamely, he agreed, "No, I shouldn't think it is. Tell me about France. What was it like during the Occupation? Did you see much of the Germans?"

"I was only ten when they came. We were very much protected, the Sisters were very good. But one of the girls— her father died for the Resistance, and others had fathers, brothers, who were killed or wounded. It was a sad time, everyone was feeling very bitter. And——" Olga broke off, her lips trembling.

"And—what?"

"Perhaps you know. About my own father."

"No. Tell me."

"Etienne de Bry Vautel. He was—— It was a bomb from a British plane. When I was told, it seemed that he must be a relative. I'm de Bry Vautel, also. I wrote and told mother. Until I had her reply I did not know that I had told her of my own father's death."

"I'm so sorry."

"I never knew him. I mean I can't remember him."

After a moment or so Vivian said "In that we're alike. I can't remember my father, either." The common deprivation seemed to forge a bond between them and as the taxi ran along Oxford Street they were holding hands.

In the train, sharing a carriage with nine others, they were more cheerful, but Vivian was slightly disconcerted when Olga revealed that she had heard a great deal about him. "But how could you? I mean, your mother's never known me except by sight, and even if she's a super letter-writer——"

"I had very few letters," Olga admitted. "But already I have been in London for two days."

"And to think I didn't see you till this morning!"

"She tells me you study occultism."

"I don't!"

"But you can do strange things, you release sufferers from pain."

Vivian laughed self-consciously. "I was hoping to start clean with you."

"I'm sorry, I don't understand. Tell me, please."

"Some other time. This is just a happy day, let's just enjoy it."

"But if we know so little of each other——" she demurred.

"It isn't easy to give a fair account of oneself."

"Of course," she pursued, "I know you have been lucky. Some rich people practically adopted you and spent thousands of pounds on you."

"Well, that's a fancy version. I was useful to some well-to-do people and that's how I had a better education than I might have had. I'm glad, of course, but on the other hand it sometimes makes me feel I don't quite fit in anywhere. I shall sort it out, sooner or later." He had a persistent premonition that the trend of his life would be decided by some external factor, which now he could not discern, even dimly.

The presence of the others in the carriage was making their conversation seem even more intimate than it might have been if they had been alone, for they talked almost in whispers. Olga spoke of her travels as a small child with her mother, "Berlin, Amsterdam, then some places I forget, always in big hotels. And then London. Just one week I remember in London, buying clothes for going to the convent. Everything black. You can't imagine how strange I feel in this." Olga touched her pale blue linen.

"Are you a Roman Catholic?"

"No. Mother sent a special contribution to a charity, every year, always insisting that I was not to be converted."

In Windsor they strolled round before lunch, and lingered over the meal before going on the river. Late in the afternoon Vivian ran the punt into a side-stream and was about to tie it up when his eye was caught by another punt sheltered by the overhanging trees. In it Mr. Trimble was embracing a woman with brassy hair. Then, realizing that he was being observed, he disengaged himself and adjusted his pince-nez. Vivian returned a blank stare, paddled swiftly, and managed to contain his laughter until the other pair were some thirty yards away. Even so, he realized uneasily that sound carries farther over water than on land.

Olga said "There's some joke?"

"That was my boss. I'll have to keep a straight face when I go in tomorrow."

As daylight dwindled and the moon turned the river to what looked like liquid platinum, a gramophone playing a waltz lured them to a smooth bank at the top of which couples were moving to the slow sentimental rhythm of 'When I grow too old to dream'. Olga murmured enviously "I have never danced."

"Then this is the perfect night for a beginning."

In his arms she felt light and ethereal, and she quickly gained confidence, following the movements with a natural sense of rhythm. Into her ear he said "You're happy?"

"Oh yes. Tonight is too wonderful to be true."

As she looked up her eyes caught the moonlight, and he kissed her mouth. When the last notes of a wailing tune died on the gramophone they still held each other, waiting for another record to begin. But the owner of the gramophone was slamming it shut. "It's finished," Olga murmured, and drew away. "Nothing will ever be beautiful again."

"Oh yes, it will. Thousands of tomorrows——"

But the magic was broken in the hurrying back to Windsor, the last-moment scramble into the train, to find themselves sharing a carriage with a noisy family party determined to indulge in horseplay. It was nearly midnight when they reached Sidley Street; when, at the doorway beside the gown shop, Vivian took Olga's hand and said "You're going to kiss me good night?"

She drew away. "When we were dancing it was so different. The cool grass, the sweet smell of flowers, everyone so happy. Even by night this street is ugly——"

The door opened abruptly and Tashy was there, clutching a dressing gown round her fleshy hips. "Come in do, Olga. I wondered where on earth you'd got to."

"I'm sorry if we're late——" Vivian began, but Olga was being hustled in and the door was slammed.

Even by night this street is ugly . . . Tashy, of all people, disapproving of a late return! Vivian went upstairs quietly, and though there was no thread of light under his mother's door he heard her voice. "Vivian——"

"Yes Mother?" He opened the door an inch or so. "You shouldn't have stayed awake. Good night." Though he could not see her he realized that she was sitting up, and he was as aware of her familiar expression of worry as if the room had been full of light.

"Don't get involved with that girl of Tashy's. I've been thinking, whatever it costs, even if I have to pay a lot for rubbishy fittings, I'm going to find a flat in another neighbourhood."

"Good night, Mother. Don't lie awake worrying."

Over the road Tashy had gone quickly into her room and with a dexterous movement, before Olga came in, had hidden the bottle of gin that had been her companion for the evening.

She challenged harshly, "What have you been up to, eh? Have a look at the clock."

"I'm sorry. You did not tell me what time——"

"I can't tell you, do this, do that, you're not a baby. You ought to have more sense. I could have gone off to sleep hours ago." Tashy yawned and then suppressed a hiccup. Solitary drinking always made her nervy. "I might as well tell you now and get it over. You know you can't live here with me, I'll fix you up somewhere, but wherever you are you'll meet rotters. All men are rotters. I'm telling you, because I want you to have a decent life. Understand?"

Olga stood trembling, silent and biting her lip, feeling tired, dispirited, bewildered.

"Get this," Tashy pursued ruthlessly, "don't give any man the chance to mess about. Don't be taken in by love stories, they're the oldest wheeze. The second-oldest is fancy stories about money, and if you believe them you'll be flat on the pavement. I'm going to find you a job. Then if you meet a chap with a level head and he's in a good position, keep him waiting a year or so and then marry him. Respectability, in the long run that's the only racket that's any good to a woman."

Olga said miserably "I'm trying to understand. You're respectable, aren't you?"

The question almost sobered Tashy. She rumpled up her coarse dark hair. Had she said too much? She wasn't in practise for inventing delicate phrases. "Yes, of course, of course. What are you standing about for? Get undressed, do, you worry me, staring like that."

Tashy flung off her dressing gown, fell on the wide divan, and in a minute or so was asleep. Olga lifted an arm that dangled to the floor, drawing up the bedclothes. In the glow of the standard lamp she saw tears on her mother's cheeks and a smear of mascara outlining one nostril; then, with a sudden pang, she realized for the first time that her own childhood was over.

CHAPTER XIV

THREE days later Mr. Linzer was standing outside the window filled with rainbows of lace and, as Vivian emerged from the side-door, he pounced, flourishing Philip Trafford's cheque. "No goot! A dud, not vort a penny. You gif me fife pounts."

"I haven't got five pounds." Vivian inspected the red superscription. "I'm awfully sorry. Of course there must be some mistake."

Linzer's shrug, his widespread open hands, dismissed all mistakes as irrelevant.

"I'll let you have it this evening," Vivian said.

"I am knowing you long time, isn't it? All right, you pring me cash zis efening, I say no more."

Vivian hurried on. Had Philip known that the cheque would be returned? Either way, it made things awkward. He himself, in his lighthearted outing with Olga on Sunday, had spent freely, and would have been short of cash until Friday even if it had not been for this hitch. There was nothing for it but to pawn his watch, the gold half-hunter that Colonel Trafford had given him on his twentieth birthday.

It was his first experience of pawning but he had heard enough of the technique. Ask for twice what you expect to get—— But he needed only five pounds to dispose of the situation, and this was the sum he asked for. The weasel-faced man behind the desk in the little cubby-hole demurred over the inscription inside the case, and Vivian walked out with the ticket and four-pounds ten. Now he could pay Linzer, and somehow manœuvre through the week.

He was about fifty yards from Trimble's when he saw Olga on the corner ahead, obviously waiting for him, and all his petty calculations blew away in the thrill of surprise. Since Sunday he had seen her once, by chance and for only a few minutes. Now, in the clear morning sunlight, she seemed lovelier than ever.

"I've found a job," she exclaimed. "At Jakeline's in Grosvenor Street."

"That's fine. When do you start?"

"On Monday. I'm living with one of the other girls. Brenda Paton—her aunt has a boarding house in Belsize Park. I took my trunk there yesterday."

"Give me the address. The phone number." As he wrote on the fly-leaf of his diary he was realizing that he would be late at the shop. "What sort of job? Anyway you'll be independent, now."

"Oh no. I am to have very little pay. Mother will pay the balance of what I need."

The information almost brought Vivian down to earth.
Life was controlled by pounds, shillings and pence. "I'm glad.
Olga, you know I want to see you often, be with you as much
as I can. You must have known it when I kissed you by the
river. You must have known—Olga, I love you, you're the
only girl I shall ever love."

That dreadful midnight in her mother's room. The shame
of what had been said, the ugly mystery beneath those few
short phrases. A horse-van clattered by as Olga said uncertainly, "You have known me, Vivian, only for three days."

"What does that matter? One knows something like that
at once or never at all. I'm sincere, Olga. I'll prove it. I'll get
on, I'll make money—I'm sorry, I suppose I've been too
abrupt." But why was Olga staring at him as if appalled?

Love stories . . . they're the oldest wheeze. Fancy stories
about money . . . Olga ran off, leaving Vivian quite mystified.
He pursued her for a few steps and stopped in confusion. He
could easily have overtaken her, but already he was late.
"Oh hell!" he exclaimed at the passing crowds, and went on
to Trimble's.

Mr. Trimble glowered and Vivian guessed the thought
behind the wobbling pince-nez. Mr. Trimble had been detected
in undignified dalliance up the river, and was suspecting that
his employee was presuming upon that situation. The atmosphere of slight tension was made no easier when a typist
came out of the office and said in Mr. Trimble's hearing
"There's a personal call for you, Mr. Mander."

Colonel Trafford was on the line, suggesting that Vivian
should call on him that evening. "Six-thirty," Vivian agreed,
"I'll be there, sir." He wondered whether the Colonel was going
to propose some further experiment with Baumgartner. Or
would it be Philip's secret visit to London? The cheque?
Suddenly Vivian realized that he would not be able to repay
Linzer this evening, for Linzer left his shop at six-thirty and
went home to the East End. Why did events combine to make
one false to the best intentions? Of course he should have
remembered his promise to Linzer. But Linzer would be
there tomorrow and the Colonel was entitled to special
consideration.

The fine weather broke in the afternoon and at six o'clock
Vivian hurried through drizzling rain to the nearest teashop.

Another five minutes' dash through rain took him to Aynham Gardens, where Colonel Trafford opened the door, explaining that his wife was playing bridge in the flat overhead. The maid had left. "We're going to manage with a morning woman," he added. "Dammit, in the end I shall be scrubbing the floors myself, a fine end to my campaigns. How's your mother?"

"Very well, thank you sir." Vivian noticed how cautiously the Colonel lowered himself into an armchair, as if unsure of his joints, yet in a moment he was up again, to stand with his back to the bare modern mantelpiece.

"Change in the weather, most exhausting. Now then— m'm, ah—— You'll know I didn't get you along just to talk about the rain. How long have you been at Trimble's, eh?"

"You'll remember, I started when Philip went to Cambridge. Then of course there was a break, when I was called up."

"And you like it? Yes, of course, or you wouldn't have returned to it. Well now, I'm going to be direct, because Mrs. Trafford will be back and I want to get things settled. You know of course, that whatever I did, I could never feel I'd completely cleared my debt."

"Really, there's no debt."

"Don't talk poppycock. Philip might have been a cripple all his life."

"Oh well. It just happened he reacted."

"So did Baumgartner. But all that sort of thing, psychic stuff or whatever it is, it's not my line——" The Colonel had a fit of coughing. "Where are my lozenges?"

Vivian handed the tin across.

"Ah, that's better. Now about this job of yours. Or rather about your future. I'm not a rich man, I'm very poor. Matter of proportion, I suppose, but it's my level that's being bled. But obviously I must do something. If the money had lasted, you'd have gone to Cambridge with Philip."

"I'm better off," Vivian said, "than if I'd never met you." But was that the truth? Tom Cray and other boys in Soho were making more than five pounds a week; men peddling nylons would spend that amount on a dinner.

"You're steady," the Colonel was running on, "and you must have learnt quite a lot about books. I may as well confess it. I have a sense of urgency. Events don't take their course, they leap at one. Perhaps it's this confounded atom scare. And of course I'm not so young. To cut the cackle, I'm giving you a few hundred, Vivian. You can buy an interest in a bookshop or do something, surely, to make the sort of headway you're entitled to."

It took Vivian a moment or so to absorb the proposition. "But already I've cost you—I don't know what."

"The money wasn't spent for your sake. Fact is," the Colonel chuckled, "I'd never have spent a penny on you for love of you, as a kid. I told Dorothy you'd be a confounded nuisance but we'd have to put up with you. Now—well, we've got to know you better. I thought of five hundred pounds. Could you do something useful with that?"

"Of course! Why, with that I could start a small place of my own. Perhaps second-hand books—I'm so taken aback I'm almost forgetting to thank you."

"That's all right. Understood." The Colonel moved to the bureau and began raking about in a drawer. "Never can find anything. Ah, here it is."

As he sat down to write his cheque Mrs. Trafford came in. The nervous tension that formerly had been so carefully controlled was now expressed in an air of haste and fluster; she was pulling off her tiny grey hat, complaining at a pin that caught the veil, as she smiled a greeting, asked her husband what he was doing, and moved across to adjust a cushion.

"I haven't seen your mother for ages. It's just no use asking her to make anything, one has to wait an *eternity*." The comment was smoothed with a smile. "It's awful how rushed everyone is, I mean we all thought after the war it would be all peace and calm, and look at us, *racked* with anxiety. Arnold, did you take your medicine? And where's Philip's letter? I know Vivian would like to read it."

"Nothing special in it," the Colonel growled. "Here you are, my boy. I've made it out for five hundred. You'll have to open a bank account, you can give me as a reference."

"Thank you, sir. I'm well, as I said, so surprised I can hardly say how grateful I am. To both of you."

"Oh, Arnold and I talked it over," Mrs. Trafford said. "We agreed completely."

"I've sometimes dreamed of having a small place of my

own. I never thought I'd have a chance of it—anyway, so soon."

"It's not a lot to start a business on," the Colonel remarked. "But you have youth and health and initiative, so good luck to you. The Lord only knows what Philip will do when he finishes at Cambridge."

Mrs. Trafford sighed "He'll just have to marry an heiress."

"Dorothy, you have the most frivolous mind."

"But you know yourself, he does depend on others. Vivian, you must be sure to let us know how you get on. What are you going to do, I mean, what business?—Oh, books. Then you *must* keep in touch with Philip, he'll be awfully interested."

He won't, thought Vivian. "Yes of course. If he sends along any of his friends I'll give them a discount."

"How clever of you to know all about business! I expect you get it from your mother. She's getting to the top in her own way. Oh dear I've lost my brooch—no, here it is. Arnold, don't you think we ought to have a drink? Those three women were quite exhausting, arguing about the two-club and the four-five no-trump——"

The Colonel went out and his wife was prattling on. Then she broke off. "I'm jabbering stupidly, I'm a wreck. You'll have to control me as you did Philip."

He laid a hand on her arm and she murmured "Of course, I was joking."

"I'm not."

She laughed artificially before she relaxed. They stood still for a full minute in silence, then she said "Well really, you do have the most soothing effect. I feel as if I'm drifting. Drifting. That's it. Perhaps I must learn to keep on drifting. I'm always trying to be on my toes."

"Drift," Vivian said. "Forget about yourself. Forget to fret about whether you're on or off your toes."

"Could I? I wonder."

And then the Colonel returned with the tray, grumbling about the mislaid corkscrew. "Really Arnold," his wife said placidly, "you worry too much, you're always so *anxious*."

He shot her a sharp glance. "*Me*, anxious?"

"Of course you are. I'll find the thing." Mrs. Trafford went out, smiling amiably, and her husband's shrug suggested that he renounced the hope of understanding her. For usually it needed only the hint that something was mislaid for her to dart about like an agitated bird, uttering exclamations of dismay.

The corkscrew was found, the sherry bottle opened, and fifteen minutes later Vivian left the flat.

CHAPTER XV

MAKING for the tube, Vivian was in a state of high exhiliaration. Olga must be the first person to know of his wonderful good fortune, for if all went well he should be in a position to marry her—no, not within a few months, but in a year. His extravagant fantasies disregarded the facts that he had known her for only a few days, that their intimacy had amounted to no more than holding hands and a few kisses, that only this morning she had fled from his precipitate declaration.

The house in Belsize Park stood back from the road. He was aware of the strong perfume of the floral border to the path; in the twilight the vegetation seemed to be steaming after the rain. The woman who opened the door was short, her hair was cut like a man's and her hands were thrust into the pocket of a masculine jacket. In her lined face her steady grey eyes suggested a slightly contemptuous attitude. Vivian asked for Olga and the woman demanded flatly "Who are you?"

He gave his name. "Her mother and mine have lived opposite each other for years."

"But," she countered stolidly, "it's just to get her away from the sort of people who live in that street that her mother's sent her here."

He let the implied insult pass, concentrating upon persuasion. "I'm not such a desperate character, you know."

"You can't see Olga."

"Are you Mrs. Paton?"

"Yes I am, and I'm looking after Olga as I do after my own niece."

"You talk as if you've got them shut up in dungeons."

She took the observation with good humour. "If I had they wouldn't be at the pictures."

"What time will they be back?"

"You're wasting your time, young man."

"I'm not. When Olga comes back from the pictures she's coming out with me."

"You're very cock-a-hoop, I must say!"

"I'm just telling you. We aren't in the Middle Ages."

"You'd be taking her to one of those Soho clubs and I'm not having it, understand?"

The accusation was a reminder of his promise to go to the opening of The Two Swords. "I won't take her anywhere she couldn't go with you. She's not working till Monday, so a late night won't hurt her. I'll be back in less than an hour and a half and then I'm taking her out. That's settled."

Mrs. Paton seemed about to contradict. He repeated "It's settled, I told you."

"I didn't agree."

"But you're going to."

"I don't know, I'm sure——"

"I do."

"I must say," Mrs. Paton frowned, "you've got a very persuasive way."

He smiled. "Could I use your telephone?"

A moment's hesitation, then she stepped back, admitting him. The telephone was on the table in the hall. There was no reply from Sidley Street and Vivian tried the workroom. "I say, Mother, I've had the greatest stroke of luck——"

His mother's voice broke in coldly "I want to see you, Vivian."

"Why, what's the matter? All right, I'll be with you in about twenty minutes."

As he replaced the receiver Mrs. Paton said "Twopence". He dropped the coppers on the table. "I'll be back, you might tell Olga to expect me."

"I'll tell her," Mrs. Paton agreed placidly.

Both his mother and Violet Bracey, her head assistant, were in the workroom in Frith Street, and as he went in he exclaimed brightly "Don't you two ever stop working?"

Then his mother's expression warned him that his flippancy

was not in tune with her mood. "You'd better get along, Violet," Mrs. Mander said. "That's three hours to be added to your overtime."

Violet found her handbag and applied a layer of white powder to her moonlike face. She had small eyes and, now she was tired, looked older than her thirty-five years. Since the death of her husband she had always dressed in black; she went out without bothering to brush the threads of cotton that clung to her. "Good night, Mrs. Mander. 'Night, Vivian."

"What's gone wrong?" Vivian asked.

His mother laid Philip Trafford's cheque on the table, and in exasperation he exclaimed "Hang it all, Linzer must have known it'd be all right. I've got the money for him."

"Then why didn't you pay him?"

"Because something quite important took me in another direction."

"I settled with him. You know I never owe anyone anything."

"Then take this." Angrily, he offered the notes.

"That means you'll be five pounds out of pocket."

"Until I see Philip or he sends it, yes."

Mrs. Mander gazed suspiciously at the money. "You must have spent quite a bit on Sunday," she remarked. "And you've still got plenty."

"What do you think I am, a crook?"

She said coldly "I wish you wouldn't do things behind my back."

"I cashed the cheque for Philip. It's a mistake, that's all. I'm not a child."

"You *are* a child if you take a bit of paper that's only rubbish and get good money out of a neighbour and make me look a fool. Come along home and I'll get your supper."

"I don't want any. I promised to go round to Johnny's." Vivian was still holding the five notes. "Are you taking this?"

"Where did you get it?"

"If you must know, I pawned my watch. But as you're so indifferent, it'll suit me better to settle up in a couple of days' time." He was angry, and doubly-angry over his own rudeness. All over a few pounds—"I'm opening a bank account in the morning and paying in five hundred, so you're safe enough."

With that he walked out. But before he reached the corner of Old Compton Street he heard his mother calling after him and he hurried back to meet her. "I'm sorry, Mother."

"You said—did you say you had five hundred pounds?"

"Colonel Trafford gave it to me. To start a small business."

"Oh. That's it."

"I was going to tell you."

"It was given to you," she murmured as they walked on. "It was given."

"Why, you didn't think I'd stolen it?" Would he ever know why she distrusted him so profoundly? "Do you want to see the cheque?"

"No, of course not. You're young to run a business——"

"Let's talk it over tomorrow. This evening I've an appointment."

"You mustn't be late." They turned into Sidley Street. "Vivian, we're moving away from here. I'm after getting a flat, a top floor in Bayswater. It'll be more of a home for you. I've to see the landlord in the morning."

"You're a marvel. A flat—in these days!" She was unlocking the door, stepping into the dark passage-way. On a sudden impulse he followed and embraced her. "Good night, Mother. You really are wonderful, you know." She seemed pleased, though always she would be haunted by some secret, ineradicable bitterness of spirit.

The Two Swords was only a few minutes' walk away, in a basement below a leather merchant's. The narrow stairs were lit by crimson-shaded lamps, and at their foot a stubby young man with a Glasgow accent was on guard. The club room retained its cellar atmosphere though it had been superficially decorated. Impossible palm trees were painted on the walls, with sun-bathing females whose poses might have been provocative if the artist had been more familiar with anatomy. About a dozen men were at the bar with several girls, a radio was blaring. Vivian greeted Johnny Johns, and said "Hullo Ginger" to the man behind the bar, who called out "I do the work and Johnny does the social stuff," then he was handed a drink "on the house". In spite of the liveliness and noise, the palms and the nudes, the place suggested a crimson-lit tomb in which the occupants were making their last protests against extinction.

Vivian said "Have a drink, Johnny," and found himself paying for seven glasses to be refilled, then as some more men arrived he slipped away to the centre of what Johnny called the dance floor to finish his own half-pint. Almost immediately he was joined by a tall sallow-faced man of forty or so with crooked eyes in a narrow face, sleek brown hair, and a thin, sardonic mouth. He had the over-tailored look of a dummy in a shop window.

"Your name's Mander, isn't it?" he challenged.

"Yes." Vivian averted his head. A puff of cigarette smoke had been blown straight at him.

"I thought I couldn't be mistaken."

"Who are you?" Vivian put down his glass. He had not eaten since lunch, and now he wondered if the drink could be going to his head, making him imagine an element of insult where none was intended. "What's your name?" he asked.

"Max Lassiter.—Convey anything to you?"

"Not a thing."

"Oh. Pity."

Yes, the insult was intentional. Vivian said evenly "Where have we met before?"

"Ever heard of the Adriatic?"

Vivian had been to the restaurant twice since his first visit with his mother. Once with Colonel and Mrs. Trafford, once with Mrs. Trafford when they came to town to buy a birthday present for Philip. "Yes, I know it," he said.

"It was there," Max Lassiter drawled, "I saw Mrs. Mander for the fourth time. One, two, three, four—you see how exactly I can count the occasions. She was with a kid with black curly hair. I see it's cut shorter nowadays."

"That was—I don't know how long ago."

"I recognized you the moment you came in."

"But do you know my mother?"

"Never spoke to her in my life."

"Then how do you know my name?" There was no reply and Vivian added "Where did you see her, before that?"

"It's all a long time ago." Max Lassiter yawned. "You see I'm about twenty years older than you are. But perhaps it doesn't matter, anyway."

"Then," Vivian exploded, "why the hell do you start talking to me?"

"Interest, my boy. Interest."

At this moment Johnny Johns came over to say "You two all right? Don't want nothing?"

"Nothing," Vivian said sharply, and walked out. What on earth could the fellow have been hinting at? Was he drunk? But he had been strangely precise about the visit to the Adriatic all those years ago. The brief interlude had been oddly disturbing and the impression of malice lingered.

From the corner of the road in Belsize Park, Vivian saw Olga and another girl at the gate twenty yards away, and as he overtook them on the garden path Mrs. Paton appeared in the doorway. Evidently she had been on the alert. Vivian hardly waited to be introduced to Brenda Paton, a stubbily-built girl with frizzy brown hair and a large, amiable, plain face. He took Olga's hand, led her back through the gate, and waved to a taxi just wheeling away from a house nearly opposite.

Olga gasped, "Mrs. Paton—— She didn't say a word!"

"I saw her earlier."

"But she's awfully suspicious. About everybody."

"I put the 'fluence on her." Vivian opened the door of the taxi, telling the driver to go to the Adriatic.

"You take my breath away," Olga murmured.

"Good." As he sat beside her he lifted her hand, drew off the glove, and kissed her finger-tips. "This is the most exciting evening I've ever had."

She remained serious. "If you can persuade Mrs. Paton you can do anything. You'll be hypnotizing me."

"Never. For one thing I *don't* practise hypnotism, and for another you'll always have me beaten. In a way it's the same with my mother, I very seldom try to persuade her about anything because I know I'd probably fail. Perhaps— I don't know, but perhaps it's the close link, affection and all that, makes all the difference. What's it matter? Darling, you're so lovely, I'm as happy as a king."

Olga was silent. He said "You didn't mind my rushing up and grabbing you like that?"

She shook her head, her expression was still troubled.

"I meant it when I told you I love you——"

"That's just it!" Olga interrupted quickly. "Do you always do everything in such a rush? Mother was talking to me, warning me, it was almost as if she knew in advance."

"Hang it all, if things have gone wrong for her, it doesn't mean they'll go wrong for us, does it?"

"I don't know. Since I've been in England, I realize how little I know. What other girls take for granted are things I'll have to get used to. I'm really only just out of school. I feel frightened if you keep surprising me."

He laughed confidently. "I'm not dangerous. But I'll remember to go gently."

At the Adriatic it seemed a happy omen that the table at which he had eaten his first restaurant meal should be vacant. Benito came forward and led them to the alcove, inquiring about Mrs. Mander. Vivian said "She's very well, though I wish she'd take things more easily."

"Ah, enthusiasm!" Benito exclaimed. "She is an artist, always her designs were so clever. She should have a studio, a magnificent showroom."

She could have, Vivian thought. Obviously the work in hand strained the resources of the cramped workroom and fitting-room. He turned his attention to the menu, envying Olga's easy pronunciation of the French dishes as they discussed the meal. "And of course," he told Benito, "we'll drink Chambertin."

"Why did he smile?" Olga asked.

"This was the first restaurant I ever knew. Mother and I drank Chambertin, and I think the old boy's got a long memory."

"There aren't many people——" Olga's grey-green eyes ranged over the tables.

"It's late for dinner, I suppose. I've lost all count of the clock."

Benito brought two wedges of golden melon and a waiter was dealing with the wine. Vivian asked "Where's Antonio?" and Benito shrugged expressively. "You mean he's dead?"

"He was seventy-eight. Time passes."

Raising his glass, Vivian smiled across at Olga. Her white-blonde hair was slightly ruffled, her eyes were bright, her freshness and youth made irrelevancies of age and decay. "Time lasts for ever. Here's my eternal love."

Discreetly, Benito withdrew. He had seen so much of eternal love—and its mutability.

Olga sipped her glass. "I wish you wouldn't talk of love," she said. "I told you, it dismays me."

"All right. I'll tell you about my fabulous fortune. I really am a lucky chap."

Love and money. She must beware of being credulous; surely her mother had experience enough for her warnings to be accepted as wisdom? "Having a job in a bookshop isn't a fabulous fortune."

"Oh but I haven't told you! I'm a capitalist and I'm going to be a go-getter. I'm opening a business of my own and the cash will simply roll in. Good-bye to being a wage-slave."

"You talk extravagantly," she said quietly.

"I don't. It's true. I've been given a cheque." He brought it out. "The Traffords have done a lot for me, one way and another. This is to give me a start—and it ought to mean *our* future. Could it?" Again, he realized, he was being impetuous, but the situation seemed to demand enterprise.

She shook her head. "I don't know. I'm feeling lost. In a strange country——"

"But it's your own country, and, hang it all, England and France aren't so far apart."

"It's a different atmosphere. And you see—I have many things on my mind. I thought I was coming home. Home, to be with mother. I never realized she lived in one room. And her life is so mysterious."

Vivian was stung by compunction. Only to someone completely innocent could Tashy be a mystery; she was marked by her years of promiscuous adventure. "I mustn't rush you, you're quite right. All I ask is that you'll trust me and believe in me, for I'll never let you down."

"I'll try," she said.

He wanted, not an effort on her part, but her spontaneous confidence "I love you and shan't ever stop loving you. I'm quite certain about that." Again there was the baffling look of secret distress in her grey-green eyes. "Oh lord, I thought this was going to be such a merry celebration, and we seem to be fencing."

As if she had not heard, Olga said "I'm going to grow up and develop and *be* someone, not just a stupid girl who's always trying to understand what ought to be like A.B.C. Up to now I've been a child. Now I'm part of the world, but it'll take years to understand it. In five years you could talk to me about love and money."

"Five years?" He was dismayed.

"I shall be wise enough by then, or I ought to be wise enough, to know what I'm doing."

He exclaimed "Does everything have to be arranged so reasonably? Where's your heart? Does everything have to be put through the sieve of logic and labelled wise or unwise? Couldn't you ever be impulsive?"

"Yes," she said, "but that's what I'm afraid of."

He tried to keep the irony out of his tone. "Then it seems that I must learn to be purely logical."

The waiter was dusting crumbs from the table and he asked for the bill. He had the opportunity, finding Benito at the door, to ask "Do you know Max Lassiter?"

"Yes."

"Who is he?"

"A general dealer—that is what he calls himself." Benito's expression was as enigmatic as Olga's behaviour had been, as he added quietly and urgently, "Keep away from him."

"I certainly shall," Vivian said lightly. The sparkle of the early part of the evening had fizzled down to flatness; perhaps he had expected too much, perhaps he was just an optimistic fool. "Good night, Benito. Thank you." In the taxi he and Olga were both conscious of constraint, and at the gate of the house she said good night with almost book-of-etiquette formality.

CHAPTER XVI

THE sign-painter was finishing the lettering over the shop in the alley-way off Charing Cross Road. *Second-hand Books.* MANDER. *Books Purchased in Large or Small Quantities.* Pausing after adding the flourish to the capital 'Q' the man glanced down into the shop and smiled cynically at the new tenant, now sorting out stacks of dusty volumes piled on the floor. As if there weren't enough old books in Charing Cross

Road, without young curly-top coming along and thinking he could make a go of still more books in a side-alley!

It was mid-afternoon. Within the shop Vivian was resisting a mood of depression caused by the chaos of dingy mounds of volumes, which had been bought at a score of auction sales. He straightened up as the postman came in, throwing a book of sermons into what was to be a sixpenny box.

"Mander?" The postman handed over two letters. "There's several for Smithson."

"Gone away, no address," Vivian said.

"Hope you'll do better than he did." The postman walked out.

One of the letters was from Philip—a request for a loan of ten pounds. Vivian tore it up, remembering how long it had taken Philip to make good the fiver that had been advanced on his worthless cheque; then he went outside to see how Sainsbury, the painter, was progressing. The sight of his own name in glistening white on bright green brought a new flash of uncertainty. Would he, after all, know how to handle the cash side of the business, make a steady profit, and continue to give his mother three pounds a week? Tomorrow they were moving from Sidley Street to a top floor in Oxford Square, just north of Bayswater Road.

He glanced along the rows of shops on each side of Orange Court. Obviously some of them had been established for a long time, but the delicatessen shop was new, so was the cheap fancy store. Their newness indicated previous failures. He asked Sainsbury, who was still elaborating his capitals, "Who had that place before it sold delicatessen?"

"Second 'and books." Sainsbury came down the ladder, a short wiry man who would have looked at home among stable-lads. He took a cigarette from behind his ear and said "Think you'll do all right?"

"Can but try. Who had that other shop—the fancy goods place?"

"Second 'and books. No, come to think of it, it was artificial flowers."

Vivian laughed shortly. "I'm glad all the failures weren't books."

Sainsbury felt almost sorry for the young fellow. Still, he didn't look hard up. That tailored tweed jacket had never come off-the-peg. He remarked "It's not many chaps of your age who can set up on their own. Needs capital."

"Not a lot. I suppose I'm lucky."

"Lucky, are you?" Sainsbury's shrewd eyes glistened with curiosity. "Not 'orses or dogs?"

"I never made a bet in my life." Vivian went back into the shop and through to the room behind it. The newly-installed telephone was on the floor and he made a place for it on the book-stacked desk before prowling back into the shop. "What a mess, glory what a mess," he exclaimed despairingly. He thought of Olga, no doubt busy on some dainty piece of work on an upper floor of Jackeline's premises in Mayfair. How long would it be before he could expect her to consider him seriously? For the present she agreed to see him only on terms of friendship.

"If it wasn't 'orses nor dogs," Sainsbury pursued, "I s'pose it was a legacy?"

Absent-mindedly, Vivian said "The father of a friend of mine set me up with a few hundred."

"Oh. A loan, like?"

"A gift." How inquisitive the fellow was. Vivian turned away.

But Sainsbury was not easily snubbed. "Oh, so a gentleman makes you a gift, does 'e? Very nice too. Nice to know a gentleman oo'll say, ' 'Ere you are, take a few 'undred, there's plenty more where this comes from'."

"Oh shut up, it's not your business." Vivian lifted a pile of books and lumped them on a shelf, shuffling a few of them into alphabetical order.

"Well, I've finished. You'll get the account from Mr. Wainwright."

"Thanks. You've made a good job of it." Vivian found two half-crowns and slipped them into the ready hand. "Something to put on a horse."

Sainsbury made a wry face, jerking on his overcoat. "Somethink to buy a drop o' somethink to make me forget my shoulder."

"What's wrong with it?"

"Kind o' rheumatism, the doctor says. It's shockin'." Sainsbury pawed his right shoulder. "O' course, it don't do it no good, 'olding me arm up to do that lettering. Fair stabs me."

Vivian hesitated. It was a year or so since he had made his last experiment in easing pain. "Would you let me do something about it?"

"You?" What did the chap think he was, a magician? "What could *you* do?"

"Come over here. Sit down and relax."

"Relax?" Before he sat on the wooden box Sainsbury stared at it as if suspecting that it was a trick contraption.

"Think about nothing. Or about something so ordinary that it's nothing. Imagine you're in a pub with a pint of beer in front of you. Your work's finished, you've got the whole evening ahead with nothing to do, absolutely nothing to hurry for."

Sainsbury's sharp eyes were full of doubt and speculation.

"Just stay quiet." Softly and slowly, Vivian repeated "Quiet, quiet, quiet."

A passer-by, glancing in the open door, saw a workman seemingly half-asleep with the tab-end of a cigarette smoking beside his boot on the littered floor. "You'll be setting the place on fire," he called.

Neither of the two in the shop heeded him. The stranger walked in and put his heel on the smouldering stub, but still they took no notice.

Vivian said "It's better, isn't it?"

"Why—yes!" Sainsbury sat up with a jerk. "It *is* gettin' better. Not achin' 'alf so much."

The man's astonishment was almost ludicrous. "Stay there for a minute. Quietly. Relax."

"I say——" began the stranger, then, deciding that both the others must be deaf, he broke off.

"It's gorn!" Sainsbury muttered. "It don't 'urt no more."

"Look here, I've saved you two from having a fire——"

"Eh?" Vivian glanced at the extinguished cigarette end. "Oh, thanks. We were rather absorbed."

"We could all be absorbed and the whole blooming town could go up in smoke." The stranger walked out in a huff.

Sainsbury rose, still marvelling. "Funniest thing I ever struck," he said. "I can't feel a thing, an' it was chronic." He swung his arm. "Not a perishin' twinge. Cor lummy, if you can take the jim-jams out o' people, what are you doin' with a ruddy bookshop? You oughter be one o' those whats-its,

faith 'ealers, not that I'd got any faith. Why, you ought to
go in for bein' a doctor."

"Couldn't afford it."

"Well I don't know I'm sure. I'm sure I don't know."

"I must lock up and get along." In Sidley Street there
would be another form of chaos in preparation for the move.

"But look 'ere, my wife's got a terrible back. I don't
know 'ow long, ever since 'er third was born——"

"I know, I know. And I can make it better? Sorry, and
all that, but I'm not in business as a healer."

"If you could do it for me why not . . . ?"

"I can't possibly. I only took you on as an experiment, to
see how it would go." Sainsbury was staring incredulously.
"It's just an occasional trick of mine, nothing more."

"Rummiest trick I ever struck. 'Ow long will it last?
The cure, I mean."

"It's not a cure. It's just temporary relief." Vivian walked
to the door. "Come on. I'm locking up." What a time to have
yielded to the impulse to help someone! So often the exercise
of his power had left him limp and spiritless.

"But think of what you *could* do, if you put your mind
to it." While Vivian found his keys and secured the door
Sainsbury ran on, "If somebody was very ill, say dyin', you
could do your stuff, I mean, if you can do what you done——"

"Oh skip it, will you? With all this nattering about your
shoulder I've forgotten to telephone—— Well, cheeroh."

"Cheeroh an' thanks a lot."

Sainsbury went off, turning to wave his hand in a wide
circle to demonstrate his ease of movement, and Vivian
returned to his back office to make his call to the firm who
were removing the furniture to Oxford Square. As he spoke
he was suddenly aware that he was not alone and, swinging
round, he saw Max Lassiter in the archway between the
office and the shop. His hat was tilted on the back of his
head, the unshaded bulb in the centre of the ceiling made
skeleton-like angles of his features, accentuating his intent
crooked eyes, his pallor, his expression of malice.

"Yes? What do you want?"

"To see you."

"Well, you've achieved your object and you can get
out."

"Oh no." There was venom in the slow twisted smile. "No, Vivian Mander. I want to talk to you. You see—I'm sorry to drag it up, but somehow I can't get it out of my mind."

"I'm not interested in your mind——"

"No? But oughtn't you to be? In case you don't know, it was your father who murdered mine."

For several moments Vivian did not take in the full import of the statement. Then, as he stared in silence, the implications of his mother's many evasions became clear.

"Your father murdered mine," Lassiter repeated. "*Now* you know how I recognized your mother. I saw her in court on a Tuesday and a Wednesday and just for a few minutes on the Thursday. This was over twenty years ago, I was about the age that you are now. She didn't wait to hear the verdict, she was in a delicate condition. You were the delicate condition."

In his confusion of horror, Vivian was surprised by the steadiness of his own voice. "Even if it happened to be true, what could I do about it now?"

"That's what I've come about. There's another angle. I've been around the West End for quite a while and I know Tashy Vautel. That daughter of hers—Olga. You're very interested in the daughter, aren't you?"

Vivian had to moisten his lips. "Leave her out of it."

Lassiter smiled sardonically. His expression was that of a fanatic marooned in some secret joyful faith. "Maybe I have a sense of humour. The daughter's quite attractive. Yes, *very* attractive. You've done me an injury—oh yes, the sins of the fathers, you know, you can't get away from it——"

"You're crazy!"

"Oh no. I'm quite, quite sane. About Olga——"

Vivian stepped forward, his fist clenched, and after a moment's tense silence Lassiter shrugged. "Surely you don't want to start a brawl?"

"Then shut up about Olga. About—what you told me, there's nothing I can do. I'm sorry. But one can hardly apologize for murder. It happened before I was born." Slowly, the realization of the nature of the 'accident' of his mother's legend was becomingly hideously vivid.

"Four months before you were born, to be exact," Lassiter said. "Three days before you were born your father was hanged."

Chokingly, Vivian muttered "Will you get out? Will you get out *now*? I advise you to get out, don't say I didn't warn you, I——"

Max Lassiter dropped back a pace and when Vivian's eyes were clear of blinding misery and rage he had gone.

CHAPTER XVII

AGAIN Vivian locked the shop door. It had occurred to him that he might discover how much truth there was in Max Lassiter's accusation, without rushing home to ply his mother with distressing questions.

At this time of the afternoon the Adriatic Restaurant was closed, and when Benito appeared at the side door he looked as if he had been awakened from sleep. A pyjama jacket hung open over old black trousers as shiny as leather.

"I'm sorry, Benito. I'm afraid you were resting——"

"Always in the afternoon. I am not so young. But come in." Benito led the way upstairs and opened the door of a sitting-room. His wife was at the table sorting embroidery silks. "Momma, this is Norah Mander's boy. You remember?"

"Norah Mander. Yes, yes. She was working with my Lisa. So she has a son who is taller than all of us. Come in, sit down, of course we are glad——"

Evidently Benito had made some gesture, for suddenly his wife gathered up her silks and went out. Vivian said "How did you know I wanted to see you alone?"

Benito's gruff voice was gentle. "My boy, I guess you are in some trouble."

"It's because you knew my mother years ago that I've come to you. Did you know my father too?"

"M'm. Let us sit down. Let us have a glass of wine." Benito went to the sideboard.

"Thanks, but I couldn't drink anything. You did know him?"

Benito nodded slowly.

"How did he die?"

Benito rested the tips of his podgy fingers on the plush tablecloth. "Your mother has never told you?"

Vivian said desperately "I want the truth, that's all."

"Your father he looked so much like you. And your mother, she is always so sweet——"

"I don't want evasions, I don't want you trying to make it easier——" Vivian finished abruptly, "Did he murder someone?"

Benito drew in a faintly hissing breath. "Yes."

"A man called Lassiter?"

"Yes. That was the name."

Vivian dropped on to a chair. How false had been that old story of an 'accident'. All these years his mother had nursed her bitter secret. "Could you tell me about it?"

It was a minute or so before Benito spoke. He lit a cigar, offered a box of cigarettes, fidgeted about the room, and sighed heavily as he sat down on the opposite side of the table. "It broke your mother's heart. So sorry we all were, but how could we comfort her? It was a tragedy too great. When she brought you here that evening, I was glad to think that again she was happy."

"I don't think she was and I don't think she is. She's always been haunted. I never even guessed why until half an hour ago. It's been—a shock. Though I always realized there was a mystery, and sometimes I thought—well, it doesn't matter now what I thought. Could you tell me more about it? If you can, it may stop me trying to imagine details, making the whole horrible business even worse than it was."

"Your father was in the war—the old war, you know, the one against the Kaiser. Then he was wounded in the head. That was—m'mm over thirty years ago, of course, but I tell you to explain everything. After the war, so much disappointment, bad times. He had some money, he imagined he was rich, somehow he found more money. Perhaps"—Benito shrugged— "yes, it was a sort of vanity. Trying to live like the smart set, *with* the smart set. Norah, your mother, she tried so hard to make him steady, she loved him so much. His ambition was enormous, terrible."

Vivian exclaimed bitterly "So he had to do a murder."

"Your father and Lassiter—Jim Lassiter he was called—

were in some schemes together. They made money, they spent it. Always I shall believe that your father was led by the other man, who was much older, who already had been in prison for some confidence trick. What happened between them no one knows, or can ever know. My opinion at the time, I remember so well, was that Lassiter had some scheme, some bad scheme, and your father would not agree to it. Perhaps he was threatened. What is certain is that they quarrelled and your father shot him. That's all."

"Even if they quarrelled," Vivian spoke explosively, "even if the old Lassiter was a monstrous crook, that's no excuse."

"No. But at times your father felt his wound. It was in the head, possibly a wound to the brain."

"But didn't that help him at the trial?"

"It might have done," Benito said quickly, "if he had been more sensible. But he would have no defence, he pleaded guilty and to the end was reckless and boasting. Today it would be different, the doctors understand a conflict, a splitting of personality, a man who is injured behaving not like himself. I explain badly. In the war, at the time he met your mother, he had been in some bad fighting, and in that he had been brave. In many ways your father was good, generous, and always kind. But so proud, so—what is the word? —arrogant, and quickly in a fierce temper."

"Well, now I know. I only hope there were as many charitable explanations as you seem to think there were."

"Vivian—I speak to you as I would to my own son. Do not be too much distressed about all this. I imagine—and I have thought often about this matter—that you are very like your father was before he was in all that violence and killing."

"Lots of men have fought and got over it. Must a war leave a lot of maniacs?"

"But that old trench warfare, lying for days and nights in the mud and blood with the dying and the dead—— Is it so strange if it affected a sensitive man. If his sense of proportion became unbalanced? After all, he had killed good men against whom he had no grudge, because that was his duty. And then to be wounded in a way that, perhaps, was not fully understood——"

"Hundreds, thousands of men," Vivian rapped, "endured all that savagery without letting it turn their brains." He broke off and added abruptly, "Thank you for telling me what happened. I didn't want to ask Mother a lot of questions. It's some consolation that Lassiter, the victim, was a wrong 'un."

"Bad, bad," Benito made a sweeping-away gesture with one hand. "Confidence tricks, and once a fire in his warehouse for which the insurance company refused to pay. He knew titled people, rich people, but some of the good hotels would not allow him inside the door. But to the police and the judge the man who is killed is not a character, he is a body. Maybe your father saved many people from unhappiness."

"It's no good, Benito, you can't smooth it out like that. Murder's murder. And I'm his son——"

Benito interrupted "This terrible thing, it happened only a few months before you were born. You understand what I mean? Until then your father was an innocent man, the change in his character, the crime, neither could affect you. You must not let your imagination confuse you, you must not feel in a shadow. Think of yourself as the son of a wounded man whose injury betrayed him at a sudden moment of fury."

"Thanks, Benito. I'm glad I came to you."

"And one more word. You spoke of Max Lassiter when you came here with the charming young lady. He too is a bad one. You must avoid him."

"I can cope with him."

"Will you now have a drink? A glass of wine?"

They lifted their glasses in silence. Vivian felt no embarrassment as the old Italian embraced him at the top of the stairway on parting, and a minute later he stepped into the afternoon sunshine. His mind, relieved of the speculations that had troubled him through most of his life, felt curiously clear, and as he eyed the crowded street he reflected that nearly everyone had some secret, more or less grave, that had to be thrust out of thought to make way for the pursuit of everyday matters. For the first time, as he passed all that remained of St. Anne's Church, he understood how his mother derived comfort from gazing at such symbols of timeless faith.

He found her folding pieces of china into newspaper, and without glancing up she scolded "You said you'd only be gone for a little while, and look at the time. I suppose you think your precious bookshop is all that matters, you leave me to do everything, you've no thought for anyone."

Her sharp words aroused only pity. Could he wonder if an old shameful grief found expression in illogical complaints? He said "You sit down, I'll pack the rest of the things."

"And break half of them."

"You know I won't. Come along." He almost lifted her to the armchair and presently, as he was stowing cups and dishes into the tea-chest, she asked what had delayed him. "I went to see Benito," he admitted.

"What for?"

"Because I met a man named Max Lassiter."

After a silence she sighed, "Well, you had to know some time, perhaps I should have told you."

He knelt beside her. "You always did what you felt was best, and I'm grateful to you—for everything. Now I know, I shan't be so impatient with you. Whatever I did, I could never make up for what you must have been through."

Her expression surprised him; she looked almost indifferent, and he blundered to his feet. "I suppose I'm an emotional fool."

"Things matter so much when you're young." Her voice was crisp, matter-of-fact. "They did to me, they do to everyone. But later on you wonder how they can have mattered so much. You remember all the tears and the lying awake, and it's as if someone else did all that. It's all gone like an old bit of toothache. One day you won't care either, about anything. But what's the good of talking? You're not even listening. I ought to be round at the workroom, they never get on if I'm not there——"

"If you say you don't care about anything, why do you bother how much does or doesn't get done?"

He regretted the question as soon as it was spoken, for he saw tears on her cheeks. But he was glad of their confession that her claim to indifference was false. And as he packed the last items of china into the box he was aware of a closer sense of intimacy than he had ever felt beyond the barrier of her secrecy.

"You're tired," his mother said. "What have you been up to?"

Intuitively, she always knew. Perhaps he'd been a fool to bother with Sainsbury's trouble. Until now the tension of anxiety had kept him alert, but now he stumbled into an arm-chair, muttering some evasion.

His mother watched as his eyelids drooped, then she moved close to smooth the hair from his forehead. Runnels of perspiration had dried on his face and his eyes were heavily shadowed; the pity and fear in her own heart were mingled in her sigh. She saw her son as a child, not a man—as a fine handsome boy with a strange, inexplicable spirit.

CHAPTER XVIII

I T was a heavy, overcast morning, and from the top floor the trees in the square were almost invisible in the mist that seemed to promise another warm day. For a moment, as he gazed out upon the grey and green, Vivian found himself half-yearning for the more vivid outlook upon Sidley Street.

This neighbourhood lacked the cosmopolitan atmosphere of Soho. Front doors were kept closed and neighbours did not automatically know each other; some of the houses gave an impression of grandeur in decay while others had been renovated recently. Nearly all were apartment houses, or let floor by floor—as this one was, but the top floor at least had the advantage of being free from the passing up and down of other tenants. It consisted of three rooms, a tiny kitchen, and an improvised bathroom. In comparison with the haphazard accommodation in Sidley Street it was luxurious.

Vivian scanned the morning paper headlines and was about to go to the kitchen with the offer of help that would almost certainly be rejected, when his mother came in with the breakfast tray. He asked "How do you like it here, now we've had a week of it?"

"Too many stairs," she said. "And it's not nearly so handy for the workroom. Bus rides every day, and the time they take."

"You ought to use taxis. And you ought to have some sort of help here."

"With daily women charging what they do!"

"Suppose I pay for a few hours help?"

E

"You'll do no such thing. I can manage. Have your breakfast while it's hot."

He noticed the grey in her hair as she leaned over the table, and she was far too thin. Nothing would persuade her to spare her energy, but he could not resist the suggestion, "Must you go to Frith Street every day? Can't Violet Bracey manage on her own sometimes?"

"No she can't. And I'll be going there until I get a better place, somewhere near Bond Street. Now you're gulping your food, there's not all that hurry."

He said evasively "I may as well get along early." Olga started work at eight-thirty and by waiting outside Marble Arch tube station he could snatch a few minutes with her, walking to Grosvenor Street. These early-morning encounters seemed to lighten the whole day. "There's more than enough to do, and one of the things that stumps me is how I'm going to get about to sales when I can't leave the place."

"You've been late every evening."

"I know. And I shall be. I'm making catalogues, sorting things out. Second-hand books don't come in dozens, each one is a separate item, and has to be priced—unless it's junk for the bargain boxes."

In the crowds pouring up the stairway of the tube he could pick out Olga's golden head before her face was visible. Then they were together, walking through the side streets of Mayfair with the sun gleaming through the haze. "Ten minutes a day," he remarked, "it's a miserable allowance. Let's have Saturday evening together."

"I'll have to ask Mrs. Paton."

"How Victorian! Olga—do you see much of your mother?"

"No. How could I? She's busy every evening, you know."

If she did not see Tashy she would not be in danger of meeting Max Lassiter; and he had not reappeared at the bookshop. His obscure taunts seemed to be without serious significance. "I say—do you know the girl in that car?"

"No. Don't you? She's waving to us."

The car had stopped and Dr. Baumgartner stepped out from the far side of it. "Vivian! How are you?"

"Fine, thanks.—This is Miss Vautel. Dr. Baumgartner."

"Let's give you both a lift. Oh, this is my niece, Susan Blane." The girl had joined them. Slim, dark-haired, with sharp features and a faintly-mocking expression in her hazel eyes, she was in a light grey suit, swinging a white handbag and her gloves. "Susan's staying with me and wants to be my secretary, but I'm curing that idea. Susan, this is Vivian Mander. And Miss—er——"

"I must go," Olga said. "I'm sorry. But I mustn't be late."

Her smile included them all as she hurried off. Vivian could hardly follow her for Baumgartner was saying, "I particularly wanted to see you, Vivian."

"I haven't long——" Olga was waving from the corner before she turned it.

Susan Blane exclaimed "She's completely lovely," and Baumgartner inquired, "And do you hypnotize her, dominate her?"

"No I *don't*."

"My dear boy, you mustn't mind a clumsy joke. Now I want to talk to you about Susan. I hear you're in business on your own and Susan wants a job."

"I couldn't employ anyone. I've only just started." Even as he spoke Vivian remembered his main problem; how to get to sale-rooms when he could not leave the shop.

"You wouldn't find Susan expensive," Baumgartner said persuasively. "She's the spoilt child of a rich father. The idea is to keep her busy and out of mischief."

Vivian remarked, "Oh, so you want to play at work?"

Susan protested "No! Just because there's a drop of money in the family I don't have to drift from one cocktail party to another till I don't know whether it's yesterday or tomorrow. I love books, you'd find me awfully civil and I'd work for you for a pound a week."

"It's a deal," Vivian laughed. "When could you start?"

"What are we waiting for?"

Dr. Baumgartner burst into a great laugh that startled a cat into dashing up a tree. "That's the way I like things arranged. I'll give you both a lift, you get in the back, Susan." He continued, as he dropped into the driving seat, "You really will find her efficient, but I warn you, she'll try to run both you and the business."

"How can I?" Susan leaned forward to interpolate the question. "Isn't this the man who can dominate anyone?"

Baumgartner smiled sideways. "You see? She can't keep

out of a conversation for a minute. Yes, Susan, he's the masterful wonder. But seriously, Vivian, I'm interested in your special gift and some time I'd like to investigate it fully. Perhaps have a demonstration before a critical and unemotional audience. Thought-transference, faith-healing, and what-have-you. Maybe it amounts to no more than a mingling of hypnotism and induced auto-hypnotism. We could experiment."

"Experiment," Vivian said, "is the word for it every time. It doesn't always come off."

"You're so honest, that's your value. You don't wrap your touch of the supernatural in a cloud of mystic claptrap. Yes, I'd like a demonstration. You could fix your own fee."

The car was involved in the Piccadilly Circus traffic. Susan said "You ought to have gone down St. James's and along Pall Mall."

"Don't be bossy, Susan. Take warning, Vivian. Which way do I go now?—Lord, these fool pedestrians!"

"Orange Court is only a sort of alley. If you'd put us down on the corner——"

As Baumgartner drove off Susan was asking questions about Olga, repeating, "Quite lovely, really lovely," but as soon as they entered the shop she inquired practically enough, "What do I start on?"

"Dust." Vivian picked up the letters fanning over the floor. "There must be tons of it. Duster's in the cupboard in the back-office. Then I'll show you how I keep the day-to-day accounts. You'd better memorize the labels over the different shelves, then an inquiry won't have you floundering all round the walls. If you go to lunch from twelve to one I'll go from one to two. I'll put out the bargain boxes and don't forget to keep an eye on them when anyone starts turning them over."

"I ought to have brought an overall."

"There's a draper's in New Street. Will this be enough?"

She refused the pound note. "I'll get it. I shan't be long," and out she hurried. During the day she proved that she could be enthusiastic, dusting, sweeping, rearranging books. She charmed an old man, who was prodding in the fourpenny box outside, into buying a two-guinea book, and in a discussion with another customer she revealed an unusual familiarity with nineteenth-century literature.

At six o'clock, as she was leaving, Vivian remarked "You're too good to last."

"Oh, but I love it. It's the perfect cure for the heeby-jeebies."

"Why, do you get them?"

"H'm." Susan took out her handbag mirror to arrange a wisp of dark hair on her forehead. "I had rather a blow. I created an awful scandal in Winchester—that's where Daddy lives, you know, when he isn't flying about the world coping with weird railways. I had a thing about Daddy's partner. Twice my age, of course. Now he's gone and married a kind of half-caste in Alexandria. That's why I was packed off to London, to get the whole thing out of my mind. Then Uncle Oscar had this brain wave of dumping me on you."

"I'm glad about that part of it."

"I still feel rather bleak. Well, see you in the morning." As Susan went out the mocking smile was again on her sharp, fresh face.

An hour later Vivian was walking through Soho. The locality would always have an attraction for him, and he had almost a sense of home-coming when he met Mrs. Glatt. Even when the shops were shut her basket seemed to be an inseparable part of her plump anatomy. She broke into a lively spate of gossip, at times so rapid that it was incoherent. A woman occupying Vivian's old room, arrested for shoplifting; Johnny Johns, stumbling up the stairs on returning from his club; Wyganowski, recently returned, involved in obscure political activities——

Vivian said "I'd like to see him, tell him where he can find me."

"Already he know, he speak of you. Tashy, she had a new frent, rich, a Greek, plenty money, then sudden the new frent is gone, Tashy don't go nowhere, is stayink in her room, she ain't so young no more. New people is your mother's rooms, is complaining already. Do I make de noise of dis street? No one else don't say nothink about de noise."

Sooner or later, Vivian brooded as he walked on, Tashy's sordid adventures would cast their shadow over Olga, if only in the shape of disillusionment. The sheltered life of the convent had left Olga so unsophisticated that she was acquiring the worldly veneer of her workmates only slowly; the shock of any sudden discovery about her mother would be incalculable.

The walk home, varying the route through the West End and Mayfair every evening, usually cleared his mind, but this evening he was still harassed as he turned into the quiet square and climbed to the fourth-floor flat, where his mother greeted him with the news that Philip Trafford had called.

"What did he want?"

"To see you. He'd been to the shop and said you weren't there. It was only a chance I was at home. One of the machines in Frith Street has broken down."

"I was out for less than an hour. He could have waited."

"I think he'd been drinking. He won't be going back to Cambridge."

"Why, whatever's happened?"

"He didn't say. I think he wants you to help him."

"Must he be molly-coddled all along the line? Didn't he give any idea of what's the matter? Where is he now?"

"I don't know. He was so excited and upset. If he comes back you must tell him to go to his father."

"There's nothing else he could do. He couldn't keep himself for a couple of days. I'm sick of Philip, I had more than enough of him at school."

"He says there's a smart young woman in your shop, you never told me——"

"Because I never saw her till this morning. Susan Blane. She's a niece of Dr. Baumgartner's, working for pocket-money. And that makes me uneasy, because she's going to be very useful."

"To be sure I'm glad. She may take your mind off Olga Vautel."

"She won't."

Mrs. Mander sighed. "You know what Tashy is. And what's in the blood is in the blood."

For a moment he was in a fury. "Each generation starts a new page. If it didn't and we inherited all the hang-overs, we'd all be bad lots." He saw that his words had stung, but still they seemed justified, and in silence he studied book catalogues while his mother laid the table for their evening meal.

CHAPTER XIX

FROM the telephone box in the lobby Philip Trafford could see the lounge, lit with an amber artificial glow though it was now mid-morning. If only he could stay here for ever, in plushy luxury, free of all obligations——

A voice said "You're through," and he heard Vivian saying, "Hello. Mander's Bookshop."

"I'm in a mess, Vivian."

"Sorry and all that, but I'm busy."

"I'm coming along for a talk."

"My dear chap, customers are bobbing in and out all the time. This isn't just a gossip parlour."

"But I'm in the devil of a fix. I can't afford to stay on here, I've nowhere to go."

"I thought you had a home——"

"What about this evening? I'm at the Superbe. Could you come along at—— What time?"

Reluctantly Vivian agreed to be there at six-thirty. Olga's absence from the usual rendezvous at Marble Arch was on his mind, all the more as a telephone call to the house in Belsize Park had not been answered. Now he rang off impatiently and went to settle an argument between Susan and a youth who had juggled a book from a shelf into the shilling box. Then he bought a suit-case full of books from a shifty-eyed Pole and noted down the titles of a list of volumes wanted by a collector of eighteenth-century works. The whole morning was full of activity, but he seized a moment just before Susan went to lunch to try again to reach Olga by telephone.

A woman with a cockney voice said that she could give no information, Mrs. Paton was out, everyone was out, "An' I'm doin' the floors, right at the top I was when the phone goes ring-ring-ring, bringin' me down all them stairs——"

Susan had been back to Cavendish Square for lunch. "I nipped along in a taxi because Uncle Oscar was lunching Dr. Turnbull and I wanted to pump them both about you and Philip Trafford. I must say, when he came in yesterday, I thought he was rather attractive. In a delicate sort of way, of course. I should think you're awfully proud of him, I mean, of what you did for him."

"I'm utterly and completely bored with him and everything about him."

"Oh, all right," Susan said sharply. She went on to suggest a rearrangement of the bookshelves, adding "I'm going to move the paper editions on to the bench inside the window."

"You've been here less than a couple of days and it's just as your uncle said. You're trying to run the show."

"But isn't it a good idea? To move the paper-covered stuff, I mean."

"Oh, do as you like." Vivian was half-ashamed of his own curtness. Susan's help was practically a gift. A minute later a voice, strange, yet familiar, called from the doorway, "Hullo there!" and Wyganowski came in.

Still wearing a shabby astrakhan cap with a huge greenish-black overcoat trimmed with fur, Wyganowski had lost none of his old air of mystery. His black beard was now even bushier than it had been when it wagged in the telling of amazing adventures, true or imaginary, on Mrs. Glatt's top landing, his deepset eyes still twinkled with good humour. "Vivian, my boy! But how the years pass, how everything changes, you are no longer my little boy, but a proprietor. We go to have a drink, yes?"

"I was just going to lunch."

"Excellent. You lunch with me. I have a proposition. Or we buy some sandwiches and go to The Two Swords, there we can talk without——" Wyganowski placed his hands behind his ears and flapped them.

Walking to the club, Wyganowski, as if from habit, told a story of a hunting exploit in Finland. They stopped at a delicatessen shop and Vivian brought out silver to pay for sandwiches, but Wyganowski hastily whipped out a handful of notes. "No, please—I have money. Plenty."

"I'm losing all my illusions," Vivian laughed.

Again in the street, Wyganowski glanced back several times until Vivian remarked "Are we being followed or something? You're making me feel as if I'm in an international plot."

"Everyone is, whether they realize it or not. But that's no reason for the man who's been behind us all the way from Orange Court."

Vivian swung round. Max Lassiter was a dozen paces away. As he came up he was smiling crookedly, his pale eyes were gleaming with malevolence.

"And how's the murderer's offspring?" he challenged, before he went on, laughing as if he had made an excellent joke.

Wyganowski stared inquiringly. Vivian said "The fellow's crazy. Come on, here's Johnny's place." But the incident had left an impression of sinister determination, underlying the apparently spontaneous taunt.

There were only two men in the club—market-men whom Vivian knew by sight, haggling over a deal in handbags. Johnny Johns, behind the bar, said that Ginger had gone to the dentist. "It's worry gives people the toothache," he remarked, "'oo ever 'eard of a cat with an achin' jaw? Cats don't worry, got more sense, but Ginger, 'e worries shockin'. Truth is you don't know what the snags in any business is goin' to be, not till you get on the inside of it."

"Too true," Vivian agreed.

Wyganowski carried their drinks to a table and as they sat down he began, without preamble, "Now. My proposition. You want to make some money, eh?"

"Yes, if it's on the level."

"Vivian, I know what you are capable of. You can be most useful to me."

"In what way?" Vivian unfolded the packet of sandwiches.

"You have power. Over other people."

Vivian felt exasperated. "Even if I said yes to that——"

"Yes or no makes no difference. You have it. I pay you good money for each one of my friends who reaches this country. They are in fact the friends of my friends, who have difficulty with passports. It is a question of persuading officials, no longer is it enough to offer bribes, for everyone is afraid, everyone is watched."

"You can't be serious! You can't imagine that I'd take a hand in wangling passports for people I've never seen?"

"You could save the lives of good men."

"I'd bungle it, even if I tried. Ye gods, I see you after all these years and you try to bounce me into something I should never understand——"

"The less you understand the safer you are. You would be simply a British student, travelling on the continent——"

"And you're the man who once advised me to be an artist!"

"Oho, oho," Wyganowski shook his massive head. "It is not now a question of a beautiful song, a graceful picture."

Vivian emptied his tankard. "I'm going to have another half-pint. What's yours, brandy again?"

Wyganowski nodded. "Perhaps if I explain more completely——"

"Don't. I'm sorry, but it would be a waste of time."

Vivian went to the bar and while Johnny was pouring out the drinks Max Lassiter sauntered in. He leaned against the corner of the bar and seemed to be lost in some distant contemplation. His very silence was oddly provocative, and Vivian swung away hastily, carrying his tankard and the brandy glass. He remained standing, wanting to get away. "Sorry I couldn't oblige you," he told Wyganowski, "but even now I can't quite make up my mind whether you're romancing, or in earnest, about the wangle you suggested."

"I'm quite serious. I wish I could persuade you."

Vivian laughed shortly. "I wonder you're not scared."

"I'm too old to worry over any risk."

"I must go. See you again soon, I hope." Vivian went to the foot of the stairs. "Cheeroh, Johnnie."

Johnnie said, with a good-humoured grin, "What about squarin' up for those last coupla drinks?"

"Didn't I? I say, I'm most awfully sorry." In some embarrassment Vivian found the coins. "Put the change in the Barnado box. I was thinking about other things——"

"O.K. boy, O.K.," Johnnie said, and Lassiter looked up to speak to the room in general. "Why all the fuss? Bilking a club isn't murder."

Johnnie was protesting at the suggestion of bilking. "Crikey, anyone can make a mistake."

"Some mistakes," Lassiter drawled, "have fatal consequences."

Vivian walked out. In Old Compton Street the air, dusty though it was, seemed comparatively sweet. He found Susan gaily flourishing a Hardy first edition that she had bought for two shillings.

"From an absolute mug. He came in with a whole case

full of trash and I spotted this among it, he grabbed the florin without even looking to see which book I'd chosen, and walked off with the rubbish.—Why, you're pleased aren't you?"

"I don't know that I am. Rather tough on the chap. Yes, I suppose I ought to be glad."

Susan laughed. "You're not cut out for commerce, anyway not for this sort of commerce, which is mostly a matter of seizing opportunities. Oh, your friend Olga Vautel rang up."

"Yes?"

"She missed you this morning because someone called Brenda fainted in the tube."

"So that was it." Vivian realized that his relief must have been obvious, for Susan murmured "We breathe again."

"Let's get on with our Fine Arts collection. Time slips away and I've got to leave promptly at six this evening." Vivian became absorbed in a pile of heavy volumes that had been lying about for over a week, unsorted and unpriced.

Philip Trafford was waiting just inside the swing door at the Hotel Superbe, and his dapper grey suit made Vivian suddenly self-conscious about his own tweed jacket and flannels. The huge lounge had an atmosphere of luxury, elegance, and laziness; this was no place for anyone who traded in shillings. Philip was pale and the mauve shadows under his eyes suggested dissipation. "Let's go in the bar," he said, "though I don't seem able to get on top of the hang-over I collected two days ago."

In the American Bar, all chromium and scarlet leather, a prismatic mirror over the rows of bottles reflected what seemed to be a thousand amber electric light bulbs. Philip led the way to a table, jerking a finger at a waiter. "We don't want to be among the rubbernecks."

So for the second time in one day Vivian felt that he was to be involved in a conspiratorial duologue. "What's all this about?" he asked abruptly.

"I can't go back to Cambridge."

"So I've heard. Why not?"

"If I do I'll only be sent down. What are you going to drink? Don't suppose they do beer in here. Martini?"

Philip gave the order and went on, "It's all rather sordid. Day before yesterday I was out with another chap in his car

and we picked up a couple of girls and drove over to New-
market. Thelma—that was one of the girls—didn't tell me
she was engaged to a chap, an awful clod called Artie something, as I was to discover——"

Vivian interrupted "Make it snappy, will you?"

"I've got to *explain*," Philip said petulantly. "You see,
we all got tight and messed about. Thelma wasn't keen at first
but in the end she got the party spirit."

The waiter brought the drinks. Vivian paid as Philip made
no move to do so, and said flatly "So you seduced the girl?"

"She was willing. The job was getting the two wenches
home. In the end we dumped one of them on the doorsteps
of her frightful lodging house, but Thelma kept blubbering
and saying she was afraid to go home. The other fellow was
fed up with driving around, it was getting late and there
was no need for both of us to be in the rough about that, so
he told me I could cope with Thelma and drove off alone. She
and I were tottering along when two big chaps loomed up
from nowhere and asked me who the hell I was. One was
her father and the other was her Artie."

Philip paused, possibly for sympathy. Then he resumed
"Thelma screamed and Artie knocked me out and that was the
last I knew. I woke up—yesterday morning, that was—and
found myself in a kind of yard where I suppose I'd been
dumped. Before I could pull myself together there was the
dam'd father again, and Artie close behind him. They'd taken
some papers from my pocket and knew who I was and said
if I wasn't out of the town within a couple of hours they'd
report me and have me charged with raping the fool of a girl.
Artie threatened to beat me to a jelly, and all that stuff, and
—oh hell, there wasn't anything for it but to collect a few bits
and pieces and make a getaway. All over a rotten trashy girl.
I stayed here last night, but what I'm going to do now——"
Philip broke off helplessly.

"You'll have to go home. Your people are bound to know
if you daren't go back to Cambridge."

"I've told you I can't. They probably know already that
I've decamped. Of course I could say the girl led me on——
Let's get out of here, it's asphyxiating. That woman's got
some stuff on that reminds me of the awful perfume of that
dopey widow at Stannet."

Guiltily, Vivian repressed a vivid memory of Daphne Langley. In the lounge Philip said "I wish you'd tootle along with me. To face the parents, I mean. We'll have another drink first, I'm feeling awfully shaken—— Waiter!"

"Why you have to keep on shooting down drink just when you need to keep on an even keel——"

"Oh shut up." Philip gave his order, and his tone changed to the familiar wheedling note. "You will come along, won't you? Be a pal. There's bound to be a scene, and you're just the one to round off the rough edges."

Vivian agreed reluctantly and they went up to fetch Philip's one suitcase. He had to borrow ten shillings to make up the amount of his bill, but it was he who called the taxi and within a quarter of an hour they were in Aynham Gardens.

Mrs. Trafford opened the door. She was deathly-white and seemed distraught. "Oh Philip! Here you are at last! I didn't expect you, Vivian, come in both of you."

Philip stood still, puzzled by such a reception, and Vivian thrust him in. Mrs. Trafford wailed "Oh Philip, it was such a shock. You're all we have and you do this to us."

In the sitting-room Philip began a lame apology but Mrs. Trafford broke in, "That doesn't matter now. It's your father. When he got the letters——"

Philip asked sharply "What letters?"

"Two, this morning. Just after the post came, your father had a stroke. The whole thing's so disgraceful, such a terrible shock——"

"You don't give me a chance to defend myself——"

"Thinking of yourself! I ought to be in the bedroom, he's not supposed to be left. The nurse has gone to the chemist's. If he's well enough to be moved tomorrow he's to go to a nursing home."

Philip was trembling as he moved towards the window. A few papers were scattered on the open bureau; he picked up a closely written sheet, glanced at the signature, and muttered "Dirty rats."

Mrs. Trafford said desperately "I must go back to Arnold." Her glance seemed to ask for support and Vivian followed, leaving Philip staring furiously at the letter in his hand. In the hall Mrs. Trafford murmured "He always wanted to be proud of Philip. If it had been an ordinary scrape—— Oh, what's the use?"

The bedroom was grey in the deep twilight. The Colonel was lying quite still and as his wife paused by the doorway Vivian crossed to the bedside. The sleeper looked very peaceful. Mrs. Trafford said "Switch on the standard lamp, he'll like a little light when he stirs."

Vivian turned the switch. After a moment or so he tilted the lamp so that the bulb shone directly on to the Colonel's calm features. They had a strange youthful appearance and the mouth under the clipped grey moustache seemed to be smiling. The eyebrow bisected by an old wound was drawn up at an unnatural angle.

"Take care," Mrs. Trafford whispered. "You'll wake him."

The Colonel was past waking. Tears were stinging Vivian's eyes as he set down the lamp; he blinked them back and wondered why Mrs. Trafford did not move. Did she realize that death was in the room? He moved to her and she only gazed at him with blank stricken eyes. Then a tremor shook her whole body and she made a wild helpless gesture, reaching out as if for support. He helped her to the chair beside the bed and slipped quietly from the room.

Philip exclaimed explosively, "Who would have thought such an ignorant oaf could write a letter that length? Full of lies, full of abuse, no one gives a darn about my version. I shall tell the old man——"

"Philip——"

Some instinct seemed to warn Philip of what he was to hear, for his voice was almost anxious. "How is he?"

"I'm afraid—— He's past listening to you."

In the silence in the room the shouts of boys playing cricket in the street came upwards with staccato clarity. Philip gulped out, "I killed him. I killed him." He broke down, blubbering noisily.

"Pull yourself together——"

"Why did this have to happen? What shall I do, how shall I get along?"

Vivian spoke quietly, "It's about time you tried to behave like a man." Then, as Philip continued his half-incoherent laments, "Shut up, you fool! Think of your mother, can't you? Didn't you hear me telling you to shut up?"

Philip gazed round in a vague way, and their eyes met. "Yes, I'll shut up. I'll—— Tell me what I ought to do."

"You'd better call Dr. Turnbull. I'll wait till he gets here."

CHAPTER XX

IT was Sunday afternoon, and Olga Vautel had to be at Oxford Square at four o'clock. She set off early, perhaps with some foreboding that she might lose her way, and indeed the tube train carried her past the station where she should have changed and she had to travel back from Leicester Square for the Central Line.

Some time, she mused, she would become familiar with London. Life at the convent had not developed either a sense of direction or individual initiative, for there the days had flowed by gently and calmly in the general assumption that everything was under divine supervision. The chatter of the girls in the Grosvenor Street workroom was a constant reminder of her lack of experience, for they had been familiar, since childhood, with the necessity of making decisions.

Such companionship was an intensive course in sophistication. It could hardly fail to arouse conflicting emotions, and now, as Olga faced the blustering wind along Bayswater Road, she found herself trying to analyse her own misgivings about her mother's veiled life. In the few days together in Sidley Street, when she herself had been even more ignorant than she was now, the atmosphere of concealment had been evident.

Some vague drift of the truth penetrated these speculations, but it had to be thrust away, rejected as an impossible, too treacherous solution.

Vivian was looking from a top window as she turned into the square and the door was flung open as she reached it. He let her in, embraced her, and exclaimed "Why, you're trembling."

"I had to hurry. I was stupid and lost the way."

"You should have let me come and fetch you. Up we go, it's quite a climb." On the first floor a radio blared over the clatter of crockery. Vivian paused to say "Now you and Mother are going to be friends, that brings us all the closer. Doesn't it, darling?"

"She didn't want to invite me," Olga said.

On the next landing Vivian urged "Couldn't we be engaged? Will you let me give you a ring?"

"No," Olga said, "not yet. Not for years. Perhaps five years."

"Why that's a lifetime! It would seem like a lifetime. Why should we wait?"

"Because I should never feel sure of myself, of either of us, until I understand the world much better. And that'll take ages."

Up another flight, and Vivian said "You defeat me. Perhaps you always will."

Mrs. Mander was standing by a table laid for tea. Her upright attitude, her black dress with its touch of white, her calm smile, reminded Olga of the Sisters who had been her tutors. But this woman, slight and small though she was, had a strong personality, a subtle air of mental independence. Vivian was bringing a trolley from the kitchen, the electric kettle was on the hearth.

"Well, Olga, how is your mother?"

The question was formal, but again Olga sensed the implication of suspicion. "She's all right, thank you."

"You don't see much of her?"

"No" Olga added quickly "of course we're both busy."

"Who isn't?" Mrs. Mander smiled and the slight tension was broken. At least, she was thinking, the girl seemed to have good manners. But what a disaster that she was the daughter of such a disreputable woman—— "Slip your coat off. Do make yourself comfortable. It's a very nice coat."

"A model. Jakeline let me have it, there's a flaw in the material."

Tea was made and as Vivian sat silent Mrs. Mander was asking a string of questions about Jakeline's. "But of course," Olga remarked, "I'm only in the workroom, I don't come into contact with the buying and selling. All the same, some of the girls who work with me seem to know everything that goes on in the showroom."

"Keep your ears open. You'd get a good salary if you could become a buyer."

Vivian laughed. "I don't think Olga's hard-headed enough."

"I want to get on, I don't want to go on being a burden on mother."

Again the atmosphere was uneasy. It was as if Tashy herself had swished through the room. Olga was relieved when she was asked to describe her life in France, to give her impressions of the German occupation. And when tea was finished Vivian suggested that they should all go and see a film. His mother's rejection of the idea did not surprise him; Olga was saying that she would enjoy it. She added "But you'll let me help to clear up the tea-things first?"

Mrs. Mander rose. "No. Thank you. But I've my own way of doing things."

Out in the street Vivian said exultantly "She liked you, darling."

"Did she? She wasn't cordial."

"But you don't know her. When she doesn't like anyone she can be absolutely acid in a quiet way. You impressed her when you were discussing needlework. I believe you know more about it than she does. Her speciality's designing, you must ask her to show you some of her drawings."

"She might think I wanted to steal the ideas," Olga was only half-serious.

"She wouldn't. She's not half as tough as she pretends to be. She'd be flattered, because she realizes you know what's original and what isn't, when it comes to women's bits and pieces. What shall we go and see? There's a good picture at the Regal."

"I don't care what. I'm happy so long as I'm with you, Vivian."

"What a bundle of contradictions you are!"

"I'm quite simple. That's my trouble. It seems to me that people get so used to hiding their thoughts that the truth strikes them as complicated."

He laughed. "I'll have to work that one out."

Three hours later, having seen Olga home, he found his mother running water-colours over sketches on her drawing-board. Without looking up she asked "What did Olga say when you told her Colonel Trafford hadn't left you a penny?"

"Why, I never mentioned the matter."

"But didn't she ask?"

"No she didn't. It wouldn't enter her head."

"Oh well, she doesn't seem to be grasping. But I do think you might have been mentioned in the will. You were given just enough to get you out of a regular job, and now you're in a catch-as-catch-can sort of business."

Her bitter mood was disconcerting. "I'm building it up. If you think I ought to give you more than I do——"

"Oh, I'm not saying that. You pay your share here."

"He left nothing to Philip, remember. Everything went to Mrs. Trafford."

"Some women have everything made easy."

Vivian laughed. "Would you like to change places with her?"

"Oh stop talking nonsense, will you? Another Monday tomorrow, we mustn't be late."

"You go to bed. I'll bring you a night-cap."

"You will not." She was rinsing her brushes and was going out when she paused to say "You're not a bad boy. Why don't you get interested in that nice girl who works for you?"

"Susan?" He checked a laugh. "No, but really, I couldn't begin."

"She's got a proper family behind her. A doctor uncle, an engineer father. Professional people."

"I know. But social levels don't worry me. And somehow I always feel as if she's just another chap about the place." Susan was not unemotional, yet she had never stirred his emotions. "Perhaps it's because she's a born organizer. Such a vigorous mind, she's almost a permanent challenge. I don't know. Hail-fellow-well-met, almost hearty—though she's no bigger than you are. It's mean to criticize, she's very useful."

Mrs. Mander sighed. "I'd like you to get up in the world. It's my dream. Good night, Vivian love."

Susan was indeed useful. On the next day the woman who usually came in to clean the shop failed to arrive and Susan set to work scrubbing the floor. Vivian remarked "You're behaving as if you're being paid half a crown an hour. Lowering yourself to the level of a well-paid job. But I didn't realize you could be so practical."

She smiled. "I'm quite versatile, really." She peeled off her splashed overall.

"Very creditable! You could afford to be both idle and dumb. If I were either idle or dumb I'd be cap-in-hand at the labour exchange. Why you do so much for my measly pound a week, I can't imagine."

She took her bucket through the office, and returning, challenged "What do you suggest I should do? If I just sit around idling I'm a parasite. If I do a proper job for a fair wage I'm taking the bread out of someone's mouth. If I work for pocket-money I'm trivial. I can't give my all to the poor, because the really needy hide their poverty till they stick their heads in gas ovens, and the cadgers go to the Public Assistance Board. I'm a victim, that's what I am, a victim of social transition!"

A voice interrupted "Who's a victim?"

Philip Trafford was in the doorway. Vivian asked abruptly what he wanted and Philip sneered "Not even a civil greeting. I thought I'd just let you know I've been literally kicked out. My worthy mother thinks it's time I made my own way in the world. Thanks very much!"

"What's it got to do with me?"

"Everything I've ever done has been compared with what you would have done in a similar situation. The fact that I'm not interested in any particular subject differs from your *admirable* concentration on the second-hand book trade. My *manners*, it seems, aren't up to yours."

Philip was adopting his mother's old mannerism of emphasizing too many of his words. "I didn't realize I was such a paragon," Vivian said.

"So I'm out on my ear while you're sitting pretty."

"Don't be a fool. I'm busy." Vivian went into the office and closed the door, but he could still hear Philip's complaining tone, while Susan seemed to be sympathizing. Then someone else was in the shop and the third voice, though subdued, sounded vaguely familiar.

Then it was recognizable. But as the dividing door was opened only Susan was there. Vivian stepped out and was

just in time to see the backs of Max Lassiter and Philip before
they turned into Charing Cross Road. "Susan!"

She came out and her expression told him that his agitation
was obvious. "That tall man——?"

"He came in once before. Just to look round. He didn't
buy anything."

"What did he want, now?"

"I've no idea. He was hanging about outside, then he
came in, picked up a book, dropped it, and asked Philip to
go and have a drink."

"But they didn't know each other?"

"Apparently not. I was rather surprised. So was Philip."

"Had the other chap heard what you two were talking
about?"

"Lordy, I don't know. Could it matter?"

"No. No, of course not. If the other man comes in again,
the sooner you get rid of him the better."

"He looks pretty wicked," Susan said. "I hope Philip
keeps his fingers crossed."

With some relief Vivian greeted a wiry little man in
bright green tweeds who had been one of the first customers.
He collected first editions of novels without particular dis-
crimination, and a pile had been set aside for his inspection.
While he was picking them over Mrs. Trafford telephoned and
Susan attended to the customer.

Mrs. Trafford talked at length, repeating her explanations
as to why she had at last dealt firmly with Philip. "He
refused to consider studying any further, he refused to listen
to Bertie Cawdell's advice. You remember. Commander
Cawdell, you used to go over to his house when you came
down to Pegwell. He and Arnold were lifelong friends. I tried
to reason with Philip, he wouldn't even listen. Then when
he sold some of my silver, that was the finish."

"You mean—he took it without asking?"

A long sigh came over the line. "He stole it. We had
a terrible scene. I couldn't stand any more. He'd been talking
about wanting to go and live with a friend of his in a flat in
Half Moon Street. I gave him a cheque—I gave him what
Arnold gave you. Five hundred pounds. How long it'll last
I don't know, and now I don't feel I care."

"I'm terribly sorry." Vivian could picture the lonely

woman in mourning at the other end of the line. He said, not believing his own words, "Perhaps this'll bring him to his senses."

"I wanted you to know. We've always been so closely linked, you did so much for him. It's all—rather heartbreaking. Some time, you must come and see me."

"Thank you, yes of course I'd like to. After all this—you've had a terribly trying time, couldn't you get away for a change?"

"I'll be giving up the flat, I think. I'm too dazed to make plans. In the Spring I'll probably go down to the cottage for good. Oh Vivian, why——?"

The unfinished question broke off on a husky note. Then Mrs. Trafford was hardly audible, "I may have made a terrible mistake. I don't know. I feel so alone. But I couldn't go on like that. Forgive me. I'm so distressed——"

He was conscious of the inanity of his sympathetic phrases. "I don't know if it would be any help if I came along now?"

What possible help could he be, unless she could find relief in dwelling upon her griefs? But she seemed glad of the suggestion and five minutes later he was on his way. The visit, as he expected, was something of an ordeal, though Mrs. Trafford hardly mentioned Philip. She was in a reminiscent mood, perhaps deliberately taking refuge in the past, recalling her social gaieties as a debutante, her presentation at Court, and the early years of her married life. Less than thirty years ago—but Vivian felt as if he were being shown an album of faded photographs of some other century.

"Just think," Mrs. Trafford commented, "my mother sacked a housemaid for buying an evening frock! And when she put an advertisement in the paper she had over sixty applicants for the place. An evening frock—— That reminds me!"

"Of what?"

"Arnold always subscribed to the Crawford Charities, and they've sent me two tickets for a dance at the Empress Rooms. I'm wondering if you could use them. I see they include the champagne supper."

"Why of course, I'd be glad of them." The tickets would provide an opportunity to entertain Olga in style without indulging in over-extravagance.

"Well, that's splendid. I'll give them to you while I think of it. I've so much on my mind, I find myself forgetting—— And you'll stay to lunch, won't you?"

"I'd very much like to. But I have to get back to give Susan Blane a midday break."

"And will you be taking her to the dance?"

"Oh no." There was a silence, and somewhat reluctantly he mentioned Olga. Mrs. Trafford seemed interested and he felt that he was floundering over his answers.

"Who are her family?" she pursued.

"Oh, she's spent most of her life in a convent."

"You mean she's an orphan?"

"Oh no. Her mother's living. Her father was killed in an air-raid in France."

"Oh. Your mother's never mentioned them."

"Well, she's busy in a very practical way, and Olga's mother's mainly interested in music." Such half-truths were more unrealistic than any of Mrs. Trafford's Georgian anecdotes.

As he rose and said good-bye Mrs. Trafford said, "I couldn't discuss Philip."

"Of course, I understand."

"I shall deal with him as I'm directed. I have messages, you know, from another sphere."

"You mustn't worry. You've given him every chance to make a success of his life, and he's muffed it. But he'll come to his senses, you'll be proud of him yet."

"Bless you for your comfort."

Vivian made an undignified exit, for he tripped as he stepped backwards over the mat. A week later, in the crowded Empress Rooms, he marvelled that he had given so lame an account of Olga. For tonight, in her long gown of cloudy net, she was looking so lovely that the memory of his inadequate description shamed him.

"You're incredibly beautiful!" he exclaimed, and still felt that he was being inadequate, paying a compliment like someone doing a bad parody of Noel Coward. But after all, he reflected as they swung into a waltz, only a poet could have described Olga in a satisfactory way. His love was none the less fervent because he could not shape it into syllables.

CHAPTER XXI

In the bright mid-morning sunshine an optimistic fiddler was playing the Londonderry Air in Orange Court. A good order had come by the post, several customers were in the bookshop, and Vivian was feeling cheerful.

Olga's arrival, at this time of day, surprised him. She went straight through to the office and when Susan took over the last of the customers he followed. "I've left Jakeline's," Olga said.

He checked the automatic inquiry 'Why?' Olga was pale, and though she was standing quite erect she had an air of hopelessness. "Don't worry, darling. You'll find something else. And even if you don't, I'm not doing so badly."

Susan came into the doorway to ask the price of a book. "Why don't you two go and have a coffee or something?"

"Well, why not, if you can cope with the rush?"

Susan laughed. "The rush has subsided."

Walking away past the bargain boxes Vivian said "Shall we have coffee—or what about a real drink?"

"I don't want either," Olga said. "Is there somewhere quiet? There's something I must tell you."

They went towards Trafalgar Square, and opposite the National Portrait Gallery Vivian suggested "We could go in there. I don't suppose there'd be many people about."

There was no one in the room of Kneller portraits, and just inside it Olga said abruptly. "I have to tell you. It'll put a barrier between us, but—— It's about Mother."

So she had been disillusioned. Vivian stared helplessly at a long-dead old gentleman with cunning eyes.

"Did you know?" Olga asked.

"Know what?" he floundered.

"About the way she lives?"

"I heard she'd been depressed, staying indoors——" His evasions had a false ring. Automatically they walked a few steps and part of his mind wondered why the members of the Kit-Kat Club, gazing from their frames, all had the same smug expression.

"I found out," Olga said, "from one of the models at

Jakeline's. She tried to be funny about it. That's—that's why I've left. I suppose I must have guessed before, but was trying not to know."

What could he say? "I suppose we all make mistakes," he hedged. "Things can't have been easy for her."

"And all she's thought of is making *my* life better, different—— What can I *do*?"

Olga looked almost like a child and he himself was feeling as useless as a schoolboy confronted by an adult problem. "Does she know——? I mean, that someone's been talking to you?"

Olga shook her head. "I've hardly seen her since I went to Mrs. Paton's. She didn't want me calling at Sidley Street, she said she—— Oh, it doesn't matter."

"Then don't let her know."

"If only I could help her."

The idea came to him as a flash of inspiration. "Supposing you and she could go away into the country for a time?"

"But how can we?"

"Mrs. Trafford's got a cottage at Pegwell, she won't be using it for several months. If I asked her to let you have it, I'm sure she'd agree. She says it ought to be lived in and, you know, she's always been quite fond of me."

Olga brooded silently. Then she argued, "Mother's used to London, I don't believe she'd go. Though of course she did live away from towns when she was young. On a big estate in the Ukraine."

"Well then! Let's see if we can work it. There's a piano at the cottage, your mother would find all sorts of things to do, she'd get a new angle——"

He broke off as two old ladies walked slowly round, pointing at the exhibits. Olga said, "Yes, she'd be lost anywhere without a piano. I might get a job in the nearest village or town, but even that wouldn't amount to much."

"I'd help over money. You'd let me. You'd be my guests. The only thing to make sure of is whether Mrs. Trafford will agree."

"I thought you'd spent all you had on the shop."

"Don't worry about that part of it." Somehow he would have to raise some cash.

"The whole thing's so awful. I thought—of course I didn't

realize you'd known all along, I thought you might turn against me." Olga glanced up. "I feel as if all those old men are spying on us, listening." She laughed nervously.

"Let's get out of here. It's time you had some lunch. You know, darling, it may not be as bad as you think. Lots of people lead unconventional lives. Just because some spiteful girl puts the whole thing crudely and vulgarly——" He saw Olga's tightened lips, and finished lamely "I'll go and see Mrs. Trafford this evening."

"Even if she agrees, I still don't see how we'll be able to live. It all seems quite hopeless."

"It isn't. I can raise a lump sum. Dr. Baumgartner as good as said if I'd give a demonstration, put on my special act, I could fix my own price."

Olga reminded him, as they were going downstairs, "You always said that you'd never—what is the word?—commercialize your gift."

"Oh, I've got over being squeamish." He had to thrust the feeling of distaste into the back of his mind as he lied glibly, "I was thinking about doing it on my own account, anyway. Why not? I wouldn't be the first to use my sort of knack."

"You were so certain you didn't want to do it as an entertainment."

"But I'll enjoy it. It'll keep me in practice." The sun had disappeared, a scurrying wind stirred the litter on the pavement. "We'll have lunch, then you and Susan can go off to a film or a museum or something. Don't go and see your mother till I've fixed everything up. Then we can go together and put the proposition as a wonderful idea, we'll surprise her into agreeing."

"Even if she does, it'll only solve the problem for a short time."

"It'll give us a breathing space, time to make more plans. Meantime I'll be building up the business. Everything will work out all right." They were steering through the crowd on the corner of Cranbourn Street. "We'll have to have a quick lunch, I'm poaching on Susan's time. That girl's a marvel. Then I'll 'phone Mrs. Trafford. But I guess it'll be a good idea to go along and see her, to put the proposition."

"It's not a proposition. It's asking a favour."

"Oh well. I've seen her several times lately. She's rather clung to me since the upheaval with Philip."

The call to Mrs. Trafford brought an immediate invitation to supper. "Seven o'clock?" she suggested. "Or later if it would suit you better."

He was there at seven. In the flat it was still difficult to realize that the Colonel would not come pottering into the room; his genial personality had somehow left its impression in his home. Mrs. Trafford, simply dressed in grey, looked strangely youthful and obviously was recovering from the anxiety that had so distracted her, accepting the breach with Philip as an inevitability.

Almost at once Vivian confessed, "I've come to ask a favour."

"What is it?" Her tone was sharp. "It's not for Philip?"

"Oh no."

"To anything else I think you can take it I'll say yes."

"It's quite a big thing I'm asking. Two friends of mine want to get away into the country for a month or so. I wondered if you'd let me rent Lane Cottage for them."

"Really—you've rather taken me aback. Who are your two friends?"

"I've mentioned them before. Mrs. Vautel, who lived opposite us in Sidley Street, and Olga."

"But why do they expect you to find them a cottage?"

"They don't. Olga's worried about her mother and thinks they ought to get away. If there's a place ready for them, Mrs. Vautel is much more likely to agree."

There was a short silence. Then Mrs. Trafford said "You must be very much interested. You've never asked for favours for yourself."

"I'm in love with Olga. As soon as my business settles down steadily, I mean to marry her."

"You're very young, Vivian."

"I'm quite sure of myself. I was on the very first day I met her. It's not that we've anything much in common, we haven't. Perhaps it's—I don't know. Instinctive. Something that couldn't be wrong."

"She's a lucky girl.—Yes, the cottage is better occupied. I wouldn't let it but I'll lend it to them."

"You're more than generous——"

"For how long, did you say?"

"Two months?"

"They can have it until I need it. I'm sure Arnold would have agreed."

"I can't thank you enough."

"I must look at the oven." Mrs. Trafford went to the door. "We're having a casserole."

"I'm putting you to a lot of trouble."

She smiled. "You're making me have a meal when I might have eaten a biscuit if I'd been alone."

"Can I help? I'm quite used to being kitchen-boy, you know."

"No. There's the evening paper. If you'd like a sherry you can pour me a half-glass. I'm almost T.T. these days."

As she came in with a tray she exclaimed "Could you imagine Philip concerning himself about any of his friends? Everything you do emphasizes the difference between you. I suppose we did pamper him as a child, but that's no reason why he should have grown up so utterly selfish. Swindling tradespeople, always making 'mistakes' and blaming someone else."

"Well, now he'll have to be self-reliant."

"He hasn't quite realized the situation, I think.—Move that mat, there's a dear boy, and we want two more dessert spoons. The sideboard drawer—— While his money lasts he won't worry and I'm sure he thinks he can wheedle me into providing more. But I shan't. It's almost as if I'm directed, as if Arnold's telling me what to do. To be stern and definite."

"Where's Philip living?"

"Sharing a flat in Half Moon Street. He doesn't come here and he's only rung up once. At three o'clock this morning, obviously he was at some party, I could hear dance music. I replaced the receiver, then I took it off so he couldn't ring me again."

Such determination was amazing. Vivian was remembering the emotional scene when Philip had staggered across the floor of the elaborate room in Curzon Street. Then it had seemed that all her affection was centred on Philip. Her endless social activities, her craze for clothes—even her indulgence in drink, had probably been attempts at distracting her mind from his infirmity. Confronted by his present infirmity of character, she was beyond such panaceas. Resignation, at least, had freed her nerves from overstrain and she seemed more natural, more sincere.

They discussed details about the cottage and Vivian made a note of the name of the man who looked after the garden, whether or not anyone was living there. When Mrs. Trafford gave him a bunch of keys he felt a sudden misgiving, realizing his responsibility, wondering if they would have been proffered so readily if the full truth had been revealed. But again she was saying that her husband would have approved her action—and he suppressed his qualms.

On the following evening he called on Dr. Baumgartner. In the first visit to the house in Cavendish Square there had been elements of adventure and comedy; now he felt like an out-of-work circus performer begging for an engagement. The doctor was at his desk with a pile of correspondence before him and in his manner there was none of his former joviality. He seemed almost to have forgotten that he had suggested a gathering at which Vivian could demonstrate his powers.

"Yes, yes," he agreed, with a touch of irritation, "I know it was my idea, and of course it would be interesting. But there's the professional angle. I have been practising in this country for only a short time. If I become involved with amateur hypnotists—why then, I'm a quack."

"I'm not a hypnotist. I've never studied hypnotism. Whatever I can do, I do as a 'natural'."

"A natural! You use a word that is applied to clowns. Am I then to become an impresario, an agent, for a performer?"

"It was you who made the suggestion——"

"On an impulse. I thought it might please Dr. Turnbull. He has been of great assistance to me."

"Then I suppose we'd better forget it."

Dr. Baumgartner seemed to be absorbed in a letter. He looked up suddenly and his blue, protuberant eyes were fixed in a penetrating stare. "Why did you revive the matter?"

"I want to raise some money. It's urgent."

"You're in debt?"

"No. It's a private obligation."

"Money is always easy."

Vivian was smiling ruefully as Dr. Baumgartner picked up

the telephone and dialled a number. Aside he said "You know Marie Franks?"

"I know the name. Wasn't she an opera singer?"

But Baumgartner was saying "Oh Marie—Oscar here. You like to give a party, ha? So you give a party. I provide some entertainment, I invite some guests, you invite your own. The expenses are mine."

Apparently the woman at the other end was asking for explanations. Baumgartner said, "You complain you are bored, this will be exciting. Yes or no? If you say no, all right.— No my dear, not angry, perhaps I am impatient. If you like it, choose your own evening." Again the woman was talking. Then, "Wednesday?" Vivian nodded. "All right Wednesday. I tell you more details when I am less occupied."

Dr. Baumgartner rose. "Next Wednesday, then, at one-two-six Chapel Street, in Chelsea. Say at eight o'clock. Of course quite informal, you go as you are, you take anyone you wish. Marie Franks is a great bohemian."

"You'll be there?"

"If I am it will be as a guest. I'll tell Dr. Turnbull in case he cares about it, and of course nothing will keep Susan away. I shall give, or send you, an honorarium."

"It's very good of you. I hope you'll be there to give me a lead. I can't see myself starting to perform stone-cold."

"You'll have all the stage management you need. Marie Franks is an artist, but now she will not sing, even among friends. She had some trouble, the vocal chords. Now, I am extremely busy."

"Well, thank you. I'm grateful."

The interview, in spite of its success, left a vague sense of humiliation. But at least the cottage was assured for Tashy and Olga; the unspecified honorarium would be useful. The prospect of the evening in Chelsea was somewhat dismaying; Vivian was wondering how he would sustain the effort, among strangers, of reproducing phenomena that had always been spontaneous, single events. He turned into a bar in Oxford Street for a drink and a sandwich.

As he ordered his second half-pint of beer his arm was touched. It was several seconds before he recognized the short elderly man who was beaming up at him. Commander Cawdell, who had been Colonel Trafford's lifelong friend.

Stout, bald, with a face almost the colour of claret, he had bright blue eyes which, now that he opened them wide, were glinting like a child's, in spite of the heavy folds of flesh above and below them; the effect was emphasized by his spectacles which magnified his eyes out of proportion to his pendulous cheeks and chin. A jovial old man, with a crimson carnation trimming one lapel of his dandyish overcoat.

"Well well. Vivian Mander!"

"You've a good memory, sir. How are you?"

"What is it, five or six years since you were last down at Pegwell? Not so long? Be that as it may, I was talking about you only an hour ago."

"You've seen Mrs. Trafford?"

"Took her out to dinner. She needs cheering up. Very sad business altogether. I should have been at the funeral, but I was in Brussels, got the news just too late even to fly back. Have a drink. Beer again? Very sensible. If I wasn't a fool I should stop drinking port." Commander Cawdell ordered the drinks. "Let's sit down. Had a bit of bother with my veins."

Vivian carried the glasses. "You're staying in town?"

"Just for a few days. I hear Lane Cottage is going to be occupied."

"Mrs. Trafford's lending it to some friends of mine."

"I'm always glad of new neighbours. But the best news is that she's coming down herself in the Spring. Settling in there."

"Yes, so she told me." The hubbub in the bar was the background to a slightly awkward silence. Vivian felt that he might be expected to give some information about Tashy and Olga, but could not find the right phrases. Either he would convey a false impression, or betray his emotions too openly. He remarked "Wasn't the cottage part of your estate at one time?"

"It certainly was. But Arnold Trafford and I—— Well, you know, we were like brothers. I practically gave him the place, with a couple of acres. I was hoping he'd come and live there, permanently, and I believe he would have done. But he got caught up in the last war again. And he wanted to keep the London flat for when Philip left Cambridge—— You know about Philip, of course?"

"Yes, I do know."

"Young fool. Messing up his chances of a career, causing tragedy and misery. Did his mother tell you about the messages?"

"Messages?"

"She believes they come from her husband."

"I didn't realize she felt it was as definite as that. But—yes, she did say it was as if he was directing her. To take a strong line with Philip. Of course I understand more clearly, how she's able to do so, if she feels she's—as it were—instructed, advised to do so."

Commander Cawdell shrugged his plump shoulders. "That sort of thing's rather beyond me. No doubt it's a comfort, after the shock she had. It's dam' bad luck Philip's proving such a disappointment. I've been trying to get hold of him. Can't help feeling a certain amount of responsibility. Hang it all, I danced him up and down when he was in nappies. I took a very good view of him in those days. And of his future."

The Commander paused, then said abruptly, "What's this bookshop you're fiddling about with?"

Vivian smiled. "It's just a small business, it's hardly got going yet."

"Why not take Philip into partnership? If it's a matter of putting up a bit of capital—I'm not a pauper, you know."

"It's not that. For one thing, the place wouldn't carry the two of us——"

"You could expand."

"In the present premises it could only expand in a limited way. But there's a bigger objection, and that is that I'd never be able to hit it off with Philip."

"H'm. Funny thing. You've meant such a lot in his life, but even when you were nippers I spotted the—what-d'you-call-it—a kind of antagonism. Jealousy on his part, I decided."

"There's no reason, even if he was jealous——"

"There's every reason. You've always been a handsome young devil, he—I hate to say it—will never look anything but a nonentity. That's one point. Then he's a clinger, and you outrage his sense of what is proper by refusing to carry him."

"That's not quite correct—if you don't mind my saying so, sir. When he was at Cambridge he felt he was a big shot and I was an outsider who might try to hang on to him. Not," Vivian added ironically, "that he was ever in serious danger of that."

"Well, perhaps my view's wrong. But again and again over the last ten or twelve years I've had the impression that he's full of a sense of injury."

"Injury!"

"You got him walking. You got rid of the wheel-chair. Such a comfortable article, with all the women crooning over it. It's thanks to you that Philip's expected to behave like a man—and every time he can't act up to it, you're to blame." The Commander finished his port, and took off his spectacles to polish them. The bar was now crowded, the hot moist atmosphere was blurring the mirrors, concentrating in trickles down the walls. "Have another drink?"

"Thanks," Vivian said, "but I've had all I want. I'll get you one."

"You won't. I've had all I dare." The Commander rose. "You may be coming down my way when your friends are my neighbours. Don't forget to look me up."

"I'll look forward to it." As he spoke Vivian was doubting whether Tashy would ever accept the suggestion of several months in the country. Another uneasy thought intruded. Commander Cawdell was a man of the world and an astute judge of character. If Tashy went to Lane Cottage he would call on her, and would hardly fail to observe her flamboyance, her automatic coquetry (mature though it was), and all the indefinable marks of her reckless years. Yet Tashy, in a way, had remained aloof from the world in which she moved; by refusing to mix with other women of the half-world she insisted on her superiority, scandal surrounded her yet no one dared to slight her openly. But his own mother, Vivian remembered as he followed Commander Cawdell's irregular course to the door, had snubbed Tashy on occasions, more by implication than by what had been said. Somehow the rebuffs had not made Tashy look foolish; she had the knack of behaving like an aristocrat who finds herself among a tribe of savages, accepting their lack of understanding as a matter of course. She was coquettish with the tradesmen and, as if she were honouring them, they served her with deference.

"Well, I go this way," the Commander was saying.

"So do I. I get a bus at the top of Bond Street. We moved out of Soho."

"Just as well. It's an ambiguous neighbourhood." They were on an island, crossing the road, when the Commander asked "If it doesn't seem over-inquisitive, who are these friends of yours who're coming down to Pegwell?"

"The girl I'm going to marry—some day. And her mother."

"Well well. I shall take an interest, a real interest."

"It isn't absolutely fixed yet that they're going. I'm just hoping they will."

"The name?"

"Mrs. Vautel. And Olga."

"Oh. French?"

"Mrs. Vautel's Russian by birth."

"They'll be a social asset. We're such a dull lot down there. Well, this is my turning. Good night, and don't forget to look me up as soon as you have the chance."

Vivian walked the rest of the way, deciding that it was hardly worth while to take the bus. He found his mother in one of her fretful moods, and her greeting was a complaint.

"You ask me not to stay so late at the workroom, and I come home thinking I'll find you here. And now it's two evenings you've been late."

"Sorry, Mother. This evening I did expect to be in earlier."

"You expected! Plans are made to be kept.—You didn't tell me why you went to Mrs. Trafford's last night."

"About nothing that could matter to you."

"Was it something to do with Olga Vautel?"

"Really—I hardly dare think with you in the room!" Vivian smiled, patting his mother's arm, trying to mollify her.

She drew her arm away. "You've been drinking, too."

"A couple of beers. I ran into that old naval chap who was a friend of Colonel Trafford's."

"The Traffords, the Vautels. First you're mixed up with people a sight too classy for us, then it's the sweepings of the streets."

Vivian controlled his rage. "Mrs. Vautel's a musician, and she happens to have made a bit of a mess of her life. It could happen to any woman. A few wrong decisions, losing grip——"

"That sort of woman is born, not made."

F

"Then," Vivian exploded, "if you assume character and behaviour are predestined, inevitabilities, how can she be to blame?"

Mrs. Mander exclaimed despairingly, "Oh why doesn't the good Lord give us children we can understand?"

CHAPTER XXII

IN the river mist drifting up from the Embankment, swirling round the corners, the houses and trees in the irregular old street had an unreal aspect, as if they were blurred illustrations to fantastic fairy tales. Walking quickly, Vivian heard only the sound of his own footfalls, for away from the main road he had passed only one other pedestrian, and there was no traffic. The evening atmosphere was eerie, ghostly, he felt almost as if he were a phantom on its way to take part in mysterious nocturnal rites.

Uneasily, he remembered that he would not be merely taking part in the affair that lay ahead; he would be conducting it, carrying the responsibility. The reflection increased his nervousness. He felt unsure of how his powers would figure in what would have to be a sustained display of them, and imagined himself being laughed out of the strange house as a charlatan. But what claims had he made? His reputation, his appearance at this evening's gathering, were due to the judgment of others. For himself, the whole undertaking, apart from the promised honorarium, was distasteful.

Every door, every gate, along this street differed from its neighbour, and most of the numbers were invisible. He turned into an open gateway, went up the short path to the door, and a dog leapt at him, barking furiously. He beat the animal off, reckoned that Magda Franks's house would be four doors ahead, and was going on when he was pulled up by his own name. "Vivian——"

Olga was standing against the dark wall. Only her face and her hair were vaguely visible as she stepped forward. "Do you mind——?"

"Mind?" he repeated automatically.

"I mean, you didn't invite me, but I couldn't bear to be left out."

"Darling!" He kissed her and realized that she was shivering. "It isn't a question of leaving you out, but I may be on the verge of making an awful fool of myself and—well, I'd rather risk it on my own. But I didn't even give you the address. How did you know?"

"I heard Susan telling Philip Trafford."

"I wish he'd keep out of the shop. It seems he makes a habit of dropping in when I'm not there." Vivian spoke irritably. "I suppose this means he'll be coming along."

"I can't see why you dislike him so."

"I could explain very easily. There are people who sap the spirit of everyone around them, and he's one of them. He's weak but he'll never tire because he'll go on draining the strength of others. Come on, it must be just on eight o'clock."

"You're angry with me."

"No of course not darling. Not with you. I'm just rather on edge."

A gush of warmth flowed out as Magda Franks herself opened the door, introducing herself with an impassioned flourish as if she were at the height of some dramatic scene. She had a deep contralto voice. "Of course I have to tell you my name, no one knows me now, no one remembers me. It was so different in Vienna. Ah, there everyone knew me. There if you did not know Magda Franks, you did not exist. Come in quickly—so. I feel the cold. Your names again? Oh, you told me." They had had no opportunity of telling her. "In any case you will have to remind me. I am old, I am stupid. I am forgotten. But tonight we have the most delightful young man, arriving presently."

The hall was like a junk shop that had been churned into chaos by mischievous children. Magda Franks led the way into the room on the left, talking continuously. "The most delightful young man, a new kind of yogi-man, a friend of Oscar Baumgartner's."

Could this, Vivian speculated as Magda Franks continued to chatter, be himself? His hostess was tall and thin, her masses of grey hair were flying loose, and in her long gown of filmy grey material she might almost have been a figure of the mist outside. Panels of net trailing from her waist caught on to various objects as she moved. Her face was hideous, masked with white powder. "You tell me who it was who sent you? Or perhaps it was Rita O'Mory?"

There was still no chance to reply, for Madame Franks was running on into a garbled story of how the chandelier had been broken. The room they were in was large, with curtained windows at each end; obviously it ran through the whole of the ground floor and, like the hall, was overcrowded with furniture. "It was Tomasino, the beast, the animal, he grows so violent."

Several people were lounging about. A small dark man, who looked like an old-fashioned organ-grinder in his tattered brown velvet suit, shouted some sort of a denial about the chandelier, and his rapid Italian clashed in a sort of duet with further accusations from his hostess. Several of the others were round a table, lingering over what seemed to have been a lavish tea-party. They were all more or less grotesque: or perhaps, Vivian reflected as his eyes steadied on the scene, this impression was created by his own surprise. Broken glass lay on the carpet beneath the shattered electric light fitment, two standard lamps were alight and here and there candles were burning, stuck to a bureau, a tallboy, the mantelpiece, without candlesticks. There was too much rich tapestry, a confusion of brocade draperies, a welter of ornaments; the contents of several elaborately furnished drawing-rooms seemed to have been assembled within these four walls.

A middle-aged woman with wispy hair, dressed like a parlourmaid in a musical comedy, shuffled in with a tray of snacks, and Magda Franks wailed "No, no. Not now, Edith. Later. For the séance, did I not tell you?" And to the room in general she cried "Will you not go away? I have other guests, I have another party, how can I hold it in this disorder, if you will not depart?"

No one stirred, except Tomasino, who laughed and swooped at the tray of dainties, filling both his hands and stuffing his mouth. Olga murmured "What are *we* supposed to do?"

"Just let it all flow by. A yogi-man, indeed. Is that supposed to be me?" Vivian no longer felt embarrassed; the situation was so far outside the range of normality that it could impose few obligations. He guided Olga towards a settee on which a youth with auburn curls was apparently sulking. When he smiled he looked like a cherub in a religious picture.

He asked "Did you get some tea? Because if you didn't my advice is to go straight to the kitchen——"

Magda Franks had launched into a new monologue on the same note of complaint. Vivian said "We've had tea. It's a bit late, anyway."

"Oh, it goes on all the time here," said the auburn-haired young man. "Magda hasn't the dimmest idea of what clocks are for. I'm Dobie, you know. I'm lurking on because she's having some kind of a faith-healing session presently. I don't mind telling you, I blush at the slightest thing, I don't suppose there's a hope in hades of getting rid of the habit."

The occasion seemed likely to develop as a ridiculous farce. "Did Madame Franks invite you here for faith-healing?"

"Actually, I was never invited at all. She was furious when I arrived, but she was in the middle of a row with that Burton woman—over there, in the vomit-making curry cloak, so I sort of oozed in, then there was the free-for-all with Tomasino over the chandelier and somehow it goes on and on." Dobie pouted petulantly. "After all, she can't keep me out, when you think what she owes to my uncle. Do you know him?"

"How the devil can I know whether I know him——?" Vivian saw no reason to be more controlled than the rest of them, "when I've never seen you before and don't even know whether Dobie's your first or second name."

"It's neither." Dobie flashed white dolls' teeth. "It's just a nickname. My uncle's Dr. Baumgartner."

"Yes. I know him."

"He was Magda's first love way back in the dawn of creation, when he was a student in Berlin. She followed him to America, and here she is. Of course she's years and years older, but she wouldn't step aside, not even when he married *the* most correct sort of English *frau*."

"So you're a relation of Susan Blane's."

"Sure. But I've never even met her. You see I'm on the German side, and we've always adored Magda, and there's a sort of perpetual feud. Uncle Oscar's quite a bohemian at heart, though of course he has to make a good job of seeming pompous."

Vivian was hardly listening, his attention had swerved to the trio who had just entered, and Olga was asking in an undertone, "What's the matter?"

Dr. Turnbull and Philip Trafford had arrived together. And immediately behind them was Max Lassiter. Vivian leapt up. "Come on, Olga I've had enough of this crazy outfit."

Dr. Turnbull was waving a greeting. Vivian strode across and challenged Lassiter, "Who asked you here?"

"My friends." Lassiter smiled unpleasantly.

"You don't know Magda Franks."

"But I soon shall."

And indeed she had swooped towards them, assuring the newcomers that they were welcome, apologizing for the disorder, urging them to be seated.

Vivian hesitated, and Olga came across to ask "Why are you so angry?"

He muttered "Do you know that man?"

"Maxie? Yes. He's known mother for ages."

"I'm beginning to wish I'd never let myself in for this. I've a good mind to slip away——"

"Well Vivian," Dr. Turnbull said, "we're looking forward to a most interesting hour or so. I wish you'd introduce me to our hostess."

"I'm sure introductions don't matter. Anyway," Vivian could not resist sarcasm, "I should hate to interrupt her."

Madame Franks was railing at the maid. "Clear up quickly, what a mess, oh how terrible it is, it was always so different in the old days in Vienna, people now have no consideration, they are animals." The attack swung to Dobie who had flung himself full-length on the settee.

"Perhaps I'm old-fashioned," Dr. Turnbull said. "Oh—— Dr. Baumgartner can't get along. He asked me to give you this."

Vivian took the thick envelope, and Dr. Turnbull moved over to Madame Franks, crunching broken glass into the carpet as he went. He was bowing, evidently introducing himself, but she swept past him to greet a small plump woman with frizzy, brightly henna'd hair, who was dressed and bejewelled as if for a state occasion. "Oh Rita darling," Magda Franks cried, "I am so glad to see you, you are an angel, you are my only true friend, come in, come in. There will be some wine. Edith! Edith! Where is the idiot? She exerts herself to give tea to everyone I detest, now she is dead." Madame Franks collapsed into an armchair, fanning herself with a vivid handkerchief.

The woman with brilliant hair said to the room in general, "I'm Rita O'Mory—— Stop it, Magda, you're making me nervous with all that flip-flapping. Oh don't tell me someone's broken a mirror! What? Oh, only the chandelier. Then we shan't be unlucky. Oh my poor feet." She sat down abruptly, still smiling.

Dobie had risen. "Music hall," he murmured confidentially. "Male impersonator."

Evidently Rita O'Mory had sharp ears. "Not me, not nowadays, not with my figure," she said amiably.

Vivian had opened the envelope. It contained five-pound notes—how many he could not discover without drawing them out, but obviously Dr. Baumgartner had been generous. Max Lassiter was moving over to Olga, who was standing beside the fireplace, where a large electric fire was glowing though the room was over-warm with some kind of central heating. Lassiter's overcoat was swinging open, he still held his hat. If Olga went to Pegwell at least she would be away from the man, whose jaunty manner towards her now suggested that he considered himself on familiar terms. But first, Baumgartner's money must be earned. In a clear voice, which betrayed none of his inner misgiving, Vivian said, "This is supposed to be a demonstration, and I'm ready to begin. If anyone has any suggestions, let's have them."

There was a flutter as everyone turned towards him. Then three new arrivals came in. An elderly man with a wrinkled brow and ascetic lips, who announced himself as "Smithson"; a younger man with a tanned, humorous face, wearing an immense plaid scarf, a pullover, and corduroy slacks; and a wizened little woman in a beaded bonnet, hugging a bulging carrier-bag, who seemed to have strayed out of a cartoonist's drawing of a charwoman of fifty years ago. Philip Trafford was still leaning against the wall near the door, over-acting a pose of cynicism and boredom. He said "You should have brought a top-hat, Vivian, and a rabbit and a cutie to hand you the gadgets."

Vivian cracked back, "Did Mrs. Allberry have to hand me any gadgets?"

"So," Madame Franks exclaimed, "it is you who gives the demonstration? Why did you not tell me? Must people deceive me in my own house?"

"I'm sorry——"

But this protest, like most of her others, was no more than rhetorical. She was continuing "It is infuriating that Oscar could not come, he makes promises, it is always the same. He declares that he is interested in the occult, yet he is not here."

"This isn't going to be anything occult," Vivian said. "And I'd like it to be clear that it isn't hypnotism either. You can call it what you like, I've never found a name for it. I've no knowledge of medical science and I've never studied mysticism —I make those comments in case anyone's interested."

"But my arm!" Madame Franks swirled her grey draperies. "Oscar tells me I am hysterical. Can you believe that? For years I have not been able to raise my arms properly, that is what I told the animal Tomasino, that is how the chandelier was broken."

All the others, except Philip and Lassiter, had taken seats, and Vivian felt that he was in the centre of a stage with Madame Franks, for now everyone was staring at them. Yet he had lost all self-consciousness.

"Tomasino said I could raise my arms, he was insulting me, telling me to touch the lowest crystal of the chandelier. How could I, I ask you, how could I?"

"And he said"—the explanation came from Dobie—"if she wouldn't touch it he'd drag the whole works down. And he did, and if I hadn't been able to mend a fuse we'd have been in the dark."

A candle, guttering into a pool of grease, set fire to a mat on the bureau, seeming to belie the statement. Dr. Turnbull rose and extinguished the flame with the base of a black marble carving. Madame Franks paid no attention to the incident. "Look," she challenged, extending her arms, raising her hands to waist-level, "so far they will move, only so far, when they are held out straight."

"Forget them for a moment," Vivian said. But she continued to lament her incapacity as he turned from her, surveying the room with a sense of increasing exhilaration. The man in the pullover and corduroys might be the first subject. "What's your name?"

"Why pick on me?" The man grinned sheepishly, pulling at the scarf he had taken off, as if to test its elasticity. "I'm George Fenmore."

"Do you know the rest of the people here?"

"Not a soul."

"Then," the query came sourly from Lassiter, "how did you get here?"

"Is that any business of yours particularly?" Fenmore stuffed the scarf in a pocket of his slacks.

"It might be, if this is a put-up show between Mander and you."

"Mander? I didn't even know that was his name. As you're so much at home, I might suggest that you act as stooge."

Lassiter stepped forward, his hands clenched, and Vivian moved to face him. Madame Franks was still wailing about her disobedient arms and as no one listened she turned hopefully to the door as it opened. Susan Blane came in with a young woman luxuriously draped in sable. The stranger had a small round face, like that of a doll, except for the nervous twitching of one eyelid. The puppet effect was enhanced by the cluster of artificial flowers worn sideways on her head.

"I hope you don't mind——" Susan was unaware of any tension in the room, "You *are* Madame Franks, aren't you? I'm Susan Blane, this is Lady Bellon. Uncle Oscar said I could bring anyone. Have you started yet?"

"The last few weeks," Madame Franks was almost in tears, "my arm has been so much worse. Soon I shall be unable to move it."

"I'm so sorry." Susan glanced across, "Hullo, Vivian." Then she turned to listen to something Dr. Turnbull said in an undertone.

"I say"—Fenmore's gaze was on Lassiter—"the chap's all right, isn't he?"

Lassiter was standing in a drooping attitude, very different from his normal arrogant pose, shaking his head as if bewildered. Vivian ordered Dobie off the settee and Dobie slid away to sit near Susan and Lady Bellon, shrugging and smiling as if to disown complicity in anything that might transpire. Slowly, with Vivian facing him and keeping pace, Lassiter walked backwards until he collided with the settee, then he crumpled to the floor.

Fenmore darted forward. "The fellow must be tight. Here, let's get him on the settee."

Lassiter lay inert, with one hand dangling, the long white fingers touching the carpet.

"That's that." Vivian took a deep breath. "I've stopped *him* being a nuisance. But I'm not here just to lay people out."

"If that's not hypnotism" Fenmore remarked, "I don't know what is."

"I know so little about hypnotism I couldn't even define it. But I hardly looked at the man, I didn't make any hand-passes, all I used was will and concentration." Vivian added, as Fenmore shrugged incredulously, "You must have had some reason for coming."

"I'm a patient of Dr. Baumgartner's. He made me curious."

"What's your trouble? I mean, what's he treating you for?"

"A bit personal, aren't you?"

"Completely so," Vivian smiled.

"I get asthma."

"Your breathing's all right now."

"It comes on when I'm in bed. After I'm asleep. It wakes me up. It's a dam' nuisance."

Vivian was reminded of Bill Ogden, whose insomnia was recorded in the childish diary kept in the old ottoman. "Supposing I tell you you'll sleep right through tonight?"

"Well, suppose you do?"

"I think you will. Right through the night. For eight hours."

"My dear chap," Fenmore exclaimed, "I've tried the old Coué system. Every day in every way I'm getting better and better. But I don't."

"This doesn't rely on your own will-power. It depends, I believe, on a psychic response—not a matter of conscious agreement. Whether I can get that response, in any particular case, is doubtful. After all, I'm here to experiment rather than to demonstrate. I feel fairly certain you'll sleep through the night without asthma bothering you."

"You're so diffident I could almost believe you. But what about the following night?"

"What you can do once you can do twice."

The old man called Smithson said loudly, "I thought we were going to have some sort of a display. Listening to you two arguing——"

With a half-humorous glance at Fenmore, Vivian said, "You're not nearly spectacular enough. I'll have to switch the bedside manner on to one of the others."

"Surely," wailed Magda Franks, "I am entitled to *some* attention? Why should everyone else be so much more important?"

The little woman in the beaded bonnet had been watching with eyes as bright as those of an inquisitive sparrow, while she had hardly ceased worrying one of her knees with a toil-roughened hand. Vivian walked across to her.

CHAPTER XXIII

CLUTCHING her carrier-bag against her chest as if to protect herself, the woman looked up with an expression of mingled timidity and anticipation. Her small dark eyes squinted slightly, her pallid skin was wrinkled, and as she spoke she revealed almost toothless gums. "Please sir, I don't want everybody lookin' at me. If you don't mind. It's not my place to put meself forward."

"Don't let that worry you," Vivian said. In fact nearly everyone's attention was still centred on Lassiter's limp horizontal form.

"It's me knees, Dr. Baumgartner, 'e said you might do 'em a bit of good, if only temp'ory-like."

"So I might." Vivian waited, relaxed, confident now that he could invoke and control his power. The woman was protesting, but in her simple mind there was no resistance; already she was accepting him, responding, stating the simple facts that were uppermost in her thoughts.

"I do for them, in Cavendish Square. I'm the daily, four

days a week it is, the other days I fit a lady doctor in with a retired gentleman."

Someone laughed. "Yes," Vivian said quietly. Now everyone was gazing at her the woman seemed not to notice or care. Her voice was a patient monotone as she recounted irrelevant events. "My daughter went off with a coloured man, a no-good coloured man, said 'e worked at the docks, 'e never worked there, not after 'e'd got 'er to work for 'im, it upset me. Then my boy losin' 'is sight, I'll never get over that. I didn't ought to be frettin' about meself, but I get a lot o' pain in me knees, an' it's an 'andicap, as you might say. Rheumatics. If I've 'ad one bottle o' medicine I've 'ad a 'undred. You can't get rid of rheumatics all in a minute or so, but it's years now. It's the pain of it when I'm down on me knees."

She was nearer to normality, Vivian was thinking, than anyone else in the room. Yet as he listened his mind was strangely absent; he was remembering the twisting lane that led up to Mrs. Trafford's cottage as he said "Even a short freedom from pain is something."

"Yes, sir," the woman agreed.

A chestnut tree had been struck by lightning and had lain across the narrow road for months, an obstruction to cars but a source of joy to two boys who could scramble and fight among the topmost branches within a yard or so of the ground. "Perhaps I can do that much for you."

"Yes, sir."

The patient, unduly respectful voice was far away, but a querulous challenge cut through the obscurity. "Are we to consider this a serious demonstration?" Then the situation became clear, sharply outlined as a contest that must be waged for Olga. Vivian concentrated, his eyes closed, his figure slack; it was as if he were absorbing the woman's pain, absorbing and then discarding it away from both of them. A minute or so passed, while everyone was silent, then as he opened his eyes he caught an almost contemptuous glance from Magda Franks. Of course she felt slighted, she had thought her own disability entitled to first consideration.

The woman in the bonnet smiled uncertainly. "I must be dreaming," she said. One toil-roughened hand stroked her knees. "There's not a twinge." She rose, her bag fell to the floor, and she retrieved it. "Bending down, too, an' it never caught me."

"I don't think we've had sufficient explanation——" Again a querulous comment came from Smithson, and Vivian turned to him.

"I thought I'd made it clear, I don't offer any explanation."

"Are you having a bang at faith-healing?"

"I've never asked for anyone's faith."

"Then it *is* hypnotism."

"It isn't. I don't even look at my subject, once I've got into my mind what has to be done. You'd have heard me saying so if you'd been interested enough to listen fifteen minutes ago."

"What about the man on the settee? You've put him clean out."

"All I did was to compel him to keep quiet. Why he's collapsed I don't know—it's some repercussion I didn't reckon with. An individual reaction, due to something in his own make-up."

"It's all dam' dangerous."

"That's what I've always thought. That's why I prefer to keep the experiments on a trivial plane. I do know that if I ease an aching bone or so, there aren't any after-effects, though of course the pain may return. If you'd like to volunteer, we might have a simple demonstration of will-power, thought-transference——"

"No thanks." Smithson backed away. "I came just out of curiosity. I expected—really, I don't know quite what I did expect. So far it's all been so—well, I mean to say, I rather thought there'd be much more of an *atmosphere*. Black velvet cloak, magic wand, all the mumbo-jumbo."

Fenmore was still beside Lassiter. He called across the room, "I don't like the look of this chap."

"I never did." Someone's guffaw told Vivian that his statement of fact had been taken for a wisecrack.

The woman with the carrier-bag said "My knees feel lovely. Will they be all right tomorrow?"

"Probably." Vivian moved away and dropped on to the chair beside the sable-draped woman with the twitching eyelid. She was older than she had seemed at a first glance, and now she was smiling almost coquettishly, with her head tilted away to conceal her small affliction.

Susan leaned over to say "Madame Franks is absolutely seething, she thinks she's being neglected."

"All in good time." Vivian drew off Lady Bellon's gloves. "Now, if you'll just close your eyes——"

As her lids drooped he saw an angular scar. "Did you have an accident?"

Lady Bellon nodded, her lips were tightened in an unhappy curve. "Tell me about it," he urged, but she shook her head and a tear loaded with dark cosmetic rolled down one cheek. "A car accident?" Her inarticulate mumble seemed to acquiesce. "Broken glass? The windscreen?"

Lady Bellon began to sob. "Why did I come? You shouldn't have made me, Susan. No one can do anything, everyone stares at the scar, it's hideous, I can't hide it."

"No one would notice it," Vivian told her.

Susan said "I've already suggested—— Wouldn't a plastic operation be the best thing?"

"I'm afraid of knives and cutting," Lady Bellon whimpered. Then she was aware that others had gathered round, puzzled and inquiring, for the discussion had been in undertones. She lifted her head, opening her eyes wide, assuming her habitual inane smile. "Let's go." Now she was speaking only to Susan, "I only came to look on, I didn't expect an ordeal."

One of her hands was still limp in Vivian's, and he tightened his hold. "You don't need surgery, the whole misery's your own invention, you know."

"You mean it's my fault?" Lady Bellon flashed resentfully.

"All your fault."

There were mutterings all round. "The tactless fool," "Most inconsiderate!" and Lady Bellon cried "I don't know how you dare!" as she fumbled for her handkerchief. A gold cigarette case and lighter and a mirror fell from her bag—a magnifying mirror, with which she could remind herself of the enormity of the damage that extended for less than an inch. She was breathing heavily, and as she tried to control herself she emitted short choking gasps, as if she were under some great physical strain. Vivian released her hand and stepped away. Now everyone was quiet, as Lady Bellon tossed her head as if she had been grossly affronted. In neither of her eyelids was there the slightest tremor. Again her mouth curved to the automatic doll-like smile.

Susan murmured "I wouldn't have believed it."

"This is pretty exhausting. I've never taken on one after another like this——"

"I'll get you a glass of champagne."

For a few minutes the room was a blur. Someone spoke to him and he nodded without knowing what had been said. He drained the glass that Susan handed him, and rose, shaking himself like a dog after a swim.

Madame Franks was exclaiming "At my own party, and no one pays any attention to me, I am nobody, I am forgotten."

"I'm sorry," Vivian apologized. "We didn't stage-manage it very well." He wiped his eyes; the room was full of humidity and cigarette smoke.

Madame Franks almost shrieked "You imagine, then, that I am a stage-manager! Must I perhaps change some scenery? Oh, this is insufferable, I do not understand what we are doing. Now we begin, eh?"

"I'm feeling that I'm finished. I seem to have laid one of your guests out, and I've worked at least two minor remedies——"

"Finished? You do not think for one moment of my arms. Can you imagine what it is for me, when I wish to make expressive movements, to be held, tied down? Two anchors hold my wrists to the floor, two anchors that no one can see and no one cares about, while I, I endure so much!"

"Oh forget it, can't you? Put your arms up, right up!" The command came out in exasperation. "Up with them and forget all that tripe about anchors."

Madame Franks gulped out a protest and he shouted at her, "Do as I say, will you?" He broke off, and repeated more quietly, "Do as I tell you. Do this." He raised his own arms.

She seemed unresponsive. But at least her complaints had been checked. He dropped his hands suddenly, forcibly, on her shoulders, which felt fat and flabby through the filmy net. "Do as I tell you. Now."

She lifted her hands, paused for a second or so in the attitude that she had declared was her limit. The others were pressing round, jostling each other. Vivian stepped clear of them all, and saw that Olga was sitting by Lassiter, watching him with a pitiful expression. The sight was infuriating; Vivian swung back and forcibly cleared the floor round Madame Franks. "Keep away, can't you? How can I get any result in a general mix-up?"

Madame Franks wailed "I thought you had abandoned me, like everyone else, not caring——"

"Oh stop blathering."

Her mouth opened—and closed without a word. She lifted her arms, keeping them level, to shoulder height, then, after a pause, straight upwards above her head. Thus she stood for about half a minute, then her arms collapsed, as if they had been the limbs of a marionette that had broken away from their strings. "No," she mumbled, "no, no, no, it's impossible, the muscles, the nerves—it's impossible." She tottered as she continued to repeat, "No, no, impossible."

Vivian caught her as she almost fell; her body felt like a sack of jelly, she seemed to have no bones. She raised her arms again and he said brusquely "You can do your physical jerks later. Where you got the idea that your muscles wouldn't work heaven only knows." He dropped her into an armchair, and, feeling only his own exhaustion and irritation, was tempted to make straight for the door. But he could not leave Olga. And now Fenmore was facing him, talking about Lassiter.

"He's never stirred, someone ought to do something. What the devil were you playing at?"

A cry from Olga stopped Fenmore. Her voice was unnaturally shrill. "He's not breathing."

As Vivian reached the settee Susan was holding Lassiter's wrist. Even Madame Franks had fallen silent. Susan said "It may be because I'm trembling myself."

"What? His pulse?" someone exclaimed.

"He hasn't any pulse."

"There was a doctor here——"

"Dr. Turnbull," Susan said. "He left half an hour ago."

Dobie tittered, "I say, it would be rather shocking——"

Vivian knocked Dobie aside, and dealt as roughly with Smithson, who was leaning over what appeared to be a lifeless figure. Then, gripping Lassiter by the upper arms, Vivian lifted him to his feet. The loose mouth emitted an incomprehensible sound.

"He'll be all right." Vivian was not sure of the truth of his own statement. So forcibly had he willed Lassiter to silence that the result—it seemed—might have been the man's final silence. The realization of the possibility, even for one so heartily detested, was appalling. He shook Lassiter violently, trying to provoke some reaction, but the man lolled helplessly, like a dummy.

Vivian said, "Keep back, let him have some air." This was what came of exploiting a power beyond his comprehension, beyond his full control. "Wake up!" he shouted against Lassiter's ear, then as if compelled by a blind impulse, he struck the unconscious man a violent blow on the cheek. Lassiter shouted, he seemed to be recovering, but Smithson cried accusingly "Hitting a man in that condition!" and Fenmore's voice cut in "He needs a doctor, not violence."

"Get a doctor, then."

Already Fenmore was at the telephone. Susan grabbed the instrument from him and through the hubbub only part of what she said was audible in the room. "But you *must*——" she was saying. Then "All right, of course I won't if you don't want to be involved, but don't forget it was you who started the whole thing——" She swung round as she slapped down the receiver. "Uncle Oscar's sending someone."

Lassiter mumbled "I'm all right, I don't want any doctor butting in. Give me a drink."

"Well, that's that," Vivian said abruptly. "I'm going. Come on, Olga."

She was not even looking at him. "I'm staying. Maxie may want some help to get back home."

"Anyone can look after him." Vivian took her hand, but she snatched it away. Her expression was bitterly reproachful.

"You've had enough." It was Susan speaking. He turned his back on her, but again she was at his side. "You're all in."

"Yes." He was overwhelmed by a curious sense of defeat, an awareness of the extent of his own ignorance and audacity. Almost automatically he allowed Susan to pilot him to the street; she had even collected his raincoat from among the garments thrown on the coffer in the hall.

"You must never do that again," she said. "It was all terribly dangerous."

Someone was calling after them. The little old woman with the carrier bag was outlined against the light in the hall. "Oh—sir! Thank you, God bless you," she shrilled.

"At least *she's* grateful," Susan said.

"Somehow that makes it even worse."

"If only you could get it all organized——"

"Is this the time," he cut in bitterly, "to tell me what I ought to do? I had to get some money, and I've got at least part of what I need. If I've done any harm you can tell me about it. But not now."

"There's a taxi——" Susan darted on to the corner and shouted. The taxi stopped, and when they were in it she asked "By the way, weren't you surprised to be paid so much?"

"For this evening? I haven't counted the money."

"Uncle was going to send a tenner. But you know, Olga's very candid, and I guessed ten quid wouldn't do anyone much good. Fortunately Uncle had just done an operation for a hundred and fifty guineas, I got him in the right mood and worked on him. He sent you seventy-five pounds."

"But—it's out of all proportion. It was kind of you, Susan."

"I owe you plenty."

"When I overwork and underpay you?"

"You've given me a chance to get back on an even keel. You don't know how rocky I was that morning we first met. If I hadn't fallen in with you I'd probably have hung my chin on a cocktail bar and kept it there for months. I really was —well, pretty miserable and incapable of making an effort."

"You did make an effort."

"M'm. Anyway I stopped being self-centred. I knew right away that you weren't too happy either. I began hoping, you don't know how fervently, that things would go right for you. It just happens that I rather like you."

Susan's sincerity was obvious beneath the forced lightness of her tone. In gratitude he touched her hand, and it was as if her intense sympathy were conveyed through her slack fingers. Suddenly he drew her to him, embracing her passionately. Her mouth was warm and responsive, and as he released her lips she was murmuring "Oh my darling—I think I cared about you from the very first, I'm such a fool to tell you."

She drew back. And when she spoke again her voice was almost prim. "That was rather stupid of us, wasn't it?"

"I feel"—he hesitated—"well, rather a cad. We'll have to forget it."

"Of course."

In some embarrassment they rode in silence until Susan said "There's a coffee stall. I'm terribly thirsty. All I had at the jamboree was some terribly sticky port."

Reluctantly, he told the driver to stop. He intended to see Tashy tonight, and had no idea of the time. He and Susan got out and were given large cups of synthetic coffee nearly at boiling point. The delay of only about ten minutes seemed like an hour. To get to Tashy, to make her agree to go away, to be sure that Olga was safely in the country—these essentials were uppermost in his mind. Absently, he noted that Susan was looking flushed, more radiant than he had ever seen her, then again his thoughts were on Olga. At this moment she was probably still with Lassiter; the best thing to do might be to return there immediately. But here was Susan, who had to be considered. She was saying "I understand what you feel about this evening, far better than you think. Don't blame yourself, for any of it. It's no wonder if you got a bit strung-up."

"I ought to have better control.—Susan, would you mind if you took this taxi home and I get another?"

"Of course not."

She had answered before his question was finished, and the radiance faded, almost in an instant, from her face. "I'm sorry, Susan. But I've got quite a lot on my mind. Would you thank your uncle? I'll be writing to him, but I'd like him to know right away that I appreciate his lavishness."

"Of course. I'll be seeing you tomorrow." Susan was stepping into the taxi and he found some silver for the driver. "Good night, Vivian.—Oh, you shouldn't have bothered."

He returned to the house in Chelsea, but though most of the party were still there, both Olga and Lassiter had left. He found another taxi and told the driver "Thirty-two Sidley Street." The whole evening was assuming the quality of a prolonged nightmare, and before he was again swinging through Sloane Square he was in fact asleep, dreaming that he was marking black crosses on an interminable wall, scoring success after success, controlling the fates of an obscure procession of people with no faces. A jolt of the taxi woke him as he was driven past the cloudy façade of Burlington House. He could have slept for no more than ten minutes, yet now his exhaustion was gone and he felt almost feverishly alert.

CHAPTER XXIV

In Sidley Street people crowding round Mr. Linzer's lace shop were being urged by policemen to move on, then as a police car forced its way through scattering groups someone said "They've caught him at last." Before Vivian had any answer to his question "Who's caught?" the speaker had been swept away in the rush for new vantage points. Mrs. Glatt's side door had opened, a tall man in uniform came out, and immediately behind him was Wyganowski, followed by a man in plain clothes.

Wyganowski was bundled into the police car, which was driven swiftly away. Now Mrs. Glatt's brother was on the doorstep, his bald patch gleaming white in its tufty ring of black hair, his shapeless cardigan hanging nearly to his knees. Vivian wove his way across and asked "What's the matter? What's Wyganowski done?"

Shaking visibly, Glatt clutched the door-frame. His thick spectacles caught the light of a street-lamp and he seemed to have two opals instead of eyes. "All these years, all these years, and we never know."

"Never know—what?"

"Some wrong kind of passports they find. He is agent, perhaps for Russia. Here in this house and we never know."

"Well, after all, he's a Russian."

Glatt muttered hopelessly, "Politics, questions, questions, for hours they question us."

Mrs. Glatt's voice came from above. "Com' in, Karl, is trouble enough, is finish."

Glatt shrugged and closed the door. Vivian watched the groups drifting away along the street, now remembering the proposition that Wyganowski had made in The Two Swords. If the adventure had been sufficiently tempting, he himself might have been involved; he had been lucky, not wise, for his new shop had been his anchor. Who would suspect so picturesque an old man, with erratic habits that inevitably attracted attention, of being an agent of any foreign power? Who were the 'friends' whom Wyganowski had wanted to smuggle into the country? And how many had he actually introduced? Such speculations were unlikely to be resolved.

Impatient though he was, Vivian lingered on the pavement. Wyganowski had been the hero of his boyhood, the adventurer, the dreamer, the man who could sing so movingly, who could tell such wonderful tales. Now he was a prisoner, perhaps the victim of his own false ideals. With a heavy heart Vivian crossed the road and rang the bell marked '*Vautel*' at the door beside the gown shop.

He had rung three times before Tashy appeared, clutching a flambuoyant dressing-gown round her hips. Her hair was dishevelled, she had put on weight, and in the near-darkness she looked old.

"Vivian! What is it?"

"Can I come in for five minutes?"

"Where's Olga?" Tashy peered out suspiciously. "She said she'd be with you this evening."

"So she was.—It's important, Tashy, or I wouldn't bother you."

"You'd better come in before the whole street starts getting interested."

He stepped inside. "The street's had plenty of excitement tonight. You must have heard the noise."

"As if I care." Tashy added, as they mounted the stairs lit only by the diffusion that came from her open door, "It's funny, I can't ever get used to the idea of you except as a kid." Her voice was harsh and yet oddly musical: the voice of a worn-out cabaret singer.

The house smelt queer, but in the first floor room the atmosphere of decay was overwhelmed by that of stale perfumes. The grand piano lent a touch of dignity to the general disorder; in the room above someone was practising a tap-dance, *tappety-tap-tap, tappety-tap-tap*.

Tashy dropped into the only chair, so Vivian sat on the end of the divan. The gas fire was wheezing and chunks of asbestos that had fallen into the hearth looked like bleached bones. On the mantelpiece there was a faded photograph of a man whose features seemed familiar. Of course, it would be Olga's father, who had been killed in an air-raid. Olga's eyes and the same proud poise of the head. The frame was propped against a gilt model of the Eiffel Tower. Tashy said "I feel shocking, I haven't even got a drink to offer you."

"I've been worried about you."

"What can I matter to you?"

"I'll come straight to the point. You know I'm in love with Olga. Very well. I've got a friend of mine to lend me a country cottage. It's simple and comfortable, and only an hour's journey from town. I want you to go and stay there for a few months."

"In the country?" Tashy was startled out of her lethargy. She found a comb and ran it through her thick dark hair.

"It's called Lane Cottage, at Pegwell in Sussex. You could take Olga and the change would do you both good."

"Well! You come here and think you can order me right out of London." Tashy's eyes, in their criss-crossing of wrinkles, were hard and suspicious, but the total effect of ravaged beauty was pitiful. "What's the idea? Where's the sense of it? Who's put you up to it?"

"No one." Vivian drew out the envelope that Dr. Turnbull had given him, and the key of the cottage. The address was on the label dangling from the key. *Tappety-tap-tappety-tappety-tap*—the tuneless noise overhead was like hammer-beats echoing on his strained nerves, yet Tashy seemed not to notice it. "It's my own idea. It's just—I wanted to make you a gift of a holiday. And this'll help with expenses."

Tashy took the envelope and extracted the notes. Pleasure and amazement contorted her bold features. "Fivers!—Ten, fifteen, twenty—— There's seventy-five pounds here."

"Yes." He spoke absently. "It was more than I expected."

The embroidered dragons and flowers on Tashy's dressing-gown writhed like living things as she rose. "I see," she said slowly, "I see. It's funny you should be so flush tonight. Just when Maxie Lassiter's made a packet."

"This is nothing to do with Lassiter."

"Well, I wasn't thinking he'd *given* it to you. He wouldn't, would he?" Tashy's smile held some obscure suggestion.

"No."

"Well, Vivian, it's very kind of you, and I'm not the one to ask where any money comes from."

He did not bother to explain; her suspicions, whatever they might be, could hardly matter. In this room the topic of money filled him with embarrassment; the sordid whispers of years of promiscuity seemed to be punctuating the overhead jazz rhythm. Tashy was saying, "Of course, with fivers you have to be careful. The banks keep the numbers——"

"For heaven's sake! Those notes were given to me by a friend. No, that's wrong, for actually I earned them." He gazed at a floral calendar to avoid Tashy's relentless stare. "Will you go to Pegwell, Tashy?"

"I can't see myself ever getting out of Soho. London becomes a habit, you get used to the streets, to the noise. It's all a help, it stops you thinking. In the early morning, when everything's quiet, I lie and think and then I get miserable. In the country it would be like that all the time."

Poor Tashy, afraid of being alone with herself. He said, "You'd find plenty of other interests. Country folk are kind."

She flashed back "When have I ever asked for kindness? I'm not in need of charity." Her declaration sounded ironic, for as she spoke she was stuffing the notes in her handbag. "It's not that I don't appreciate your offer."

Here was a moment for domination—but he felt that he had no power, his inner strength was spent. "I can't force you."

"And once you were the clever boy who could make anyone do anything."

"I wish you'd go. It might be an escape from your worries for a time, then when you came back everything would fall into a new pattern. Think it over, Tashy. I'll come back tomorrow morning and if you won't go—well, I'll just have to collect the key and return it to its owner."

She seemed inattentive. "Why, I didn't even thank you for the money," she exclaimed. "However you got it, it's lovely of you to let me have it. I don't mind admitting it, I've been hard up lately. Somehow I—I don't know, I've lost heart, I suppose that's it."

Perhaps he could persuade her. One more effort might do it. He moved close and laid his arm under hers, cupping her elbow in his hand. "Go to Lane Cottage, Tashy."

"I won't go," she said, "I wouldn't think of it."

The tap-dancing hammered erratically overhead. For a moment or so as he concentrated upon Tashy her face, so close to his own, blurred into a misty semblance of Olga's. But how different, in reality, they were! Tashy might have been symbolized by an overblown crimson peony; Olga by a delicate pale golden rose yet to attain its full bloom. Tashy's voice cut into his reverie. "I don't know," she was saying, "there's nothing much to stay for. I can't be more miserable there than I am here. I might as well go. After all, you say it's not far away, I could always come back. I'd leave my things here. But I'll miss the piano."

"There's one there, I should have told you. Then you'll go?"

She shrugged in a resigned way, and rose. "It's a funny do, isn't it, getting a cottage lent to you? How did you work that?"

"It would be too long a story." As he stood up he had a flashing memory of the drawing-room in Curzon Street, of Philip tottering from his wheel-chair, Mrs. Trafford in the doorway, the Colonel behind her—— "It doesn't matter, the details are a bit dim by now. All I'm thinking of is that you're going to Pegwell. Make it as soon as you can, I'll get the address of the woman who goes in to clean and let you have it. There's a part-time gardener, the owner keeps him on whether or not anyone's there."

"I haven't actually said I'll go."

"But you *are* going."

There was a silence; even the tap-tap of the dancer overhead had ceased. "Yes, I'll go," Tashy said.

He was at the door. "Good night, Tashy."

Again only the glow from her room lit the stairway. Her voice, harsh and sarcastic, followed him, "In a moment I suppose I'll wake up. I've been so near-crazy I've been afraid I'd get delusions."

The street was now deserted except for some vague figures on the corner, and the freshness of the night air seemed to dissipate the uneasiness of the past twenty minutes. Everything was going to be all right. Yet it was with a keen awareness of problems unresolved that Vivian made for Piccadilly Circus and ran down the steps of the tube station to telephone.

A strange voice answered him, and then shrilled "Miss Vautel!" The air in the kiosk was humid, reeking of stale breath and cigar smoke mixed with the familiar tang of the underground. It was over a minute before he heard Olga's sharp question, "Who is it?—Oh, did you ring before? I've only just got in."

"I've been with your mother. I think it's all settled, I persuaded her and she says she'll go."

"Go?"

Was Olga so forgetful—or so indifferent? "To Pegwell, the cottage we've been talking about."

"Oh, of course."

"Try to go within a day or so. The sooner the better."

"So much seems to be happening——" Olga broke off, and added "Philip and Maxie and I left just after you did, we went to The Two Swords."

"That's no place for you! And with those two."

"We didn't stay twenty minutes."

"To think that I was just round the corner—— If I'd known I'd have come and collected you."

"I'm glad you didn't, Vivian. It might have been awkward. You see, I know so much more than I did."

"About what?"

"You."

"Is it too late to see you?"

"It's ten to twelve. Mrs. Paton hates the 'phone ringing so late."

"Well, so long as you don't believe anything Max Lassiter says, even till tomorrow."

"M'm." The sound was non-committal. "I'm really more sorry than angry."

"For heaven's sake," Vivian exclaimed, "about what?"

"The way you've injured Maxie."

"I must say you seem very protective about the man. What the devil have *I* ever done to harm him? He came to the thing this evening to be a nuisance, he made that plain right away. What I did was to avoid an argument which might have developed into a brawl."

"It's not this evening I mean. You might have told me, about your father and his."

It was a moment or so before Vivian replied; his lips felt unnaturally stiff. "Are we going to reproach each other about our parentage? For all you know my father may have rid the world of someone better out of the way."

"Defending murder! You haven't any heart."

"For heaven's sake, Olga! I hate this arguing over the 'phone, in a few hours you seem to have changed——"

"I *have* changed," she broke in, "every day, every week, ever since we first knew each other. I must go to bed now."

"You'll call in the shop tomorrow?"

"Perhaps. You always have Susan."

"She's nothing to do with us." Yet in an emotional reaction he had embraced Susan. "I want you, I love you, Olga, you don't realize how much."

"After talking to Philip and Maxie I see everything so much more clearly."

"So much more crookedly."

"I really must go to bed."

"Olga——" he began desperately. But the receiver at the far end was replaced.

Vivian stepped out of the kiosk. In the underground circular hall belated travellers were hurrying for their trains. Three drunk men clinging together lurched along, looking like one monstrous creature as they staggered, fell, and recovered. One, who must have been an acrobat, turned a couple of somersaults, and the others, trying to control him, found themselves embracing his ankles while a face peered backwards from between their shoes. The grotesque incident intensified the effect of nightmare that had permeated most of the evening; perhaps, Vivian reflected, one had no personal control and the total nightmare had to proceed to predestined awakenings.

A girl in a tight black dress and a fur cape was adjusting her tiny hat, which had a white pompom on the front of it. The pompom bobbed about, came closer, was beside him at the foot of the stairway to the street, and then a wheedling cockney voice told him he looked lonely. Up a few stairs with the pompom keeping level, and he was feeling in his pocket while part of his mind speculated as to whether his seventy-five pounds had been thrown away on a hopeless situation. "Yes of course," he said, "if you'll tell me what you expect. I mean I wouldn't want to disappoint you——"

"You'll treat me all right. I can always tell." She was smiling, telling him she lived in Long Acre. "Only a few minutes walk even if we can't get a taxi."

He saw her clearly in the light of Piccadilly Circus with the Guinness advertisement flashing over the white pompom. Dolly Hart, who had dragged out a meagre existence as a waitress when she had the room next to Wyganowski's, snuggled her silver fox round her pointed chin, and giggled, "I wondered if you'd know me again."

He was staring in dismay. Once she had seemed so much older, so grown-up when he had been a schoolboy. "I always used to think you'd find a fairy prince," he said.

She laughed. She had perfect teeth. "You were a comical kid. I never would have thought you'd grow up to be a fly-by-night. Come on, it's this way."

He need not confess how slight had been his experience. "Everything's out of focus tonight," he remarked, and she was looking puzzled as he slipped his arm through hers. "I'm very glad you came along, just when you did. I was quite romantic about you when I was ten years old. I wanted to be heroic for your sake. It's queer how this is giving me confidence, you haven't changed."

"Haven't I?" Her voice was squeaky with surprise.

"No. You're the same. The real you will always be gentle and kind."

"That's right, ducks. Ever such good friends, like we always were." Dolly weaved her way expertly past the groups outside the Corner House.

Yes, she was gentle and kind. And so wise in contrast with his bungling, excitable love-making. In the early hours he tiptoed down the furtive stairs into Long Acre with a mingled sense of relief and treachery. The air was cool and sweet, calming to his confusion of emotions, and he breathed deeply, gratefully, as he hurried through Leicester Square. Luck was with him, for he arrived in Regent Street just as one of the night-service buses pulled up. A clock struck four as he used his latchkey, and he reflected that it was as well that his mother had relinquished her habit of waiting up for him.

He dropped on his bed to take his shoes off—and woke four hours later, still fully dressed. Another day—to which yesterday's events would contribute a hangover of complications. A faint misgiving assailed him as he stripped for a bath, a memory of warnings uttered by one of the masters at school, then he remembered that Dolly Hart had touched on the same subject. She had taken care of him. Altogether, she had been quixotically generous, for in his pocket he found the two notes that he had given her.

CHAPTER XXV

THE smoke from the train spread a mauve smudge across the
bleak fields and suddenly a blackbird sang loudly, as if
encouraged by the thudding rhythm of the engine. In the
garden beside the small station snowdrops and crocuses
offered their promises of Spring. The air was keen, though
after a hailstorm the sun had appeared as if to make a half-
hearted apology.

Vivian walked hastily, impatiently, until within sight of
the thatched roof of Lane Cottage on the slope away to the
left, then he strolled at a more leisurely pace up the winding
by-way, in which every twist and undulation had become
familiar during his visits to the Traffords.

Olga and Tashy had been here for three weeks. He had
been fully occupied, but he could have broken away; the
underlying reason for the delay in making this first call was
a kind of pride. He had given, to the limit of his resources;
surely, he had argued to himself, he would receive an invitation,
some definite indication that he would be welcome? Olga, in
the three days that elapsed between Madame Franks's party
and her departure, had been elusive; he expected her to write.
His own letters were answered by the briefest notes, and it
was Tashy, writing about some account that had come in for
bulbs, who had inquired *'Why haven't you been to see us?'*

The lane took an S-bend and now he could see a woman
in the garden ahead. She was muffled up in a large tweed coat
and had a scarf over her head, but another glance assured him
that it was Tashy, who was talking to someone behind the
clump of holly trees. As she laughed, Commander Cawdell
stepped forward—recognizable only by his stocky figure, for
a tweed hat was crammed low on his head and the upturned
collar of his coat concealed his lower features. Then Olga
appeared in the porch, pulling on her raincoat as she came
out. Vivian waved, then all three were waving back, and Olga
ran down to meet him, her Wellingtons slipping on the wet
path, her hair streaming back from her glowing face.

There was a moment of uncertainty as they met. They
kissed almost formally, both conscious of the two in the garden.
At such a reunion, Vivian felt, he should have found something

significant, even poetic, to say, yet he found himself uttering the banal questions, "How are you getting on? How do you like it here?"

"We love it." She threw back her hair, gold silk against the sackcloth of the sky.

"You might have written, darling."

"You were angry with me."

"Me, angry with *you*? My dear, as if that could be possible." Olga was gazing at him quizzically and he added, "I admit I didn't like you getting mixed up with Lassiter."

"We've gone over all that. He's an old friend of Mother's, I could hardly cut him, could I?" A shadow flickered across Olga's grey-green eyes and she seemed to take refuge in evasion. "Was it a bitterly cold journey?"

"No.—I hardly recognized your mother in tweeds and woollies."

"She's bought quite a lot of things in Horsham. She sold her diamond wrist-watch there to raise some cash, Cawdie was furious with her when he heard."

"Cawdie? Commander Cawdell?"

"He's going to give her another to take its place."

"He certainly seems to be—— How shall I put it? Taking an interest." The Commander was handing Tashy a small posy as he and she went into the cottage.

"She amuses him," Olga smiled. "He spends quite a lot of time here, or we go over to his place. The loveliest old house."

"I know. I went there when I was a kid."

"It makes me feel I'm in an old-time film. The house-keeper in black satin and the antique butler, everything done so quietly and beautifully."

"And expensively." Vivian moved forward to open the gate, which had swung downwards as Olga came through it.

"He's becoming so romantic about Mother I'm beginning to feel I'm their chaperone."

"Don't let's hurry. I wish we could stay and talk for an hour."

"You weren't listening."

"But I was." Uneasy speculations thrust themselves forward. How much did the old naval man know or suspect of Tashy's past? He was a man of the world, keen witted and shrewd beneath all his bluff amiability. Almost with a sense of treachery Vivian found himself remembering the scandals of Sidley Street, the sly leering comments, the heads thrust out of windows as Tashy flaunted along with some new admirer who might last for a few months at most. Her life had marked her, as life marks everyone from the clerk to the playboy, from the yokel to the diplomat. Could the transformation be so complete that a man who had known all sorts of women in every continent could be hoodwinked? Life, it seemed, had a trick of outraging logic, but it was impossible to believe that Commander Cawdell, if he had recognized Tashy for what she was, would indulge in a promiscuous affair—in these particular circumstances. Lane Cottage belonged to the widow of his oldest friend, he himself had often declared his respect for convention. "I'm glad," Vivian felt that his remark was inane, "if you're finding the neighbours sociable."

"Not all of them. Not that we mind. Mother spends hours every day at the piano—and Cawdie appreciates that she really can play. He ran us into Horsham yesterday and bought a whole stack of music and ordered lots more."

"We've had these few minutes—and we've used them up leaving everything that matters unsaid."

"Everything that matters?" Already Olga was in the porch.

"Couldn't we walk round the garden, round the house? Anywhere to have you to myself."

"They won't mind," she said lightly.

A car was standing near the garage, under a leafless tree. "Cawdie's," Olga remarked.

"What I wanted to say—— You probably guess. Olga, darling, will you marry me as soon as you come back to London?"

He could not fathom her thoughts as she caught at one of the overhanging branches, bringing down a shower of cold drops which made her exclaim while still she avoided meeting his eyes. "I know I haven't much to offer," he went on, "but things are improving all the time. And anyway I'm my own boss, which means that every bit of energy I put into the business is something invested for us. You know I love you. Now and always."

"I wish you didn't."

"Darling!" In dismay he seized her hands, but sensing her reluctance, released them.

"Ever since that evening at Madame Franks——"

She left the sentence unfinished, and he said, "I know what you feel. That it made a barrier between us. In a way it did. But I still feel the same—I mean, I couldn't understand your going to a dump like The Two Swords with Lassiter and Philip Trafford. That's all over."

"Maxie knows you're jealous of him. No, not jealous. Envious."

"Envious!"

"He's doing very well."

"I don't give a hoot *how* he's doing." And why should Olga care? At times she was disconcerting, incomprehensible. "Let's forget him."

"Of course," Olga spoke musingly, "you've put me deeply in your debt."

"That's—forgive me, but it's quite ridiculous."

"You've done something really amazing for Mother. She's altogether different, her awful depression's gone. I believe, for a little while at least, she's really happy."

"I'm glad, of course. But darling, you haven't given me any sort of an answer."

"I can't."

"But—I do so urgently want to make our plans definite. We can't just drift. Life's too precious, too short." Vivian smiled, "I'm glad at least that you haven't said I'm too young to be taking on responsibilities."

"It isn't that."

"What, then?—There isn't anyone else?"

"You know there isn't. But I feel so uncertain, I mean deeply uncertain, as if it would be wrong to force myself to a decision. Don't you understand, Vivian?"

"You're unsure—of me?"

"No, no. Not that at all. But ever since I've been back in England I've realized how backward I am—in understanding people, life, everything. At Jakeline's the other girls seemed so much more poised, so familiar with situations that just puzzled me. Of course I learnt a lot from them, I'm not really stupid, but it'll be a long time before I feel I've really found my bearings. To know when it would be sensible to laugh instead of being shocked. Perhaps I should have laughed when Philip told me what a bully you were at school——"

"He didn't say that?"

She nodded. "I was shocked. If I'd had more experience, if I'd been like the other girls in the workroom I'd have thought of something smart as a reply."

"Heaven forbid! Darling, you mustn't go on thinking that those girls you happened to work with set the absolute standard of behaviour."

Olga sighed. "I can only develop as I go along. That's what I'm telling you. I need a lot of time to get more knowledge, balance, a chance to sort out everything. Supposing you turned out to be quite different from what I think you are?"

"How could I? With you I'm completely sincere."

"Sometimes I wish I'd never left the convent. It was so safe, it went on year after year being just the same."

"Like death. Or being in prison. We're free and of course everything that's alive must change and develop. Together, we'd grow into each other's lives."

She said suddenly, like a small child, "My shoes have sunk right into the mud."

"I'm terribly in earnest, Olga. Come on, let's get back on to the path.—It's such a precarious sort of time, with all this talk of a cold war, another real war. If we don't get married soon——" He could not voice the dread, 'We may never be able to.' This long argument, with the wind lashing up the hill, had produced a sense of fatalism. And how powerless he was, with Olga, to exert the persuasion that had won him so many disputes—when the triumphs had been worthless. He could not approach her objectively, forcing his will upon hers; with her, as with his mother, there was a spiritual bond that might neutralize any attempt at domination. And he wanted her willingly, gladly, not as a conquest unable to resist psychic compulsion. "I suppose I must try to be patient," he said.

Tashy called "Olga!" and appeared round the corner of the cottage. In a maize-coloured pullover and tweed skirt, apparently wearing no make-up except lipstick, she still looked unlike the woman who had lived in Soho. "Hullo,

Vivian. We've been wondering how long you two were going to stay out here and freeze."

"I'm all muffled up," Olga said.

In the lounge Commander Cawdell seemed to be thoroughly at home. "I'm ready for tea, if no one else is," he remarked.

"Vivian must be more than ready," Tashy said.

Even in her intonation there was a subtle change. "You're looking well," Vivian told her.

"Without so much of this?" She ran a hand lightly over one cheek. "I feel fine, I could stay here for ever."

Olga said, "I put the kettle on ages ago, it'll be boiling itself dry."

The long narrow room with its low oak beams seemed to have shrunk. But how well-remembered was its atmosphere of welcome. Logs were blazing in the open hearth, the flames throwing their bright glow over old oak and leather. Tashy had draped an oriental shawl across one of the armchairs; Vivian remembered having seen it in her Soho room. Her personal possessions were strewn everywhere, as if she had transported as much as possible of her London background to make herself feel at home. Tea was laid on the low table that the Traffords had brought from their Curzon Street house; there was a photograph on the mantelpiece of Philip holding a cricket bat nearly as tall as himself.

Vivian followed Olga to the kitchen. "I wish your mother *could* stay here for ever," he said.

Olga's glance was enigmatic. On the table spread with a blue-checked cloth a tray was loaded with cakes and sandwiches. "Would you take that in for me?"

Was she avoiding more private conversation? As he took the tray to the lounge he was again wondering how much the Commander knew or guessed about Tashy. She was pinning a crimson winter rose on his tweed lapel and he was looking as sheepish as a schoolboy flattered by a film star. Could he imagine himself in love with her? Many a man was more romantic in maturity than in youth. But in Tashy's half-world love had been a meaningless word, a matter of brief simulation. Vivian had a disturbing memory of her walking along Sidley Street with an oily-looking elderly man, disputing as she swung her ostentatious furs, and did not realize that he was

G

frowning as he returned to the kitchen. Olga, buttering toast, inquired "What's the worry now?"

"I'm puzzled. It's nothing. I often realize how little I understand people." He could not voice his thought. It's all so artificial, like an unlikely situation in a play.

There was a knock at the door as they were all sitting down to tea, and Mrs. Standish, the vicar's wife, came in without waiting to be admitted. She was a heavily-built, forthright sort of woman. She used no make-up, but the crimson triangles below her wide-set eyes seemed to have been painted on, crudely, without shading. Her hat and tweeds were as shaggy as her dull brown hair. Vivian remembered that even as a boy he had perceived her stupidity; she had always insisted on kissing him, ruffling his hair. She was greeting Tashy, and obviously they were on the friendliest of terms. Then she swung round, exclaiming, "Why—surely I've seen you before?"

"I've stayed here several times."

"Of course! You're Vivian, Philip's friend. How sad, oh dear me how sad about his poor father!"

"Yes."

"He's in a better world. Gone to the angels. I do hope Mrs. Trafford's bearing up."

"She's taking it very bravely."

The Commander was slumped into his chair, ignoring everything but his own cup of tea. Mrs. Standish sat beside Tashy, accepting a cup and a sandwich, but still her attention was on Vivian. "How handsome you've grown! And you've still got your curly top-knot."

He resisted the invitation to sarcasm. Would she have expected him to have lost his hair before he was twenty-two? Tashy was smiling, "It's just too bad the way the men seem to get all the natural waves. A perm never gets the same effect."

Commander Cawdell grunted. "You don't need any effect but your own." His expression was almost fatuous. Then Mrs. Standish involved him in a discussion which ranged over honey, a dog's kennel, the division of dahlia tubers, and a Chinese shrub that had withered on someone's rockery.

Tashy's interpolations made the old man chortle, while Mrs. Standish kept exclaiming "Was that a joke? I must have missed it." The three-sided conversation emphasized the suggestion of familiarity, of understanding, between the two who had met less than a month ago. Vivian touched Olga's fingers each time he took a cup from her to pass it to one of the others, but she was so silent, so remote and absorbed, that he began to feel like an interloper, a stray caller whose interests could not penetrate the intimate circle. If only he and Tashy and Olga had had the place to themselves they might have talked about their affairs, could perhaps have made some plans beyond the brief tenancy of this cottage. He had contrived this situation, yet felt that he had no command of it. Even his suggestion of a stroll round the garden, made directly to Olga, was seized upon by the others and in the near-darkness the five of them trooped over the crazy paving, round the lily pool, and along the network of muddy paths that seemed designed for sunny weather, intimate companionship.

Suddenly Mrs. Standish announced that she must go. She smirked at Commander Cawdell and Olga, rubbed cheeks with Tashy, and hesitated. "I used to kiss *you* good-bye," she said.

Vivian cut in almost too quickly, "That was a long time ago."

As she went, the Commander was suggesting that the four of them should have supper at his house, adding, with his eye on Vivian, "I could run you to the station on our way back."

Our way back. Vivian said stiffly "It's very kind of you, sir." Obviously he was going to have no further opportunity of talking freely to Olga, and he had had enough of the embarrassing quartette. "I rather thought of an early train."

"What's the hurry?"

"My mother's not too well," Vivian said.

"Oh. I'm sorry to hear that."

Tashy laughed, "She'll recover." To the Commander she added, "Pale as a ghost, always has been. I never got so much as a mouse's squeak out of her, but I'm certain she's got the strength of a lion."

Vivian bit back a comment. His mother was physically frail but her spirit was indomitable. A cold wind was brushing across the bare garden; he was glad when Tashy and Olga decided to go in to fetch extra wraps.

CHAPTER XXVI

"Change your mind," Commander Cawdell said. "We're having a goose for supper. You may remember Mrs. Tappin's cooking."

"Yes, of course." Vivian stifled what he recognized as petty pride. "Well—thank you."

"I'm glad of the chance of a word with you." The Commander pulled a pipe from his pocket and the flare of the match lit his plump, benevolent face. "About Philip. I saw his mother again after I met you in town. She's still determined not to have anything to do with him."

"I know. He has himself to blame."

"But he's not steady enough to stand on his own feet. He was slobbered over as a nipper, I'm not surprised he's never caught up. I was his father's best friend, you know that. In a way I feel—well, hardly responsible. But what the devil is to happen to the young fool?"

"I don't know," Vivian said. "I don't see him. I'm busy."

"He's getting mixed up with the wrong set. Filthy types."

Another silence, as the Commander applied a match to the pipe. "Well sir, Philip's got to face up to life some time. If he's continually helped he'll expect continual help."

"I asked you before. Couldn't you take him into your business?"

"And as I said before, I couldn't."

"Who's this chap Lassiter?"

"But—— You don't know Lassiter?"

"Well, I wouldn't say I know him. But of course I spend quite a lot of time here."

"You mean——?" Vivian broke off the unnecessary question.

"I was here the first time he came down. The day Philip brought him. Look out! You're on the snowdrop bed."

In astonishment and anger Vivian had stepped back. "So Lassiter comes down here!"

"I gather you don't like him?"

"Most certainly I don't."

"Any definite reason?" The Commander asked.

A light shone in an upper window, Olga's head was

silhouetted before the curtain was drawn. "It's a personal matter," Vivian said.

The Commander moved towards the garage. "I must say he rubs me up the wrong way. What's his business? What does he do?"

"I hardly know. I'm told he deals in surplus army stores and that sort of thing."

"The way the wind's blowing, no army stores will be surplus."

"I know little, and care less, of what the man's doing. I'm told he's making money." Vivian spoke bitterly for he was caught up in an entanglement of unhappy speculation. Why hadn't Olga mentioned the visit of those two, when their names had cropped up? And apparently Lassiter had been here more than once. Was the duplicity that had governed Tashy's life to be adopted by her daughter? The suspicion was intolerable.

The Commander was saying, "Perhaps he's a shade better than those pretty boys who find Philip's flat such a convenient rendezvous. But it's an odd friendship. Lassiter must be— what? Forty-three, four. Or more?"

Vivian ignored the speculation. "I wonder whether I'll ever be free of Philip!" he exclaimed. "If I'd had any sense, when first I had the bad luck to run across him, I'd have left him in that wheel-chair. His mind, his attitude, have never been anything but crippled. The crippled body was probably a stroke of kindness on the part of nature. If only I'd known what I was taking on! And now he brings the scum of Soho to hobnob with Olga."

"We've got to remember," Cawdell's voice was even, non-committal, "Tashy has known Lassiter for years, and she raises no objection. She's a very discerning woman."

At the window, with the light behind her, Olga had seemed to wear a golden halo. Was she no more than a stranger, Vivian speculated, an illusion draped in his own romanticism? Impossible thought! Equally unbearable was the suspicion that he, who had been pitying the older man's blindness, was being deceived, deliberately, for some reason that he could not discern. Olga might have swerved away from the topic of Lassiter merely to be tactful, to avoid acrimony. Even if this were so, she had revealed an unsuspected flair for duplicity. She, who was so appealing when pleading her own inexperience!

The Commander was busy with his car, flashing a torch into the open bonnet. Vivian remained where he was, brooding over Lassiter. Twice before the other man's will had collapsed under domination, so surely he could be dissuaded from pursuing Olga? As the torch snapped off the dark garage was suddenly the frame for a clear vision of Lassiter—determined, cynical, quite inhumanly ruthless. "Oh—Olga!"

She had approached unheard, so absorbed had he been in imaginary conflict with a man over forty miles away. "You're unhappy," she said quietly.

"Can you wonder?" Vivian exploded, not caring whether or not he was overheard. "I love you and need you, and we don't seem to have any sort of chance. There was a time, in London, when we seemed so close to each other, when we trusted each other. Now we're far apart."

It seemed part of the nebulous conspiracy of secrecy that Tashy should arrive at this moment, flashing her torch on her sheepskin boots. The Commander backed the car, turning it beside the garage, and Vivian went to open the gate. It seemed to him as he dropped into the back seat beside Olga that she was wrought-up and nervous, almost dismayed at the opportunity for something like a tête-a-tête. And, fearing his own conjectures, he could not ply her with questions. He held her hand, fancying that she was glad of his forbearance. Or was he torturing himself needlessly?

The evening seemed to be out of tune, as the afternoon had been. Even Swann, the butler at North End, behaved unnaturally, performing his duties with stiff formality as if he had only just taken up his post and wished to make a good impression. Was he resenting Tashy's intrusion? One could not penetrate the wrinkled mask of perfect civility.

"Coffee in the drawing-room, sir?" Swann intoned.

"Yes, yes." The Commander rose as Tashy did. "Well, Vivian, Mrs. Tappin used to call you her sweetheart. If you'd like a word with her, now's the time."

In the kitchen Vivian found only a girl with mouse-coloured hair wound in tight plaits round her bovine, amiable, freckled face. With a vacant smile she said that cook would be back at any moment, but it was fully five minutes before Mrs. Tappin appeared, rather stouter than she had been, with hair now yellow-white. She was as formal and non-committal as the man Swann had been. The atmosphere of friendliness had gone from the kitchen that formerly had gushed merriment, jam tarts, and spoonfuls of cream.

"Have you still got Boofles?" Vivian thought the reminder of the dog might bring a smile to that pursed mouth.

But Mrs. Tappin shook her head gravely. "He's gone. It's a long time, and things change."

"Yes." A brief, uneasy silence. "We all felt Colonel Trafford's loss."

"There's not many like him. Things change, they do, what with strangers about, people who don't know one thing about the country, people who traipse in and out and bang the piano."

So she was openly antagonistic. Vivian said "I expect you know that Mrs. Trafford's going to settle down at Lane Cottage? Later on, of course."

"*She's* a lady."

"Well, I mustn't keep you." He made abruptly for the door, nearly colliding with Swann.

Mrs. Tappin raised her voice. "You don't happen to know when Mrs. Trafford's going to take over?"

"In a few months. She herself doesn't know exactly."

"And how's Mr. Philip?"

Checking the first answer that occurred to him—'Drinking too much and hobnobbing with effeminate men', Vivian said "He's well, so far as I know."

"Your friends are a different sort."

"I didn't know you knew any of my friends. Do you?"

Thus challenged into the open, Mrs. Tappin turned to snap at the freckled girl, "Get on with the washing-up, do, 'stead of gaping at what isn't your business."

In the drawing-room Tashy and the Commander were near the piano, turning over sheets of music. Olga was by the fire. It was a charming scene, softly warmed by the glow from two standard lamps; the older people so obviously happy. Olga, slender and flowerlike, apparently deep in thought, A charming scene—but again Vivian had a sense of exclusion. He drank his coffee quickly, refusing a liqueur. "I think I'll be getting along.—No, I'll walk, I'd much rather. Thank you very much."

Tactfully, the Commander said something about fetching a cigar, and went out. His absence of a minute or so gave Vivian the chance of being confidential with Tashy. "I don't know how you're fixed for money. I hope you don't mind my asking? Because if you're short, of course I must do something about it."

"Skip it." Tashy flashed one of her bold smiles. "We're not spending much down here."

"You'll stay for as long as the cottage is available?"

She shrugged. "I'm making no promises."

"I'm glad you're——" Just in time Vivian checked the phrase 'adapting yourself', and finished, "finding everything all right."

Cryptically, she said "It's like going back thirty years."

"Well, good-bye." He hoped that Olga would follow him to the hall. She did so, but Tashy came with her, seeming as determined as any old-time chaperone that they should have no chance of privacy.

The Commander spoke from the door of the dining-room. "Good-bye, my boy. Next time you must make your visit a longer one."

"Thank you. I'd like to." There were more conventional phrases of farewell as Vivian opened the door. Then he was out in the drive between the tall dark firs, heading for the station, with the feeling that the afternoon and evening had merely widened the rift between Olga and himself. Why they had been unable to re-establish their earlier relationship he could not discern.

Less than two hours later he was discussing the visit with his mother. It was a relief to express some of his conjectures, though his partial secrecy and her obvious attitude —that he was being foolish to allow himself to be so disturbed —were further exasperations.

"Those two," said his mother, "are getting above themselves, thinking they're too good for you now they're livng like gentlefolk."

He knew that she was wrong. Even Tashy had too strong an individuality for petty snobbery. "You've given up disliking Olga, though. Haven't you?"

"I never did." Three pins were adjusted, readjusted, in a length of satin. "I'm sorry for the girl. There's something— yes, you have to admit it, something very sweet about her."

"I always knew you'd come to realize that. But now she's all at sixes and sevens. Losing her job, and finding herself dumped in a place different from anything she's ever known. Mother——"

"You're going to ask me a favour," she said in a resigned tone.

"When they come back, would you give Olga a job, for a time, anyway?"

"I don't know, I'm sure. She's a good little worker and she's got nice taste. I don't know but what she mightn't be useful. But I wouldn't want to be mixed up with Tashy. Where *she* is there'll always be trouble. If I've said so once, I've said so a hundred times. She's just an adventuress."

"She's no longer young——"

"My eyes get tired. They're worse than ever." Mrs. Mander folded her work as if to pack up the argument.

"Olga could take over a lot of the delicate work. Anyway, with the prices your customers are paying you don't have to keep on so late."

"It's a habit, I suppose."

He felt it would be tactless to press the matter of Olga's employment, better to leave the idea to take root in his mother's mind. "You ought to get out more. To the pictures, or theatres."

"That's all you young people think about. Pictures. Gaiety. Gadding about."

He could afford to smile at the baseless accusation. "I'll take you to the pictures tomorrow, if I have to drag you there. What's your choice? Studio Two? Or there's a new thing with Alec Guinness starring, I've heard it's good."

"I like to be quiet on a Sunday. I've got a lot of new orders, that workroom isn't really big enough. Violet Bracey does her best, but next week's going to be a drive against time."

Indirectly, she was arguing in favour of employing Olga. He said "Olga will be back in two months or so."

"Maybe." With a shrug his mother rose. "From all you say, that old fool of a neighbour of theirs won't let Tashy go. It seems he's properly hooked."

"He's not a fool. And if he's serious, then everything may be quite simple."

"No it won't. Not with a woman like Tashy. You can't say simple in the same breath with her name. When you're older you'll understand that no one, man or woman, can put down the past as if it's a photograph they've been looking at. The life you lead soaks into you, right through and through. Oh well! When are you going down again?"

What was the good of a visit like today's? "I don't know," Vivian said. "I suppose I'll wait till I'm asked." He began to unlace his shoes. "Next week I'm going to see Wyganowski."

His mother was silent. As if she had voiced some criticism he added, "If he'd been up to any real mischief, he'd have been sentenced to more than three months."

"Three months or three years, he's in jail. I never trusted him."

"I don't understand him. But I trust him. I like him."

"You've got queer taste. Well, I'm off to bed."

CHAPTER XXVII

EACH time the door of the bar revolved Max Lassiter glanced towards it. The traffic beyond seemed to vibrate the rows of bottles against the mirror wall, jarring his nerves. He was having lunch with Philip Trafford, and this—he reflected sourly—could well be their last meeting. Philip might have been useful in profitable schemes; his appearance was disarming and he had never had to diguise his original accent. But he was soft. Soft, soft, Lassiter repeated to himself as he watched Philip entering, taking his time, with the casual manner that was so natural, so assured—and so exasperating to one who used just that manner as a necessary veneer. Blackmail was a word that Lassiter never used, but in the practice of it he often had to be more gentlemanly than any gentleman. His various forms of confidence trickery allowed him a wider choice of character. At the moment he was merely being himself, but still he could not relax. For he, who had never allowed emotion to interfere with his interests, was at the mercy of bitter hatred, an illogical hatred that he recognized as such without being able to purge himself of it.

"Hullo," Philip said. "How's Pegwell?"

"I've only been down once since I saw you. I'm letting it ride. What'll you drink?"

"I'll have a sherry. It'll have to be a quick lunch. I've got a chap coming round to my place."

Lassiter ordered two drinks. "I suppose I wouldn't know the chap?"

"It's Redlink."

"Advertising?"

"The one I know is the son of the advertising chief."

"Oh. Eric Redlink. Plenty of this." Lassiter rubbed a middle finger against a thumb.

"Seems to have. I'm not money-minded."

"He's one of those. I suppose you know."

Philip's pallid cheeks flushed. "He's very interesting. As a matter of fact we're thinking of doing a motor tour through France as soon as the weather improves."

"With him paying all exes?"

"If you want to be offensive——"

"My dear chap, no. So long as you know what you're playing at. His last pal was a chorus boy." Lassiter made a mental note of Redlink; later on he might pay a dividend. But at the moment he himself could feel no interest in anything but his overpowering obsession. "Let's get along to grub. I'm taking you to the Adriatic. It's not smart but the cooking's good."

"So I've heard." Philip added that his mother liked the place.

"Oh. I should have thought it was too bohemian for her. Too mixed."

"When my old man was alive, Vivian Mander took them both there. My people were pretty well off in those days. The slum kid was showing off with his flush friends."

The Adriatic staff had changed, and a new young waiter showed them to their table. Then Benito emerged from the kitchen and went from table to table, smiling, assuring himself that everyone was satisfied. Lassiter greeted him, "Hullo Benito. Here we are again." The tone was deliberately insolent.

Benito turned his back.

"You're popular," Philip snickered.

"As a matter of fact," Lassiter smiled crookedly, "I rather enjoy baiting people."

Uneasily, Philip studied the menu. He had been flattered by the invitation. Lassiter was experienced, a successful man of the world. Until this moment he himself had not considered what might be the motive for this meeting. "I'm not hungry," he said. "I don't know what's the matter with my appetite. Of course I've never been really fit."

Like an old woman, whining about his health, glorying in his weakness—"Try a bowl of bread-and milk," Lassiter suggested. "I'm having the chicken. I say, doesn't that blonde with the dago remind you of someone?"

"Where?—No, I can't say she does."

"A bit like Olga Vautel."

"She's older than Olga," Philip said.

Lassiter felt that he had been reminded of his own middle-age. He remarked "Amazing how Tashy's gone all country-lady. Even those tweeds that fit all wrong and look just right. Hardly any paint and none of the old mascara. Tashy's a clever bit of goods. Of course she lived on a big estate somewhere in Russia, when she was a kid."

"I thought she was just an old Soho floozie."

"So she is. But her father was someone. It makes a difference." Lassiter began to eat, then laid down his knife and fork. "The only way to have a bang at Vivian Mander is through *them*."

Philip looked up, startled. The thought occurred to him that he might be lunching with a madman. The light eyes of the man opposite glittered with malice, his thin mouth had an exaggerated twist. It was the face of a visionary—of a man seeing visions not of glory, but of evil.

Lassiter continued, "I want to get busy before they get back to town. Now I've got the car I can run down there any time."

"Yes, of course. But I don't quite see what you're getting at. Is it Olga you want?"

Olga was desirable. But unresponsive. Her feelings need not be considered so long as Vivian Mander was attacked, so long as he was made to pay off old and more recent scores.

Lassiter's gaze was strangely intent, as he said "I'm a careful worker. Steady and patient. I never tire."

"Aren't you being rather dim?"

Lassiter smiled. "I don't know if I'm guessing wrong, but I've an idea you're not in easy street."

Philip twiddled the pepper-pot. "I had a few bets. It's amazing how the money goes. I'll have to soften my old lady."

"You won't need her if you've got Redlink. In the meantime if chicken-feed is any help, I could manage a few pounds."

Philip had taken too much pepper, he almost spluttered "I'd be very grateful. As a matter of fact——"

Listening to Philip's troubles would be so much waste of time "If you've got to get back to your place we can't have any long stories. What I've never understood is just how you and Mander got so involved. You're not out of the same sort of stable. If you give me the low-down on that, I'd have something to work on. It's just too silly, that story of faith-healing, jiggery-pokery."

Philip tried to concentrate on his food, but he felt sick. He watched a party entering and a couple continuing their flirtation as they walked out. Again he met the eyes of the man across the table, and noticed the spasmodic twitch of the lids. Instantly the significance seemed obvious. And if the man was a dope-addict, then he might indeed be dangerous. But his venom was directed against Vivian; indeed, Vivian was their common enemy. The upstart, the imposter! "You were saying, you could lend me a few pounds——"

"If you can tell me anything worth while, I'll give you a tenner." Lassiter thrust away his plate and ordered two more beers with the cheese. "How did Mander get in with you?"

"Through soaping up to the old folk," Philip improvised. "His mother was my mother's dressmaker. Vivian did fool them that he'd done me a bit of good. Of course, I had a dud leg, but I'd have been able to walk anyway, in time. It just happened that I did walk, for the first time for a year or so, when Vivian was around. A stroke of luck for him, of course, because that was the beginning. The old man must have been off his rocker. He fixed Vivian up with clothes, paid for his schooling, gave him a packet to start that bookshop. So now he's in clover."

Lassiter spoke impatiently. "I knew all that. What I want are details. This dominating, as you've called it. It's fake, it's a twist. He could be run in for getting money on false pretences."

Reluctantly, Philip admitted, "He never set out to make anything out of it, until he did that stunt at Madame Franks. He got seventy-five quid for that."

"And who the devil produced the seventy-five?"

Philip explained, adding "Susan Blane doesn't invent yarns."

"A doctor. And a German. That's certainly interesting." Lassiter's eyes narrowed, and now he himself was conscious of the twitching of a lid, dabbing at it with his handkerchief.

"I think I get your idea," Philip said. "But Baumgartner wouldn't back up an idea of false pretences."

"Let's look at it another way. The doctor—what's the name?—Baumgartner, could be in a devil of a mess. It's hardly professional to pay an amateur hypnotist to perform."

"They won't admit it's hypnotism." Philip drank some of his beer, then studied his cheese with distaste. "I feel shocking."

"There must be something behind it all. Why should any doctor encourage that sort of thing?"

"I don't know. I don't care."

"Have you got a line on the Franks woman?"

Suddenly Philip was seized with terror lest he might be involved in some manœuvre that would land him in disaster.

"Actually," he blurted out, "it isn't fake. I mean, what Vivian does. It's genuine enough, I've seen too much of it to be mistaken. I admit it's always annoyed me. But you yourself had proof enough. You were as good as dead until he punched your jaw and brought you to your senses."

"I'll bring *him* to his senses. That old chap Cawdell is wealthy, isn't he?"

"He's got oodles. But what's he got to do with it?"

Lassiter prodded into a jar of pickles before he said "He's absolutely fascinated by Tashy."

Philip started. "You mean she's carrying on her old games?"

Lassiter shook his head. "She's discovering the charm of honourable intentions. He's giving her hothouse flowers and handing out the never-too-late-to-love stuff. After all, Tashy's handsome, if a bit battered. Cawdell's well over sixty and wouldn't expect a smooth maidenly cheek."

"I still can't see what the hell it's got to do with us."

"My dear boy," Lassiter used the tone of a patient school-master, "when you're as old as I am you'll know that the more angles you investigate, the better you can work. But what I was asking you for was the info on Mander. If you've known him all your life and don't know a thing against him, either you're a fool or he's a ruddy angel."

Philip opened his mouth to speak, then closed it. The devious workings of Lassiter's mind were beyond him. It seemed that now there should be a chance to take Vivian down a peg or so. But somehow Vivian had always been in command of situations in the past and now this lean, unpleasant bounder masquerading as a gentleman was in command of the moment. The consciousness of inadequacy, both physical and mental, boiled up sourly. Perhaps this was the time to prove that he, too, could assert himself. The words came out explosively, sharpened by his underlying fear, "I hate Vivian Mander, but at least he's never sneered at me. Take that expression off your face. You've got money, but you've never yet earned any honestly."

"Silly boy," Lassiter's interruption was a murmur.

"Oh yes," Philip could not restrain himself, "I get about the West End and I hear quite a lot."

"You drivelling idiot," Lassiter still spoke quietly.

"Now you think you're going to chisel-in on the Tashy-Olga outfit. You're a blackmailer and if you think I'll help your blackmail——"

"Don't be a drip." Lassiter turned to a waiter and remarked that the Stilton was good. He seemed unmoved by the attack, as indifferent as if a fly had been buzzing against the ceiling.

But Philip was growing heated in his vehemence, "You're a blackmailer. If you try anything, even if I'm helping Vivian Mander, I'll put a spoke in. You rotten crook, you scrapings of God knows what sort of gutters."

"Just a moment, kiddo, just a moment." Lassiter's face was dragged by a perverse smile, his eyes were slits of malice, "you've been no dam' good to me, you don't know anything. I thought you might have given me a line to work on. You haven't. So before you say too much about me, to me or anyone else, just remember what I told you. I'm a careful worker, and when I work I sometimes make people uncomfortable. *Very* uncomfortable. I don't care for the word blackmail, so you can drop it. If I decide to dislike anyone, I don't get tired before I settle with them. Understand?"

The sardonic smile was more than Philip could bear. He had to pretend to blow his nose, for tears were stinging his eyes. Lassiter was saying "You'd better pull yourself together, otherwise you may lose your fascination for Redlink. He's used, so I've heard, to the most attractive companions." Two pound notes fluttered on the table as Lassiter rose.

He strolled out. Almost automatically, Philip picked up the notes. The waiter came across and scribbled the bill. It was for sixteen shillings; Philip picked up two shillings change from a pound and tried to rise. His legs seemed to be made of wool. He gripped the edge of the table, got to his feet, took one step, and fell back on his chair. He was shaking with fury and anxiety, and now his tears overflowed. He would never be able to assert himself, never, never, never. Lassiter, Vivian, the chaps he had known at school, his own mother, all despised him. He had only one friend. Redlink.

And here he was in a second-rate restaurant, striving to get to his feet to keep his appointment with Redlink. Again he tried, and was able to move towards the door. Benito came after him. "You're not well, sir? A taxi, perhaps——?"

Philip staggered on to a chair. "I've got to have some-one—— Someone to see me home." In his misery he thought of Vivian. Vivian was his best friend, after all, and could always work a miracle. He would tell Vivian that Lassiter was planning some desperate mischief. "Benito——"

Benito was ready enough to telephone to the bookshop, asking Vivian to come. "Of course, sir. Always he was your good friend, your mother has assured me."

So Susan picked up the telephone in the back room in Orange Court. She beckoned Vivian "Philip's been taken suddenly ill. He's at the Adriatic. He wants you to go there right away."

"I won't. Tell him to get a doctor, an ambulance, any-thing."

Into the telephone Susan said, "Yes. Just a moment——"

Then her glance was reproachful, "He only wants someone to get him back to his flat."

"He always wants someone to get him everywhere. I'm through with him."

"If you don't go, I will," Susan flared.

"I'm not stopping you," Vivian snapped.

"You're forcing me to go. If I go, I shan't come back."

"You needn't."

As Vivian walked angrily back into the shop Susan was saying "I'll be there in less than ten minutes. Tell Mr. Trafford. This is Susan Blane." She slammed down the instrument, put on her coat, collected an attaché case in which she kept personal oddments. Vivian was looking out of the window, his back was to her as she said "Do you want a pound in lieu of notice?"

"You're being quite idiotic." He swung round. In Susan's flushed face a scar by her mouth, usually hardly visible, was a chalk-white zig-zag.

She seemed about to retort, but suddenly darted to the door. And as she sped past the window Vivian had a sense of relief. Her services had been almost a gift, but her sentimental interest in Philip had been exasperating. Now he was done with both of them. A faint sense of disloyalty began to tease the back of his mind. Philip's father had founded this business and Susan had been its second mainstay; yet now he could feel no gratitude. The whole enterprise might have been a mistake. Few customers came in during the afternoon, and he imagined the small business crumbling, failing. Then as he was locking up he was struck by a flash of perception, so keen, so vivid, that it seemed like a mystical revelation. He had never belonged here; the trend of his life had been on a wrong curve. Second-hand books in Orange Court had represented nothing more than a marking of time, an irrelevant preamble. He had yet to find his true vocation.

The damp murkiness of the evening struck against his face as he opened the door, then he saw a vaguely familiar figure just outside. It was Sainsbury, the sign-painter.

Sainsbury said, "Ah, just caught you. I meant to come along before this."

"What for?"

"My shoulder. You remember, you put it right. I've never 'ad so much as a twinge ever since. You ought to be a specialist

I told you so didn't I? You ought to set up in 'Arley Street, worth more than a guinea a box, you are."

Vivian turned the key. "I'm glad you're all right. I'm in rather a hurry."

"O.K., O.K.," Sainsbury's disgruntled voice followed him. "I only wanted you to *know*."

For the first time Vivian reflected seriously that, had circumstances allowed it, he might have chosen the medical profession. All his tentative faith-healing had been on the fringe of a medical man's functions. That he had often succeeded and sometimes failed was neither here nor there. Deep within himself there had always been the impulse to heal, to relieve pain. Only the exasperation of today's events had caused him to deal so tersely with Sainsbury. He turned back to make amends for what amounted to a snub, for the man had come along full of gratitude, but Sainsbury had disappeared.

Even if the money were available, it would take over five years to become a doctor. Idle thought, ineffectual dream! He brought his mind back to reality, wondering how he could develop his trade sufficiently to pay an assistant who would need a living wage. Hopes of marrying Olga now seemed even more remote; her trip to the country, instead of forging a stronger link between them, had alienated them. His second visit had been even less satisfactory than his first, for Olga had seemed more elusive, more resentful of his attempt to re-establish their former intimacy.

CHAPTER XXVIII

I T was a fortnight before Vivian heard anything more of either Susan or Philip, but on an evening that had turned suddenly warm after the chilly early Spring day he arrived home to find the telephone ringing. He let the *burr-burr* continue while he kicked off his shoes, for a blister was stinging his heel, then made a swift move as it occurred to him that his mother was the caller.

Philip's voice came over, sounding childish and defiant.

"I just wanted you to know I'm glad you were such a swine when I needed your help," he said.

"Is that all?"

"Because," Philip went on, "you did me the best turn you ever did anyone."

"Oh well, that's that." Perhaps this meant that Philip would no longer make appeals when he was in difficulties.

"I'm at Bognor, with Susan. She's in the next room, we're in digs and she's looking after me."

"Well, that's fine."

"We're getting married in three weeks time. She understands me."

Vivian's patience failed. "She's always wanted someone to boss. I wonder if she realizes what she's taking on?"

"That's all the gratitude you show me."

"Yes, that's all." How familiar was this puerile argumentative mood of Philip's, which had no aim and could never reach any useful conclusion.

"You'll be sorry," Philip was trying to make his tone impressive. "There's something you don't know. I was going to be on your side. I swear I was."

Talking as if they were at one of their old games of Red Indians! Vivian put down the receiver, opened another window, and went to the letter-box. The caretaker in the basement distributed the post throughout the house, and an envelope within the wire-mesh attached to the banisters bore Wyganowski's erratic writing.

The usual prison notepaper, with regulations printed on the front page, recalled Wyganowski's offence. He had been in possession of two passports whose owners could not be traced, and no doubt—Vivian thought—they had been destined for foreigners who wished to enter Britain, political refugees or men who might be in danger from the expansion of Russian control in eastern Europe. Wyganowski's activities had remained mysterious even under the searchlight of legal investigation. But evidently, in view of the shortness of his sentence, he was not regarded as a traitor, and no one who knew him could suspect him of any but benevolent motives.

The letter announced that he would be released on Friday. *I go to a room, second floor over The Two Swords, you come and see me, Saturday afternoon perhaps?*

Vivian went to the kitchen and made himself a snack supper. His mother would be late, for she had another rush of orders on hand. Surely she must be making quite a lot of money? The thought reminded him of the unsatisfactory state of affairs in Orange Court. It would be impossible to carry on without help, for by being tied down he was missing auction sales and his stock was dwindling. Again he considered whether, if Olga would marry him, they might run it together—but how could he ask her to share so precarious an existence? Besides he would want her to stay at home—and this thought was a reminder that the home had yet to be provided. Perhaps after all he was presumptuous, to be so deeply, so finally in love at his age.

He read part of the evening paper, but a curious sense of anticipation, almost of premonition, distracted his attention. It was as if the very air of the snug room were whispering a warning. He rang up the workroom, and his mother's tired voice scolded him for his anxiety; she hoped to be home by nine o'clock.

All the evening his vague apprehension persisted, though he told himself that there could be no cause for it. He tried to deride his uneasiness, telling himself that he was like a hero in a thriller who receives supernatural warning that some lovely lady is tied to the furniture in a burning house. Tashy and Olga would be back in London in less than three weeks; he must try to get to Pegwell again on Sunday and this time he would insist on discussing future plans.

When his mother came in she was drooping with weariness, and her condition provoked him to a false assumption of good spirits. She had had an evening meal, she said, and was going early to bed.

As she went she spoke gently, "Don't worry, my boy. Things don't go too smoothly for anyone. But you'll see, we'll manage them in the end."

"Why do you think I'm worrying?" Her smile indicated that the question was foolish. "Of course, you knew I was a bit edgy."

"Don't I always know?"

The shadows under her eyes were mauve with fatigue. "You get to bed," he said, "we'll both be brisker after a good night. It's this sudden muggy weather that's getting us down."

Olga had written few letters but there was one from her in the morning, and the news it contained was startling. Tashy and Commander Cawdell were engaged, were going to be married quietly in a month's time at the registry office in Horsham, and would then be going to Cap Ferrat for a fortnight before returning to North End. Tashy would be staying with Mrs. Standish at the vicarage for a few days before the wedding.

I am not going to live with them, Olga wrote. *I want you to come and see me at Mother's old room on Wednesday, a week from when you get this letter. I am going up to collect some of her things, she does not want to see that place any more. I will explain everything then.* She signed herself simply *Olga,* with no personal phrase or endearment. The postscript was *Four o'clock at Sidley Street,* so evidently she had not absorbed the fact that he was alone in the shop, and that four o'clock would be an awkward time.

Somehow, of course, the appointment would have to be kept. Vivian passed the letter to his mother, who adjusted her spectacles, read the single page without comment, and passed it back. On her way to the kitchen she said quietly, "It's what I expected. Tashy's making herself comfortable."

Vivian followed and stood in the kitchen doorway. "If Olga doesn't live with them—Mother, you *could* find a job for her? You've been saying you'll have to take on another hand, anyway. If you did—well, it would be a real link, until I'm in a better position."

"Until you can marry her, eh?"

"Of course that's what I mean," Vivian said quickly.

His mother pursed her lips and he waited anxiously for her comment. "Well, with Tashy making herself respectable, at least Olga will have a sort of family at her back. I never disliked her. If she wants work, I'll take her on. I pay my girls properly."

"Oh Mother, it's good of you. I can't tell you what a difference this makes——"

"Do you think I can stand talking all the morning? Let me get the breakfast, we've got to hurry."

Mrs. Mander ate a square of toast and drank a cup of tea hastily. Vivian was still eating when she was at the door ready to go out. She paused to say, "I never told you, the only time I had five minutes alone with Olga, she made a queer remark. She said she'd never marry anyone until she's twenty-five. She's got into her head that she's very young for her age."

"Yes, I know. She's always worrying because she was taken care of like a child until she started at Jakeline's. She's shy and timid. She only wants encouragement."

"Example does more than encouragement. And look at Tashy!" Mrs. Mander shrugged and went out.

From the shop Vivian dashed off a letter of congratulation to Tashy, and seized every possible quiet interval to write at greater length to Olga. The cool tone of her missive, he was trying to persuade himself, was due to her preoccupation with her mother's affairs; it did not restrain him from ardent phrases among his more practical messages. In a week he would be seeing her in London, would be making arrangements for her to remain, she might even take a room in one of the apartment houses nearby in the square so that they could spend most of their evenings together.

Such reflections cast a glow of optimism over the next few days, and he dealt enthusiastically with his business. It was nearly two o'clock on Saturday when the last customer finished picking along the shelves, then he had a quick lunch before going to The Two Swords. How strange that Wyganowski should have chosen to live over the club! Vivian reflected that Johnny Johns must be thinking him a poor sort of member, he had been along only four times since the club opened. The fact that a visit might involve an encounter with Max Lassiter would have been enough to keep him away, apart from other considerations.

(How often had Lassiter been to Pegwell? In future Olga would have more protection than she had had from her unaccountable mother.)

In Wardour Street, along Old Compton Street, Vivian recognized many familiar faces. The neighbourhood retained its charm for him, he could have found his way by the odours from the various shops. He went in the open door that bore the sign 'THE TWO SWORDS. *Members only*,' and heard the hum of conversation from below. Apparently Johnny Johns was busy. The first floor consisted of workrooms, now closed, and on the second floor a strange name was scribbled on a card stuck to one of the doors. Vivian knocked at the other, it was flung open, and Wyganowski grasped him in a quick, strong embrace. The old man was much thinner, his once-monstrous beard was trimmed to a point, and his wrinkled skin had a bleached look. Behind him, by the window, a shabby young man with a dark skin and crinkly hair was standing in a curiously alert attitude.

"Vivian, my boy! Come in. It is like years, no? But always we are friends, always shall be. This is Mark Torgler, he is from Bulgaria, not so long arrived, his grandfather was a friend of my sister, many many years ago. We all go out together, have some coffee, eh? You are thinner, Vivian my boy."

He laughed. "You haven't gained any weight." (Why was the strange young foreigner so nervous?) "It's good to see you again, Wyganowski."

The old man put on an exaggerated air of secrecy. "Now I must be more careful," he whispered dramatically. "Once they know me, always they know me. They take those passports, but still Mark gets here. It is clever, you know."

"Very clever," Vivian agreed drily. Mark Torgler, who might have been a poor student, or an unprosperous young schoolmaster, looked crushed rather than dangerous. Vivian asked him, "What are you doing in this country? Any plans?"

"So far, I live on charity. I do not like charity."

Torgler spoke English slowly, as if rehearsing each word before uttering it. Wyganowski said, "Now I am free, I shall arrange something. Come, we go out, we have not yet eaten. You are both my guests. I have money."

"I had lunch twenty minutes ago," Vivian said.

"Then you talk, you tell us the news, the gossip. Oh it is good indeed to be free, to be here." Wyganowski glanced round the bare shabby room, with its narrow bed, one chair, and crude washstand, as if it represented undreamed of luxury.

"Yes, I suppose one doesn't appreciate freedom until one's tasted the other thing."

They went to the Chinese Restaurant nearly opposite Mrs. Glatt's. Loo Wong bowed courteously, his expressionless almond eyes on Wyganowski. Vivian drank pale tea from a tiny cup while the others fell on their chop-suey as if they were ravenous, and it was he who did most of the talking. Before the end of the meal the arrangement was made; Mark Torgler would help in the bookshop for a nominal wage until he could find a better post. "So," said Wyganowski, "he establishes himself, and he will gain a reference. It is important for him to be correct."

Vivian remarked "But he won't be able to live on a pound or so a week."

"I am his uncle," Wyganowski said. "Mark, my boy, you must remember to call me uncle. If you are good, I give you two pounds a week, Vivian also will give you two."

"I'll be doing well out of the arrangement," Vivian said.

"We all help each other. It is necessary, in the world how it is. A friend of Mark—we now call him Dick Richards, for we have all forgotten what name he had, he too must find a place to establish himself. He studies English all day, all night. Perhaps you can think of some idea, Vivian?"

Disconcerted, Vivian said "I can't, off-hand." After a moment or so he added, "Are you going on—how shall I put it?—importing people into this country?"

Wyganowski shook his head. "Perhaps one more, if I can do it. Do not laugh, it is the son of a dancer who was my sweet friend thirty-eight years ago. And he is now thirty-seven. She——"

"Yes?"

Wyganowski fumbled with a cruet. One great tear ran down the furrows of his cheek and trembled on a hair of his beard. It was Mark who explained, "She was in Buchenwald."

"Oh. I'm sorry."

"She lived for a little time afterwards. Now——"

Wyganowski blew his nose loudly and stuffed away his handkerchief. Mark reached across the table, gripping his hands, speaking in a language that Vivian did not understand. Wyganowski smiled wanly. "I am an old fool," he said.

Mark muttered, aside, "She was shot on the day I was not. I mean, I was for the shooting also, but I escaped. I could not help her. She was a patriot, she was delirious, she was screaming all that she believed, no one could stop her. So——! For such a few words, for only an idea that does not conform, such things happen."

"I suppose we don't realize what goes on." In embarrassment, Vivian was trying to pour from the teapot that had been empty for some time. Presently, when Wyganowski was puffing a cigar, Vivian ventured to say to Mark, "I'd like to be clearer about your politics. I mean—and I hope I'm not being tactless —I'm wondering why you couldn't have got here in the ordinary way." He broke off as he saw Mark's expression. He looked like a sullen, ill-used, frightened animal. Worse, he seemed to be suspecting that some trap was being laid. "Some time or other," Vivian finished casually, "perhaps you'll tell me."

"Yes."

Wyganowski interposed, "I know your thought, Vivian. You speculate whether you are doing wrong to take Mark, whether you are perhaps on the wrong side of the law. Mark will do no harm to this country. And humanity is bigger than the law of any country."

"It only occurred to me," Vivian remarked, "that lots of political refugees get in on the level, and aren't sent back. Naturally," he smiled to temper the criticism, "I'm a bit perturbed at the thought of forged passports and wangling and all that sort of thing."

"It is more complicated than that. Mark is not political, but his two brothers are. I should say—*were*. To tell you everything, it would take long and it would not be wise. You need not worry, it is better just that you employ this boy because you need an assistant. If he steals your books, I replace them. There, my hand on that!"

As Wyganowski shook hands vigorously Mark smiled for the first time, and as he did so his skeleton face became like that of an elfin, though the dark eyes retained their melancholy. And now Wyganowski was insisting on going to The Two Swords.

"I could think of better places to go," Vivian said.

"But we must have a drink. And by now the pubs will be closing. Come, this is a reunion, one cannot have a reunion without a glass." :

The club was full of the usual Soho idlers and more prosperous looking men, with four or five women among them. Instantly, Vivian noticed Max Lassiter, standing apart with his glass in his hand, seeming quite remote from his immediate surroundings. He met Vivian's quick glance with no sign of recognition. Then he smiled absently, finished his drink, and walked out.

Vivian said "Hullo" to Johnny Johns, who was behind the bar with Ginger Parley. Johnny said "You're a stranger."

"Sorry. But life is real, life is earnest, you know."

"That Lassiter, he's gone very queer."

Vivian said flatly, "Has he?"

"Got plenty o' smackers, it don't worry me 'ow 'e gets 'em. But the others can't stand 'im, I want to keep 'im out. If you'd come in oftener, it looks like you'd do the trick."

"I couldn't care less." Vivian was reflecting that in four days' time Olga would be in London. She must never come here, she must never be where Lassiter was likely to turn up. With a shrug that dismissed some uneasy speculations, Vivian called above the hubbub to ask the other two what they wanted to drink.

The three of them were sitting in a corner, watching a quarrelsome pair who were gambling at a pin-table, when Vivian was struck by an idea that seemed likely to solve most of his difficulties. Wyganowski was in funds and was anxious to settle Mark Torgler safely in England. Why shouldn't they take over the bookshop? As a going concern it should be worth more than he had put into it.

He put the question in the most casual manner. "How would you like to buy my business, Wyganowski?"

"Buy it! What would I do with it?"

"You could let Mark run it for you."

"My dear Vivian, Mark has yet to learn his way about."

"That won't take more than a week or so."

"And what would you do?"

"With my experience, at Trimble's and on my own, I could find a decent post almost anywhere. I want to get away from London, settle in some other town, away from all this." Leaving London would be the surest way to prevent Lassiter from trying to keep up his association with Olga.

Wyganowski laughed away the suggestion. "If I own a bookshop, then there might be inquiries."

"I'd sell for what I put into the place. If you don't want it, I'll advertise it."

Still the old man shook his head. But when they parted

two hours later he remarked, "In that idea of yours, after all, there might be some advantage. You are serious?"

"Think it over," Vivian said. "I'll do the same. I'll know my own plans more definitely by the end of next week." He told Mark where to come on Monday morning and bade the two of them good-bye.

It was five o'clock. The workroom in Frith Street was only a few minutes walk away and he decided to call there on the chance that his mother had not yet left. He found her at her desk. The three sewing-machines were under their covers, the place had a tidy, folded-up appearance. Some watercolour fashion designs, pinned to the wall, bore the trade name that his mother was now using—Madame Noreen.

"Still at it?" he remarked. "Oh, accounts. You ought to let me help."

"Mr. Carruthers does the books. I only send out the bills."

Carruthers was her accountant. Everything seemed to indicate how greatly the dressmaking business had expanded. He saw that his mother was studying what looked like a legal document and, glancing over her shoulder, discovered that it was the lease of premises in Bruton Street.

"I'm moving on quarter-day," she said. "But there's a clause I'm not sure about. Dilapidations. Do you think it's fair?"

"Why—the rent's five hundred a year!"

"I'm making dresses that cost thirty guineas apiece. You can't bring many of that class of customer to this neighbourhood. But I've got a show to dress, and that'll be a good advertisement, with my name on the programmes. A girl at the Slade is paying for her art training by designing my models."

"You certainly do go ahead. Remember your one handmachine in Sidley Street?"

"I was giving my work away. Why, to get anything as good as I do for them, as original and stylish, my customers would have to go to one of the big houses. Or Paris, and pay twice what I charge them."

Vivian smiled ruefully. "Why do I bother with books, all in terms of shillings? I think I'd better come in with you, and call myself Monsieur Vivian."

"You'd only be a nuisance."

He leaned over to touch her hair lightly with his lips. "I'm sure I should."

"I was asking you about that dilapidations clause."

"So you were. But I don't know, I haven't the experience. You'd better ask your Mr. Carruthers."

"That's what I shall do."

"I see you'll have a showroom as well as workrooms. Bruton Street will be ablaze. Madame Noreen in neon lighting."

"I don't go in for splash, I go in for quality," she said.

"As if I didn't know that by now."

"I'm getting a woman to help at home. The kitchen sink doesn't go with a proper manicure, and I do get tired."

"You don't think you're taking on too much?"

It was a moment or so before she answered, "No, I know what I'm doing. Don't lean on that parcel, it's a roll of velvet." Mrs. Mander thrust the lease into a drawer and drew down the roll-top of the desk. "I suppose I can call it another week," she sighed. "It's Saturday as soon as it's Monday, the time flies."

"And you've hardly taken a week's holiday for years. I say, Mother—with a Mayfair place you'll want an assistant who can speak fluent French."

"You're on about Olga again."

"Of course! She'd be a terrific asset."

"We'll see. I've got to get in there first. Fittings are going to cost something. Let's get home, I want my comfortable slippers. You're always saying you'll take me out to the pictures or somewhere but you never do."

He leapt at the suggestion, without reminding her of her almost invariable refusals. "Of course. I'll see if I can get some theatre tickets."

"No you will not. If I go to the theatre I'd want to dress properly for it, and I can't be bothered. We'll go to the Odeon at Marble Arch and chance what we see."

"We'll have a bite at Berti's first, it'll save you cooking. Well well, you're moving out of here and I've been thinking of a change——"

"What change?" she interrupted sharply.

"Oh nothing definite. Just ideas waffling about in the back of my mind. I'd tell you if they jelled."

"I do wish you wouldn't use slang. Half the time I don't know what you're talking about."

He took his mother's coat from its hanger and held it for her. To a stranger their argument might have sounded like a dispute, but it was a part of her affection for him, to inflect most of her talk with a scolding tone—as if she still had to train him not to grow up like his father.

CHAPTER XXIX

MARK TORGLER was twenty-nine and had been a schoolmaster. He hardly looked his age, though six years ago his wife and baby had died of starvation in the shambles of Europe. So much Vivian learnt, forbearing to question further, for obviously Mark had known enough of tragedy to be spared the torment of recalling details. He never complained, but once, reading the title of a book on the joy of living, he was stung to the exclamation, "I don't hope to live, I have to accept survival."

He proved himself adaptable, and Vivian felt no misgiving about leaving him in charge of the shop while he himself went to keep his appointment with Olga in Sidley Street. It was one of those dry Spring days when the wind is a reminder of how much litter can accumulate in London streets. Dust and grit and fragmentary garbage blew up from the gutters, men clutched their hats on their heads, bare-headed girls had wild-flying hair.

Olga opened the door beside the gown shop, and even in his delight at seeing her he had a faint sense of foreboding. The only other occasion when he had entered this door was to persuade, or rather, compel Tashy to go to Pegwell. But somehow the door was a symbol of Tashy's sordid past, and though she was marrying so advantageously, he could not suppress the inexplicable fear that her past might in some way shadow the future. He was about to embrace Olga in the hall, but she moved away swiftly, and now he was following her up the stairs.

"Mind the curve," she said. "The stairs are narrow on that side, and one's trodden right through."

"Yes, I know." It was as if even their voices were echoes of former questionable ascents. "It's about time they had it mended."

The room looked bare and the gimcrack furniture was coated with dust. A standard lamp was burning, though outside the gusty day was still bright; Tashy's old curtains, thick and secretive, nearly covered the windows. "You haven't even kissed me," Vivian said.

"No." Olga moved still farther away.

Startled, he queried "I haven't done anything to offend you?"

"No. But I'll have to explain."

She was still standing, looking curiously rigid in her severe green coat. Obviously she had just combed her hair, it was like a curved sheet of light-gold metal. Her face was pale, rather drawn; she looked as she had done after an attack of influenza. "You're not ill, are you darling?" Again he moved close to her.

"Please, Vivian——" her gesture of rebuff was almost desperate.

"Whatever's the matter? I just don't understand all this. Is your mother all right? You must be glad she's marrying the Commander, he's a fine old man, she'll be comfortable and well cared for. And happy, if she realizes her luck."

"Yes. That's just it."

"So that leaves us. Well, we're all right. I've been thinking of moving away from London. But Mother's taking a place in Mayfair, she wants you to help her there. So we can see each other often and we shan't have the awful feeling that I've had about the cottage. You seemed so very far away, and I was never quite sure whether I was welcome. And I never had you to myself."

"Of course you were welcome," Olga spoke almost primly.

"Oh well, it's pretty well all over now. Where are you staying tonight?"

Olga said sharply, "I'd better tell you straight away. Then you won't go on day-dreaming."

He tried to say, Tell me what? But a lump in his throat strangled the words.

"I'm going to marry Maxie Lassiter."

"You——? You're *not*."

"I am. I'm sorry——"

"It's impossible!"

"I'm sorry. I know I'm hurting you."

"But you don't, you *can't* be in love with him."

She burst into tears. "I don't understand love, I don't know what it's all about, I'm bewildered. It's all—I don't know, it isn't really part of my stupidity. Please—Vivian, don't look at me like that, I can't bear it."

"My darling——" He took her hand but she snatched it away. "I can't have you making this awful mistake. Let's sit down—— There. Don't be so distressed, we can sort everything out."

She shook her head dolefully as he lodged on one arm of her chair, "Please, let me just hold your hand, please let me. I can't begin to tell you what a shock you've given me. For heaven's sake, how could you think, even for a moment, of doing such a thing?"

"It's no good, Vivian." She tried to free her hand.

"Don't struggle against me, please talk to me, tell me, only tell me *why*."

"It would be much easier," Olga mumbled, "if you didn't ask questions."

"It's the most incredible thing I ever heard. Lassiter's a wrong 'un, it isn't just that I'd be losing you, I'd know you were doomed to absolute misery."

"No." Olga sighed deeply. "It's settled, there's no changing it."

"But can't you give me any *sort* of reason? Of course I know Lassiter's been running down to the cottage, I thought it awful cheek on his part, but I was so counting on everything being straightened out once you were back."

"He didn't come down often," Olga said weakly.

As if the number of his visits could matter, in the light of this situation! "You know I've loved you, Olga, ever since I looked down from that window over the road and saw you with your mother. Coming across to see us. I could tell you every detail about yourself at that moment, it was all fixed in my mind for ever. I became a man on that day, though you only let me kiss you as I might have put my lips to a

Bible to take an oath. I loved you then and I love you now, and you're *not* going to marry Lassiter."

Olga slid her tongue over her dry lips, and again drew away her hand. "Could we be calm about it?" she murmured.

"Yes, by all means," he said tensely. His heart was thudding and a trickle of perspiration ran down his spine. "Yes, let's be calm. I feel as if we've both side-stepped into some horrible nightmare. I want to get back to where we were, to reality."

Olga was silent and he had to exert all his self-control not to lash her with further pleadings and remonstrances. Wildly, he raked his mind for some simple phrase that would convince and win her, but his imagination failed. Outside in the street a brass band struck up a travesty of the *Knightsbridge March*. Olga made a gesture of distress. "Oh, that *noise*."

He moved to close the window and as he turned she said quietly, "I don't love you, Vivian. I told you, I don't really understand love. But oh Vivian, darling, I feel more tenderly towards you than to anyone in the world. And of course I'd always trust you, completely, absolutely."

"Well, then——?" He was even more deeply mystified.

"I don't know how to explain. It's—well, of course, it's all to do with Mother. I know such a lot now, about how she went all wrong. She was in hell, a worse hell than those religious Sisters ever told me about. She grew up in a wild lovely place, her marriage went wrong, then she got crowded into this street and lost heart, she felt she'd never escape, never get back, and she gave up caring what happened to her."

"Yes, of course I understand all this. But——"

"Then you lent us Lane Cottage."

"I didn't lend it. It was my accursed powers of persuasion that got it for you. If only I could use them on you! Even now, even with what you've told me, you're too much part of me."

Olga seemed not to be listening. She pursued, "And she was back in the sort of place she really belongs to. Cawdie loves her and she's terribly grateful. He's going to marry her and make her safe and she'll be happy."

"Yes, yes, I know all that. I'm more glad than I can say. But that doesn't mean *you* have to make a mess of your life.

It leaves you quite free, and I'm full of plans. I've been feeling so optimistic, so sure of the future, in the last few days. There's not a thing for you to worry about—if only you'll forget you ever had the insane idea of marrying Lassiter."

"It's not insane——"

"You're not going to marry him. That's definite. Darling, I'll be patient, so very patient, so long as you're mine in the end."

Olga rose suddenly. "I'm going to marry Maxie," she said quietly. "If I don't, Mother won't be able to marry Cawdie."

"That's sheer nonsense!"

"No, it isn't. You see, Maxie knows everything about her. Everything. And Cawdie doesn't."

The implications of this reasoning penetrated slowly into Vivian's mind. He choked out, "You mean he's threatening her? Threatening to talk? The dirty blackmailer!"

"That's a horrid word. All he did—well, he said he was just putting it to me as an angle."

"An angle! That blasted film actors' word! I'm sorry, darling, but we aren't concerned with 'angles'. Lassiter can't force you to marry him by any hold he's got over your mother. It's preposterous, it's worse than all the old stories of wicked squires foreclosing on—— Oh, I forget how that goes, but this is here and now, and this is you and me, and you're not marrying Lassiter."

"It's arranged, Vivian. I asked you to come here just so I could tell you, and say I'm sorry. It would have been much easier to write. But—well, I knew it would be a shock to you. I'm very, very sorry."

"It isn't true." Vivian had to clear his throat. "Things like this don't happen."

"They do, you know." The voice that cut in was coldly sarcastic. Lassiter was in the doorway.

Vivian leapt up. He said quietly, "Olga belongs to me. You know that."

Leaning against the doorpost Lassiter snapped his lighter and tilted his head to puff out cigarette smoke. "I knew there'd be a cry-baby scene. That's why I came along. If you've done with all the explanations and blubbering—— Come on, Olga, we'll go."

H

"Don't, Olga! You can't——" Instinctively Vivian moved between the other two.

Lassiter came in. "Olga!" He jerked a thumb and Vivian sprang at him. He checked his movement, facing the man. One moment, or just a few moments, and perhaps he could exert his will-power. Anything to gain a little time——

But Lassiter was not waiting for any such subtle form of attack. He swerved a fist armoured by a knuckle-duster. Vivian lunged back, but still the metallic blow caught him. And another. Through the blur of fading consciousness, with blood streaming down over his eyes, he heard Lassiter's voice as a semi-articulate purr. "I didn't want to do that. But I'm not having any more of his hypnotism stuff. I believe in clean fighting. You can't fight clean with a murderer's son."

The end of the sentence was repeating itself, like a faulty gramophone record, with a murderer's son, a murderer's son.

"Olga—— Olga." Vivian did not know if he had blurted her name aloud, or whether it was just a silent prayer. And then the darkness came down, mercifully obliterating pain.

Two yellow oblongs against dark purple. A sweet horrible taste . . . Blood. The oblongs were windows. Night time, Tashy's room, and more blood running down his face as he moved. Vivian dragged himself up, wondering in his distorted consciousness why the standard lamp was not still alight.

Then, dimly, he discerned its shape, flung over as Max Lassiter had used his thug's weapon.

Painfully, slowly, stubbing his toes, Vivian made his way to the kitchenette across the landing, and splashed cold water against his face. Automatically, he fumbled for a towel, then used his handkerchief. Olga had gone with Lassiter, that knowledge revolved in his fuddled mind. Olga with Lassiter. If he had to go to any extremity, those two must be parted.

"Is there something wrong?"

He was leaning against the wall, gasping painfully. A shadow moved on the landing. He gulped out, "Yes. An accident." Several deep breaths, the shadow was shrinking away as if scared. "Please, would you telephone for me?"

The shadow was a woman. She said sharply, "It's none of my business."

"If you could telephone—— The number—— I can't remember. Noreen, Frith Street."

"Maureen?" the wraith said.

He spelt the name, painfully, and moved a step or so. The darkness swung over in blinding flashes of colour. "If you could help me back into the front room. A chair——"

"It's nothing to do with me," the dim voice repeated. But his arm was taken, and as he was piloted into the front room he heard the exclamation, "The light's gone. Fused."

He seemed to sink into billowing pillows, all surrounded by pungent perfume. Whoever had helped him had reeked of some odious scent, and it clung in the dusky air. Now he was alone, feeling increasing pain as his senses returned.

"It's nothing to do with me . . ."

He thought he was imagining the repetition. But two people were in the room, and he heard his mother's voice, so faint that it was on the very edge of audibility, "What's wrong, what's happened? Oh why isn't there any light?"

Then her hand gripped his. "Get me home," he said.

She was kneeling in front of him. His head dropped forward against hers. "Something hit me," he said, "I'm stunned, I'm stupid. I'll be all right. Only get me home. I must clean myself up. Then I've got to find Olga."

"You'll come right home and stay there. I'll get a taxi. Wait till I come up and fetch you."

His mother's tone was harsh with anxiety. Then he realized that he was alone.

CHAPTER XXX

THE electric light shade hanging from the centre of the ceiling swayed to and fro, for both a window and the door were open. Vivian leaned back in an armchair, glad of the fresh breeze blowing in from the square; his bandaged head was aching, but his mind was clear. He only had to wait for Dr. Barnett to leave, then he himself would be able to set off. The doctor seemed to be taking a long time over washing after inserting stitches in a cut that extended from one eyebrow to the roots of the hair. Now the bruise on the other cheek was more painful.

A pretty sight I shall look! thought Vivian. His mother and the doctor were talking in undertones, and as they both came in the doctor said cheerfully, "How's it feel, eh?"

"Much more comfortable, thanks."

"I want you to take this——"

Without reflection, Vivian swallowed the tablet and drank from the glass his mother handed him.

"You'll be all right after a good night's rest."

Suddenly alert, Vivian exclaimed, "You don't mean——? Was that some sort of a sleeping tablet?"

"No need to be horrified. You've had a shock, and——"

"But I don't want to sleep." Vivian added desperately, "I've got a hell of a lot to do."

The doctor was snapping his bag shut. "Take things quietly for the next three or four days at least. I'll have a look at you on Friday, though I don't anticipate the slightest trouble. Next time you fight, pick on a chap about half your own size."

Obviously the remark was intended as a witticism. Vivian smiled stiffly. The doctor was being shown out. There was no time to lose, Olga must be found and—by whatever means might be necessary—parted from Lassiter. But as Vivian rose he swayed dizzily.

His mother, rather oddly, was remaining on the landing. He said "I'll just get my jacket."

"I'll get it for you."

"Don't bother. I have to go out, you know."

"You will not go out."

"Mother, *please*! I got this crack from Lassiter and he went off with Olga. I've just got to find her."

"Tomorrow——"

"As if I can wait till then! He thinks he's going to marry her."

"Did you say—marry her? Lassiter?"

"I can't stop to explain."

"Don't you realize, you'll fall asleep on your feet if you won't lie down."

"I've got to stay awake." As he spoke he tottered. "Some black coffee might do it."

"You'll come in your room and lie down."

He continued to plead, to argue, almost to threaten, as he was urged towards his room. Certainly it was a physical relief to be on his bed, but he was trying to resist the drowsiness already making him feel helpless. His mother asked, "Where do you expect to find those two?"

A suspicion struck through the dimness. "Was it you who told the doctor to give me that sleeping tablet?"

"For your own safety. After all you said in the taxi— You scared me, Vivian. Where will they be? You've got to tell me."

Even in his present condition he was aware of the anxiety in her voice. He shifted, tumbling a pillow on to the floor. Then he began to talk volubly, without knowing whether he was being coherent. "She came up from Pegwell, she might have been going back, but she must have told Lassiter she was meeting me. I don't know where they went, I couldn't stop them, I was clean out. She might be going back to Pegwell, she might go to Mrs. Paton's, I don't know where else . . ." He was drowsing off.

The question seemed to come from far away. "Where does Max Lassiter live?"

"In Denman Street."

"The number?"

"Don't know. She . . . thinks she's saving Tashy. Tashy. Lassiter knows too much about Tashy. He'll keep quiet if Olga . . . It's to injure me, he's capable of anything, if . . ."

"Don't worry. You're nearly asleep."

He was striving to get up, but knew that he hardly moved. "Strong black coffee . . ." he mumbled vaguely. Then he realized that he was alone and, for the time being, quite helpless.

In the sitting-room Mrs. Mander was clearing up bowls, towels, oddments of bandages and cotton wool. Then she swept some things from the top of the old ottoman that had been brought from Sidley Street, and opened it, turning out books, tattered bundles of letters, photographs and dozens of other oddments, the sentimental relics of a lifetime. She found what she wanted, and after a glance into Vivian's room, to assure herself that now he was sleeping soundly, she telephoned to a car hire firm and put on her hat and coat.

She took some money from a metal box in the secret drawer of her bureau, and sat down to wait.

Earlier, she had been agitated, for the message from the unknown woman in Sidley Street had been a shock. But now she was calm, and as she considered the events that had led up to this situation, they were as definite and unemotional as if they had been facts recorded in black and white on a card index. Without her overwhelming love for her son, her boy born in grief and bitterness, all would have been without significance. Her self-reasoning had as its lode-star spiritual rather than material ambition, and throughout Vivian was in the centre of the visionary scenes.

He had always been so easily popular with nearly everyone he met, and his peculiar psychic gifts had earned him easy admiration. Was it for these reasons, rather than for the old tragedy of their two fathers, that Max Lassiter had conceived so ruthless an enmity? The more important point emerged, that this crisis was a humiliation necessary to Vivian's development. Without it he would have pursued his casual way, pottering with his bookshop, exerting his gifts of healing and will-power as the fancy took him, perhaps marrying Olga, frittering away or disregarding his incalculable potency for beneficence, for relieving sorrow and pain.

A sigh escaped the waiting woman. She was unaware of it, unaware that it may have expressed a momentary regret for her own voluntary renunciation of life. She was remembering that she had once been happy, and had been still young when Vivian was born. Her years of effort might now bring their reward. For Vivian, sobered and humbled, might now be pliable, ready to accept guidance rather than follow his own unambitious—or at the best, limited promptings. If her own life had not been so absolutely devotional—well, she reflected with a faint inward smile, she might have enjoyed many trivial pleasures. And no doubt her son would have met with average success.

Average success was not good enough for the handsome little lad who had chalked his scores of mastery on the walls of Mrs. Glatt's top floor.

The street door-bell rang. The car had arrived. Mrs. Mander switched off the light and hurried downstairs.

It was full daylight when Vivian stirred. The flat was

quiet and a glance at the clock told him that it was after nine. His mother had probably left for her workroom, and it was with a sense of despair that he realized the night had passed without his having been able to do anything to find Olga. With his head pounding, he let the bathwater run while he went into the kitchen to put a kettle on. Then he splashed cold water over his head recklessly, soaking the bandages, and swallowed two aspirins.

The morning paper had not been picked up from the landing. Usually his mother glanced through it before setting off. He opened the door of her room and there she was, in a dressing-gown, yawning as if she had overslept and could not yet regain full consciousness. In recent years she had been having her hair tinted—"good for business", she always said —but now it was flying loose and with no touch of make-up on her pale face, she looked pitifully faded.

Her smile flashed on. What courage she had! "What I need is a cup of tea," she said.

"It's made. I've got to hurry. To think I've let the whole night go——"

"You've no need to go chasing after Olga——"

"I'm going to. It would be waste of time to argue."

In the sitting-room the telephone rang and he went eagerly to answer it. But it was only Mark Torgler, inquiring why he had not turned up.

"You carry on," Vivian rapped, "I may be along later or I may not."

"Mr. Wyganowski is here. He wishes to see you. He will purchase this business, if you are willing to sell it."

"I can't discuss it now. I've more important things to do." Vivian slammed down the receiver.

His mother was behind him. He said, "Wyganowski wants to buy my bookshop."

"Good! That's splendid! Oh really, I'm glad."

Even in his distraction he was puzzled by such enthusiasm, but he could not delay. "I'll slip into the bath and get dressed."

"How's your head?"

"Not too bad."

"Vivian—I've told you already, there's no need for you to go looking for Olga."

"But there is!"

"I'm telling you, there is not. Will you always go on thinking I've no sense? The dear Lord knows someone had to do something last night, without waiting for this morning. A girl must be taken care of, whoever she is."

"I don't understand."

"She's perfectly safe. Did I ever lie to you?"

"Never. But——"

Again the telephone rang and this time it was Violet Bracey ringing from Frith Street, to say that the decorators had called with samples of wallpaper for the new Bruton Street premises.

"Wallpaper!" Vivian exclaimed impatiently.

His mother seized the telephone. "It's important. I told them I must have John Lines——"

"But I can't wait to hear what you meant——"

"Be quiet, do. How can I listen to Violet?"

Impatience set his skin tingling. His mother was saying that the decorator must leave the samples. Lady Glaize's cocktail suit must be delivered this afternoon. Violet must telephone to Paris for the chiffon for someone else's gown. Something about bridesmaids' dresses and a traveller from Archway Supplies. It seemed that such trivialities would keep the conversation going for hours.

"She's a good girl, is Violet." Mrs. Mander turned from the telephone. "I must get along there. But after last night— I didn't get much sleep."

"You told me Olga's safe but you've left me puzzling—— Don't you realize what she means to me?"

"If you'll not get so excited, and you'll sit yourself down and keep calm, I'll tell you."

With exasperating deliberation Mrs. Mander went to the kitchen. There was a clink of china. Then she called out "Sakes alive, the bath's within an inch of overflowing!"

"I'm sorry," Vivian said. He noticed, absently, that the ottoman had been turned out. Oddments were stacked around it and he thought how strange it was that his mother should have chosen such a time for tidying up—or rather, for creating disorder.

She returned carrying a tray. Of course he would have to let her recount whatever news she had in her own way. He sat gripping the arms of his chair, turning his eyes from the window, for the light this morning seemed painfully brilliant. "Well——"

"If Max Lassiter had the idea he was going to marry Olga—Vivian, you're not in a draught?"

He rose and slammed the window down rather than delay over an argument. "There!"

"Of course," his mother said, "the first thing was to find her. She wasn't at his flat in Denman Street, it took me an hour to find the place, not knowing the number, and when at last I got in two detectives were there, waiting for him. He's in real trouble this time, the woman on the floor below said——"

"Olga wasn't there, that's all that matters to me."

"All right, all right. She wasn't at her old lodgings, Mrs. Paton's. Then I went back to Tashy's room, she wasn't there, and that woman who found you injured let off some terrible language at being disturbed. Then I went to Lane Cottage."

"You went *there*!"

"I had a car. Olga wasn't there. But Commander Cawdell was. I had ten minutes alone with Tashy and I made her agree that she had to tell the Commander a few things about the life she'd led in Sidley Street."

"I don't see what that's got to do with it."

"You'll realize when you're older, my boy" (there she was on that old theme!), "that everything's part of a pattern. Of course she argued, but she gave in."

"It doesn't seem possible——"

"It was better for her to tell him, than for me to have to explain what sort of a criminal she'd had visiting her down there, what sort of a man she'd let her daughter get engaged to. That would have been something he couldn't forgive, no matter how infatuated he was. Anyway, there it is, he had quite a lot of her story. It's queer——" Mrs. Mander looked up reflectively, "but you can't get away from it, good breeding's a wonderful thing. Generations of good behaviour—— I could see he was shocked, staggered, really. But he kept quite steady, he never raised his voice. He said 'Tashy, do you really wish to tell me all this?' And of course she said yes, she'd rather be frank than have any fear of discovery hanging over her."

"It all sounds crazy. And what it's got to do with you. Or me——"

"Oh, there's plenty of plain reason in it. You see, I'd shown her these——" Mrs. Mander reached for her handbag and extracted two newspaper clippings. "And even you'll agree they've got a lot to do with Olga's future."

The cuttings were torn at the edges as if they had been stuck into a book and then removed. The size of the print seemed to indicate that they were many years old. PICTURESQUE WEDDING. Vivian read the three paragraphs hastily and turned to the second item, which consisted of a photograph and a caption.

His mother was saying, "I used to keep cuttings about anyone I knew, and stick them in a book with the family snapshots. Many's the time I've nearly thrown the whole lot away——"

"*Max Lassiter and Charlotte Haynes*," Vivian read.

"It's a miracle I never burnt the rubbish, years ago. I've had it over twenty years." Mrs. Mander frowned slightly as the tip of her little finger rested for a moment on the photographed group, "That one—the best man, that's your own father. The picture was taken eight days before he was arrested. You can see, he's not a lot older than Max. And that's James Lassiter, with his elbow right in the bride's bouquet."

"But is she—the wife, I mean—is she still alive?"

Mrs. Mander nodded. "He left her in no time. She was Roman Catholic, brought up very strictly, and wouldn't divorce him. No one could persuade me she'd ever do anything so he could have divorced her. I've often wondered if she was dead. After all, it's a long time. But it's not many months since I saw her name in a Sunday paper. Charlotte Lassiter, there's not likely to be two of them. Her teashop in Manchester was burgled."

"So if he married again——"

"He wouldn't stop at bigamy."

"He'd stop at nothing," Vivian exclaimed, "to injure me, though God knows I've never done him any harm. It's he who's always come along to provoke me—that doesn't matter, but to think of Olga——" he broke off, appalled, as his mind absorbed the possibilities. "Does Tashy know about this?" He threw the clippings on the table.

"She does now. But whether or not she knew before I proved it, she's always known what the man *is*. She's not the first he's blackmailed."

"I'm quite—staggered. I wouldn't have believed that she'd be ready to sacrifice her own daughter. Good God, what a horrible business!" Vivian began to pace the room, but the movement jarred his forehead and again he stood still.

"I've always told you, Tashy's a bad woman. I'm glad Olga's so different in looks, we'll hope she's as different in character."

"She is. I'd stake my life on it."

"Well, I kept my word to Tashy. I didn't tell Commander Cawdell she knew Lassiter was a blackmailer who'd lived on women. That *would* have put him off, and well Tashy knows it. I just said it was lucky I had proof of Lassiter being married. Anyway, the Commander was hardly listening, there's no doubt he'll be fool enough to marry Tashy, in spite of everything." Mrs. Mander added grimly. "She ought to be grateful, there's no one can blackmail her now. Lassiter's wanted for a big confidence trick, and he can't know they're after him, or he'd have got out of Soho."

"But where did you find Olga?"

"It was after midnight when I got back to London, of course the car had to break down and we were a mile from a garage. I went to The Two Swords, because you'd said you'd seen Lassiter there, but it was all closed up. Then I went back to Tashy's old place, and I woke half Sidley Street before someone came down and said there wasn't anybody in Tashy's room. I went up to see for myself. And coming down I ran slap into Olga and Lassiter at the street door. They'd been to some night club. I grabbed Olga and had her in the car in a flash. *He* couldn't do anything, there was his taxi driver still there, and the driver of my car, and several people were passing. Olga was sobbing, but everyone thought she was my daughter, and I let them go on thinking it. Then I told her about Lassiter's wife, as we drove off."

"Drove—where?"

"To Violet Bracey's place. She's got a couple of rooms over a grocery shop——"

"Is Olga there now? What's the address?"

"Just a minute." Mrs. Mander began to straighten a pile of fashion papers as if she had just realized that this detail of tidiness was important. "There's something I wasn't going to speak of till after I'd moved into Bruton Street. But we'd better get it settled now."

He shifted impatiently. "There's only one thing I'm thinking of——"

"And don't I know that? That's why I'm going to ask you now, while perhaps you're feeling a little gratitude."

"More than a little. I'll never stop being grateful. To think while I was sleeping like a hog, you were rushing about, working miracles!"

"Well, you can show your appreciation by doing what I want. You know I've been saving this last twenty years?"

"I rather thought you must have been."

"It's been with a purpose. I've always had it in my mind that I want you to be a doctor. It's what I've worked for and prayed for, it's what the good Lord meant you to be."

"It would take years!"

"Five years, or not very much longer. It's my dream, Vivian, it always has been. If you won't do it, I might have saved myself all the worry, and the trouble of working till all hours."

"But—Mother, it wouldn't be fair on you! I'm grown up, independent, in a few years I ought to be helping you."

"Yes. Later on you'll be helping me, as likely as not. I'll give you time to think it over, while I get dressed. I've got the money, and Dr. Barnett, who stitched up your silly head, will give you all the advice you'll want about starting with your studies."

"Five or six years, and I'd be completely dependent on you."

She came across, smoothed a lock of hair from his wound, and rested her hand lightly on his head. "It's me who's dependent," she said softly. "I've got no one else."

He rose as she went out. Perhaps it was the turmoil in his mind that made him suddenly so acutely perceptive of details, seeing as if for the first time the shabbiness of the old sewing-machine that had whirred in Sidley Street, the bundles of patterns on top of the bookcase, the model ship on the mantelpiece that he had made for his mother when he was twelve, the cane work-basket that might have belonged to any old cottage woman. Olga was safe; he would be seeing her today, this morning. As for the proposition that he should study medicine, his mind was made up, as if automatically, without any conflicting advantages and disadvantages. His mother had merely reminded him of his true vocation while making its achievement possible. His precarious powers of domination, his flashes of faith-healing, would be submerged in years of hard study; later on, with the solid basis of science, they might be of inestimable value.

His mother came in, fully dressed. He said quickly, "Of course I'll do as you want. I'll study medicine. I only hope I'll justify all you've done for me."

"That's settled, then." Her tone was matter-of-fact but her face lit up with delight.

"Thinking of all you've done—I'm overwhelmed. You seem to take it for granted that every hour you've been awake has been spent in working and planning, and never for yourself. You've cheated yourself of every pleasure, you've let the best years of your life slip by. How secret you've been, too. And how brave!"

She shrugged casually. "I'm satisfied. I've got what I wanted. Who can say more than that?"

"This means it'll be years before I can marry."

"What's worth having is worth waiting for."

How trim and efficient she looked, in her small black hat and stylishly cut coat! She picked up her handbag, and paused, gazing at the two newspaper clippings still on the table. "Olga's seen those. So has Tashy, so has the Commander. You'd better burn them."

"But they're the evidence——"

"They won't be needed any more. Lassiter's finished. Whatever those two detectives were waiting for, it's something serious. The police had been there in relays for several days. He's on the run and they'll get him."

Vivian struck a match. In an ashtray the clippings, dry with age, burnt in one momentary flame. "You haven't yet told me where I can find Olga."

"Is it ten o'clock?"

"A couple of minutes to."

"Oh well. I shan't be kept long."

"Kept? What's delaying you?" He was suddenly aware of his mother's mood of alert anticipation. And now she was smiling. "What happens at ten o'clock?"

"I'm not having you rushing round to the workroom. And I know you won't stay quiet and give that wound a chance to heal until your mind's at rest."

"You're absolutely right——" There was a knock at the door and Vivian leapt to open it. He and Olga remained as still as statues for several seconds, gazing at each other as if rooted by some enchantment. Her sudden appearance was like a fantastic conjuring trick, a miracle, it was as if the slightest movement might shatter the illusion.

Olga's face was pale, her grey-green eyes were darkly shadowed, but she was holding her head high as she came in.

In emotional crises, it is often the superficial details that seem obtrusive. Vivian found himself asking "What's happened to your coat?" From elbow to cuff, both the sleeves of Olga's green coat were oddly stained.

She looked down. "Oh. Yes. I tried to wash it out but it stuck. You see, I put my arms round you, yesterday, when you were unconscious."

Suddenly Vivian was embarrassed by his own appearance. Unshaven, in his old dressing-gown, with his forehead and one cheek a patchwork of bandage and plaster. "You put your arms round me. And I didn't know——"

His mother's voice, crisp and practical—"Here we are, hanging about as if we've got all the time in the world. Olga's coming along with me, I don't mind saying she'll be quite a help, with the rush of orders and the move and one thing and another."

Olga seemed to be studying the ashtray in which the burnt newspaper clippings had curled into a tiny cornucopia. "Don't fret," Mrs. Mander added more gently, "I'll wait downstairs for you. Don't keep me long. And make Vivian promise he'll take today quietly. Perhaps he'll take some notice of *you*, he's never been anything but a bother to *me*."

Mrs. Mander went out. With her head still bowed Olga was obviously trying to control her emotions. "I've been—you'll never understand how miserable I've been. I knew——" her voice failed.

"I do understand. My poor darling!" Vivian took her hands.

"I *hated* him," she said quietly. "I've been so bewildered."

"How you could ever have thought of sacrificing yourself . . . Oh, let's both try to forget it! I'm only grateful that you told me in time."

She came readily into his embrace, but was shaken by a sudden outburst of weeping. He soothed and comforted her. "I'd like to keep you, never let you out of my sight again." At the back of his mind was the thought—five years, six, seven? He sighed. "It'll be such a long time before you're really mine."

"Must it be?"

He smiled ruefully at the irony of the situation. Until now, it had been Olga who pleaded for delay. "Yes. This isn't the time for explanations. But now we're both sure, aren't we, that we belong to each other?"

Her eyes, moist with tears, were questioning. "Of course we belong."

Again he embraced her, tenderly, gently, controlling his trembling eagerness. Never again would they be completely apart, isolated from each other, as they had been yesterday when they sat together in Tashy's room in Sidley Street.

Three minutes later two slim figures were crossing the square, stopping to wave up to him, and he recalled the Sunday morning when first he had seen Olga—looking upwards, as she was doing now, from a street to an open window. Then, his heart had seemed to miss a beat at the sight of her, and now he knew that his instinct had been prophetically true. She gave a last glance and smiled before turning the corner of the railings, and he was left gazing at the trees in the square. On the branches the first buds were opening, glinting gold with the promise of later abundance.

Twelve years ago childishly, he had called a window his spy-hole on the world, and now, automatically, he was standing in the same attitude, his head lowered, his finger-tips thoughtfully pressed together. But his contemplation was not so clearly of the visible scene as of the inner recesses of his own heart, while his reflections flowed calmly, merging into their logical interpretations:

The leaves on the trees below will flutter for a few months

*in the interminable cycle of the seasons. In the phases of human
life there is no such circling repetition; each movement is a tangent,
which may strike a point beyond imagination. For everyone,
humble or exalted, the possibilities are infinite. And anyone with
a precious gift—such as scientific talent, artistry, genius, even so
nebulous a faculty as psychic power—must make a proportionate
contribution to the eternal plan.*

Vivian turned from the window, heavy-hearted at the
knowledge that he must renounce his immediate personal
aspirations, must impose patience upon his passionate love.
Yet in retrospect, in ten or twenty years time, how well
worth-while the sacrifice might seem! As if dropping a
telescope, he swung his mind from the fanciful future to the
realistic present; he must go to Orange Court, to set about
disposing of the concern that had been no more than a
stumbling adventure in a wrong direction. The way to his
true vocation would be longer, more arduous—but his progress
would be guided by a steady star.

THE END